PAULINA VAS(

Broken Luna

Book 1 of the Broken Trilogy

CHAPTER 1 – WHAT NOW

"LUCY!" I heard Alpha Ranger roar at me through the house.

I was folding towels in the laundry room located in the basement of the pack house. My hands began to tremble as I hear him yell, **"GET YOUR SORRY ASS UP HERE!"**

I quickly raced up the steps and nearly stumbled over my own feet. I entered the kitchen to find Alpha Ranger standing next to his girlfriend, Miranda. She was tall, blonde and beautiful, but she was ugly on the inside. I graduated high school three months ago, and although Miranda tormented me in school and made me miserable, I still liked going. It was a break from my chores and being the pack slave.

I also miss eating every day, even though most kids hated school lunch, it was often the only meal I had.

The kitchen smelled great as the cooks prepared breakfast. My stomach growled loudly at me; I haven't eaten in three days. I only get table scraps and leftovers, since werewolves have big appetites, I often go days without eating.

"Yes Alpha." I nodded my head down in submission.

"Lucy, I'm only going to ask you once, did you take Miranda's iWatch?"

My mind was racing, and panic started to set in. She

was accusing me of taking her iWatch. What the hell would I do with an iwatch? I don't even know how to use electronics; I've never had any.

I'm not a thief! Even if I don't have much besides my raggedy old clothes, I would never steal from anyone. My eyes filled with unshed tears. "No Alpha, I would never."

"She's lying babe, Lucy's the only one who's been in my room. I think she needs to be punished." Miranda screeched.

Ranger stared at me and for a moment, his beautiful blue eyes seemed to flash sadness, but it was quickly gone. He stood tall, well over six feet, jet black hair, muscled body with his arms folded across his chest. I felt a strange pull in my heart. I wanted to beg him not to punish me, to tell him that Miranda was wicked, to make him see the truth, to touch his chest! Wait, what am I thinking? Touch his chest? He was twenty-five, looked like a Greek God and still had not found his mate. Of course, everyone wanted to touch his chest!

Ranger was stone faced for a moment before he spoke. "Lucy, as punishment you will not have any food for the next three days, thievery will not be tolerated around here. You're lucky I don't throw you in the hole."

He walked out of the kitchen and left me standing there alone with Miranda.

"Watch yourself loser. I'm going to be your Luna soon and when I am, I will have the power to do whatever I want to you."

I turned around and went out the back-door walking towards the woods. Some of the wild berry bushes still had fruit on them, if I was lucky, I might be able to eat a handful before I returned to my chores. I was responsible for cleaning the pack house and all the laundry. There was no way for me to sneak food from the kitchen, I was entirely at the mercy of the left-overs and scraps that I got a few times a week.

When I reached the woods, I sat for a moment on a big fallen tree log to take some deep breaths. I enjoyed breathing the fresh pine smell as a cool breeze blew through the trees. I shivered for a moment in my baggy shirt and yoga pants.

I was small for a she wolf and thinner than I wanted to be. I was five foot, three inches tall with striking amber colored eyes. My skin was fair, and my hair was waist length and dark.

In a few weeks from now, I would finally be eighteen and experience my first shift. I only hope I'm strong enough to handle the first shift which can be very painful and takes a lot of energy. I was also hoping to meet my mate soon and be saved from my daily abuse.

"Please Moon Goddess, have someone kind and loving paired with me. Someone who won't reject me and will love me regardless." I silently prayed.

Our pack was attacked by rogues four years ago. My father was a warrior and was killed during the attack along with my younger half brother and sister. Benjamin and Brianna were twins that belonged to my father and his second chance mate Ursa, they were playing in the front yard when the attack occurred.

They were only eleven when they were killed. Ursa is my stepmother and has never really treated me well. I was a spitting image of my mother and reminded her of my father's true love. My mother died when I was a baby, no one ever talked about her, and I only have two photos of her.

When the attack occurred, I was cleaning the attic and organizing the boxes up there, just as Ursa had told me to do. I had done everything she had asked me to do and tried to gain her love and affection, but she never liked me. She faked being nice to me when my father was around and only tolerated me. Now, she had an excuse to really hate me, she blamed me for the death of her children. Ursa often said I should have been watching them in the yard and keeping them safe. I was only fourteen, unable to shift or do anything. Sometimes I think she blames me for surviving and wishes I had died that day. On occasion, even I find myself wishing I had died that day too.

After my father and siblings were buried, Ursa threw me out of my father's house which had belonged in the Michaels family for generations. The house was rightfully mine, but the Alpha did nothing about it. Ursa also happens to be Miranda's aunt, being cruel runs in their blood.

Ranger's father was Alpha Knox LaRue, he was good friends with my father, who was his best warrior. Alpha Knox had also lost his mate, our Luna, in the same rogue attack. He took pity on me and gave me a nice room at the pack house. He was always nice to me.

Two months later, Alpha Knox's oldest son Ranger, became twenty-one and took over our pack as Alpha of Dark Moon. Ursa's niece, Miranda, hated me and she was a popular girl because she was the daughter of our Beta, her brother Max is now the Beta. Miranda turned all the kids against me, and I had no friends. The few friends I had started avoiding me. I became a loner and the pack punching bag in two short months of losing everything, my family, friends and home.

Alpha Knox lives in the Alpha family home a few miles north of the pack house and is rarely seen around. I assume he's either become a hermit or is traveling. Ranger doesn't have a Luna yet, because of this, Ursa became Ranger's house manager and runs the day to day operations of the pack house. She immediately moved me out of my comfortable room at the pack house and down to the basement in the Laundry room.

I was pulled from my thoughts when I heard some footsteps behind me and turned around to find Miranda standing there with her minions.

"What now?" I asked feeling annoyed.

"Someone needs an attitude adjustment. Let's give this little thief what she deserves." She smirked back.

I was always so busy with housework, that I was never allowed to train. I was weak and they preyed on weakness. I tried to run back to the pack house but was grabbed by Beth, a mean girl with a hard punch. She punched me in the mouth and split my lip wide open as I hit the tree behind me. When I landed on the ground, all five of them started kicking me all over. I tried to curl up in a ball and protect myself as much as I could.

"Look at her, she's so weak." One of the girls said.

"She needs to be put in her place." Beth said.

"You're sad and pathetic Lucy, no one is ever going to want you." Miranda spat.

Someone landed a hard kick to the back of my head and I saw stars. The forest was spinning, and I couldn't see straight, everything was blurry. From a distance I heard a familiar male voice call out, "What's going on? What have you done?"

I felt warm strong arms lift me up and carry me as the darkness pull me under.

CHAPTER 2 – MY LIFE

I opened my eyes and saw the sterile room I was in. I was at the pack clinic, but how did I get here? I tried to lift my head, but it felt so heavy.

"Lucy, you're awake." I heard Dr. Baker say.

I tried to sit up, my head was spinning, and I felt nauseous. My side was aching, and I was sure I had broken ribs. Werewolves tend to heal pretty quickly, but I haven't gotten my wolf yet so the healing will take a while, though certainly not as long as humans.

"Easy there, you've got a concussion and two broken ribs," Dr. Baker confirmed. She's been treating me my whole life. She was in her late fifties, had her brown and gray hair pulled back in a braid and had warm brown eyes.

"Lucy do you remember what happened?" She asked.
I closed my eyes and remember the beating, "Miranda and her friends." I sighed; my voice hoarse. My throat felt dry and my eyes found the pitcher sitting by the bed. Dr. Baker poured me a glass of water and handed it to me.

"You've been asleep since yesterday, you need to rest up and eat something Lucy. I'll have Jane bring you something to eat."

I've been here since yesterday? Who brought me here? I was about to ask Dr. Baker, when I remembered my punishment. If Alpha Ranger finds out they gave me food, I would surely end up in the hole this time. Oh Goddess, what about my chores, Ursa would see to it I was punished again.

My anxiety was bubbling inside. "I need to get out of here." I cried as I hobbled for the door. I was still wearing the clinic gown when I spotted my shabby clothes sitting on the chair by the door. I moved into the bathroom to change into my clothes.

I looked down at my body, I was covered in bruises complements of Miranda and her minions. I couldn't bring myself to look in the mirror right now. I'm sure I looked as bad as I felt. I just needed to get my clothes on and get back to my chores as quickly as possible. I struggled to get my legs in my pants and pull them up.

Dr. Baker urged me to lay down and rest, but it was no use, I knew I would have piles of laundry and angry pack members. I didn't need them hating me even more. Life was hard enough as it was, I was just trying to survive.

"Please, at least eat something Lucy." The sympathy was clear on her face.

"I'll eat at the pack house." I lied. "Thanks for everything Dr. Baker." I called rushing out the door.

When I got outside the sun was setting, I was squinting, my eyes felt sensitive to the light. I've been here since yesterday morning, shit! Alpha Ranger was going to be pissed, it was my job to deliver fresh towels, linen and laundry to all the rooms at the pack house. I also cleaned the rooms and made the beds. My absence would have been noticed.
I approached the pack house from the back, there was

a pool party in full swing. I was never allowed to attend, so I had forgotten all about it. This was the last pool party for the year as we entered fall.

The pups were running around chasing each other with water guns, having the time of their lives. Families were gathered around eating and enjoying each other's company. The music was blaring, the drinks were flowing, and the barbecue grills were grilling. The burgers smelled absolutely delicious and my stomach growled at me again reminding me it's been days since I've had anything. I felt so weak.

I put my head down and tried to walk towards the door as quickly as possible without being noticed. There was a wild game of chicken fights going on in the pool and I hoped everyone was distracted enough not to see me. Times like this I wish I was invisible.

Beta Max was standing at one of the grills closest to the door and saw me. "Hey Lucy, how are you feeling?"

I looked up at him, frozen for a moment, did he just speak to me? He asked me how I was feeling? This was Miranda's older brother and he seemed genuinely concerned when he asked me. This must be a cruel joke, there's no way anyone in this pack cares about how I'm feeling. I wasn't sure what to say, before I could speak, I heard Miranda yelling. "Hey look, the little thief is back."

The music was cut, and everyone turned to stare at me. "Give it a rest Miranda!" Beta Max nearly growled at her. She was perched on top of Ranger's shoulders in the pool, they had paused their chicken fight game with several others. She was wearing a skimpy red bikini leaving nothing to the imagination.

I started walking for the door when Ranger called out, "Lucy." I turned to look at him and saw a look of disgusted in his eyes as he looked me over. "We need fresh towels." He growled and went back to the game.

"Yes Alpha." I turned to leave and get those towels. Before I could take another step, our Gamma and Delta, Blake and Cole, grabbed my arms and dragged me to the pool. "No! No! Please don't." I cried, but it was useless. I was tossed right into the deep end and I couldn't swim.

I struggled to the surface for some air and heard everyone laughing. I was going to die, and they were laughing. I was bobbing up and down choking on chlorinated water. My ribs were hurting, and I just didn't have the energy. I sunk below the surface and didn't have much air left in my lungs.

I felt a familiar strong set of arms reach around me and pull me up to the surface. As he lifted me out of the pool, I noticed the laughter had stopped. Beta Max was carrying me towards a pool lounge chair. He set me down and handed me a towel.

I looked down to find my wet shirt was now see through and clinging to my body. I pulled the towel close to my chest and uttered "Thank you." To Beta Max.

My head was spinning, it was Max who had saved me in the woods and carried me to the clinic. Should I say something to him, but what? Before I could even muster the courage to say something, I caught a glimpse of Ranger making his way to us. I quickly stood up to leave.

Ranger stepped in front of me, staring at me with those beautiful blue eyes. I could feel the heat and power radiating from his body. His jet black hair was dripping water down his amazing chest and I felt my heart start to race. The left side of his chest and left arm was tattooed with tribal type of designs. His wash board abs on full display before me. Blush creeped up my cheeks and heat throughout my body just looking at him. Why does he affect me so much? Maybe it's an Alpha thing?

He closed his eyes and inhaled deeply. After a moment he opened his eyes with a smirk on his face, he looked down at me and quickly yanked my towel back. His eyes gazed at my breasts as they darkened with lust. I felt my breath catch in my throat. My nipples became rock hard. My breasts were a humble C cup and I had curves in all the right places, but I never felt attractive because I'm too skinny.

He began drying himself off with my towel. "I'll go get some more fresh towels." I squeaked as I crossed my arms over my chest. I'm pretty sure I heard a low chuckle as I walked away. I must have looked like such a fool.

When I reached the back door, I saw Beth, Miranda's minion who helped beat me up standing at one of the barbecue grills turning over burgers. She was in training to be a warrior and she's been mean since she was a pup. She had shoulder length red hair and was very muscular. She locked eyes with me and gave me a wicked smile which promised pain in the near future. I hated her and felt my anger flare. I looked down at the coals burning in the grill, suddenly sparks and flames jumped out burning her arm.

Beth screamed in pain and immediately ran for the pool to cool off her arm. She already had her wolf so her arm would be healed by tomorrow. I smiled, it felt good to see her in pain, even if it was for a short while.

I made my way through the kitchen and down the hall to the basement door. I carefully went down the stairs with my head still throbbing. The front half of the basement was used for storage and shelfs full of cleaning supplies. The back half was a laundry room.

I went to the laundry room and grabbed a basket of clean towels. "Look what the cat dragged in." Ursa sneered from behind me.

"Hello stepmother." I responded.

I felt a sting across my face as she slapped me hard, reopening my split lip. "Don't call me that, your father is dead and I'm no longer his wife." She spit at me with venom in her voice.

"I've had to arrange for a few omegas to come in and clean the rooms for the last two days since you disappeared, you ungrateful child."

"I'm sorry, Ursa." I looked down at the floor, "Alpha wants me to bring fresh towels out, please excuse me."

"I'll take them. You will stay here and not leave until the laundry is caught up and complete." She yanked the basket of towels from me and left. Moments later, I heard the basement door slam shut and the lock tumbling from the other side. She locked me in the basement.

I'm a pack slave, this is what my life has become and now I'm trapped down here for who knows how long.

CHAPTER 3 – HUNGER

The good thing about being locked in the basement is that the bullies in this pack don't usually come down here looking to torture me.

I was in the back of the basement, in the laundry room. It was a big room, with four industrial sized wash machines and four industrial dryers. There are two huge laundry shoots at each end of the room that drop the laundry down to me in the basement. This room had everything you need for laundry; a stack of laundry baskets, a large clothes rack and hangers, ironing board, folding table, and a big laundry sink. It even had a dog bed.

In the corner of the laundry room, on the cement floor, was a large green dog bed and tattered old blanket. This was my bed. I slept in the laundry room and on cold freezing nights, I would dry clothes to try and stay warm.

Next to my bed was a plastic tub that had all my belongings in it. My old clothes, a stuffed beige colored wolf my father had given me when I was little, a couple of books, a broken clock radio that I kept because the radio still worked and an old tote bag.

I kept the tote bag buried at the bottom of the tub; it contained my mother's necklace, a bottle of pain medication that Dr. Baker gave me two months ago, my dad's old hat and two photographs. One photograph was of my parents at their mating ceremony and the other of my mom holding me hours after my birth.

I have nothing else in this world. No money, no friends and no family. Hopefully I will have my mate soon, but it could take years if your mate isn't in the same pack. If my mate isn't in this pack, I don't know how I'll ever find him. If he is from this pack, he might not want me.

I've considered running away many times, but I don't know where I would go. Being a rogue is dangerous and living amongst humans would require money. Deep down inside, I know I can't be a laundry maid for the rest of my life. Speaking of laundry, I should get busy with it.

The carts under the laundry shoots were piled high with dirty laundry. I typically wash twelve to fifteen loads of laundry a day, and now I was looking at double. I wheeled one of the big carts to the washers and started loading the machines full, separating clothes, linens and towels.

Once all four machines started washing, I decided to take a shower and wash the chlorinated smell out of my hair. Just outside the laundry room in the basement, was a small closet sized room with a toilet and a hand sink. There was a tiny corner shower that was hardly big enough for me. In fact, it may have been a large floor sink, intended for washing mops, but was used as my shower.

I turned on the water and stripped my wet clothes off. I held the spray nozzle in my hand and stood in the shower with my eyes closed. I thought about Beta Max, and how he saved me twice now. Thinking back, I can't remember a time that Max was ever mean to me.

He had the same sandy blonde hair and green eyes as Miranda, and he was built like a tank. Max was handsome and had a warm softness in his smile.

I washed my face first, then my hair and finally my body. I turned off the water and wrapped a towel around myself. I brushed my teeth and got dressed. Ursa wouldn't allow me to have a blow dryer, so I must towel dry my hair and pull it back in a ponytail. My stomach growled at me again. I went to the laundry sink and cupped my hand to sip cold water. It's been five days since I've eaten anything, and the hunger pains have me hunched over. I plopped down in my dog bed, my hunger wouldn't let me get comfortable or nap.

An hour later, I was moving the clothes from the washers to the dryers. I sorted and started the next four loads to wash. I was lightheaded from the lack of nourishment and tried to steady myself.

I could hear laughter coming from the back of the house. I walked over to the other side of the basement, to the tiny window looking out at the back yard. It was dark out, but I could see people gathering around a large bonfire as the pool party died down.
I stood at the window and watched Blake and Cole feed the fire with logs. A few pups were left, and they had long sticks with marshmallows on the end they were roasting. I saw couples cuddling by the fire and wondered if I could be so lucky one day. I remember toasting marshmallows with my dad, everything was so different when he was alive.

I stared out the window for a few more minutes, I couldn't take it anymore. I decided to sneak out the

tiny window in the laundry room to look for food. I stood up on the dryer and quietly slid the window open. Any normal person would never fit through it, but I was small and underfed.
I slipped my head out first and quickly scrambled out the window. My ribs were burning in pain. I ducked behind a bush by the window to make sure no one was coming. Once I was sure the coast was clear, I ran towards the family homes and cabins closest to the pack house. The exercise left me feeling faint. I stayed in the shadows and watched.

I was standing behind a tree when I heard the back door open up at the house, I was near. I crouched down low and waited. A young boy came outside with a bag of garbage and put it in the trash a few feet away from me.

Please Goddess, do not let him catch me here. I stood frozen, not daring to breath. He looked like a nice kid, about eleven years old, I wondered if he would give me food if I begged. No, no, I couldn't risk asking and having the Alpha find out.

He went back inside, and I waited a few minutes before I ran towards the trash. I lifted the lid off and ripped the bag open. I removed the empty milk carton from the top, an empty bakery box, before I saw leftover dinner scraps. I dug into the spaghetti and meatballs that had been scraped off dinner plates, with bits of leftover salad.

I felt like a disgusting dog eating trash but the hunger pains in my stomach were driving me to do it. This isn't the first time I've had to dig through trash to eat, but hopefully, it will be the last time. I turn eighteen in two weeks and when I get my wolf, I should be able to hunt for food.

I spotted a piece of garlic bread that didn't seem touched, I lifted it to my mouth and devoured it practically moaning as I chewed. I was starting to feel full when I felt someone watching me. I looked around but didn't see anyone. I placed the lid back on the trash and ran back to the pack house.

I ducked behind the bush closest to the laundry room window again and waited. When I was sure no one was coming, I wiggled back down through the window on top of the dryer. I closed and locked the window before I jumped down off the dryer.

I went to the bathroom and brushed my teeth again and washed my face. I finally felt better as my stomach was full. I walked back to the window on the other side of the basement and stood on my tippy toes to look out at the back yard again.

The fire was dying down and Miranda stood close to the fire. I watched as Ranger walked over to her with a beer in his hand and started kissing her. His free hand squeezed her ass and she immediately jumped up to wrap her long legs around his waist.
She started running her fingers through Rangers thick beautiful hair. I wish I could run my fingers through his hair.

Ughh! What is wrong with me? It must be an Alpha thing; every unmated female would have to be blind not to want him.
"MIRANDA IS SUCH A SLUT." I mentally screamed in my head. She wasn't even his mate.

And that's when I saw the flames from the fire pit rise ten feet high for a moment and drop back down. Miranda was screaming about her hair getting singed and the next moment Blake and Cole were holding the garden hose and dousing Miranda and the bonfire down with water.

CHAPTER 4 – UNEXPECTED

I opened my eyes and saw the sun rising through the little window. I was feeling groggy from the pain pill I had taken last night to help with my ribs. I groaned and tried to stretch in my dog bed.

The cement walls and floor made everything feel cold down here. I walked over to the dryers and started them up to help warm up the laundry room. I stood next to them when I changed my clothes to keep warm.

I didn't have any pajamas, so I had to sleep in my clothes from the day before. My clothes consisted of random hand me downs from the pack. My shoes were pretty worn down, they didn't look like they would make it through the winter.

I was still standing by the dryers when I looked up and noticed a brown paper bag in front of the tiny window. The bag wasn't there last night when I crawled back through the window. Someone placed it there early this morning. I climbed on top of the dryer and slid the window open. I wasn't sure if I should take the bag. What if it was a trap or cruel trick?

I looked out the window and didn't see anyone. I wish I had my wolf already so that I could sniff the bag or maybe catch a scent. I reached my trembling hand out carefully and slowly picked up the bag. I sat down on top of the dryer, still holding the bag. A few moments passed and I was still staring at it, unsure of what to do. I took a deep breath and decided to look inside. Muffins, blueberry muffins and they looked delicious. I was debating eating them when I heard the lock tumble to the basement door. I jumped off the dryer and quickly stashed the bag behind the washer machines. I moved to the pile of clean towels on the folding table and started folding them, trying to look normal. Ursa appeared in the doorway of the laundry room with her arms crossed. "You need to restock the spare shift clothes at the tree line this morning, then get back here and finish the laundry."

"I'll do it now." I reached for the basket full of spare shifter shorts and shirts. She followed me out of the basement, and I went out the back door. I walked towards the forest with the basket in hand. It was nice being out of the laundry room and feeling the morning breeze.

In the distance, I could see warriors and pack members training at the training field. Alpha Ranger's big black wolf also stood out to me; he was training with a group of warriors. Beta Max was still in human form and turned to look in my direction.

I continued for the tree line and stepped in the forest. Everything was beautiful and green; I inhaled the fresh smell of pine and earth. I walked from each designated tree and placed spare clothes in small wooden boxes. When wolves shift back to human form, they're naked, spare clothes are placed just passed the tree line for them.

As I bent down to fill the last wooden box with clothes, I noticed an eerie silence in the forest. It was as if time stood still and even the wind was holding its breath. I heard a loud howl from behind me and many paws running fast through the woods in my direction. I was sure they would be at the tree line in a moment and I couldn't outrun them, so I climbed up into the pine tree.

I heard Ranger let out a loud howl from the training grounds. Fear bubbled in my chest. I looked down and saw red eyed wolves. Rogues! They were rogues and we were being attacked.

I gripped my arms around the tree and tried not to move or panic. I could hear clothes ripping and wolves shifting. I counted about fifty rogues. A large gray wolf stopped near the bottom of my tree; he was sniffing the laundry basket I had left. I stopped breathing and hugged the tree tightly, praying he didn't look up.

He shifted back to human form and was standing fully naked. "Come out, come out, wherever you are." He sang as he walked around the tree.

I wish I had the ability to mind-link with the pack so I could scream for help, but I couldn't because I didn't have my wolf yet.

"I spy a little dove in the tree." He called out.

I gasped and he laughed. He jumped up and grabbed the bottom branch and pulled himself up. He was moving pretty quickly up the tree. There was nothing I could do except climb down the back of the tree before he could reach me and make a run for it. I took off running and before I could gain speed, I was knocked down to the ground with the rogue laying on top of me. My broken ribs were aching.

"Leaving so soon?" He said flipping me over to face him.

I was pinned beneath him and he leaned into my neck to take a deep breath. "You smell delicious little dove." He growled as he tore open my shirt and bra exposing me to him.

"Please, please don't do this, I'm a pack slave." I cried.

"Then no one will care *little slave.*" He coldly said and clawed away at my pants.

I tried to fight back but it didn't faze him at all. I brought my hands up to his face in an attempt to scratch at his eyes, but he slapped me across my face, and I screamed out. I was no match for him.
"Feisty little thing, I like that." He grabbed a fist full of my hair and his other hand slid down between my legs ripping off my panties.
"Stop! Please don't." I sobbed. My lip was bleeding again, and the tears were clouding my vision. This can't be happening. He was going to rape me.

He positioned himself between my legs and I felt his hard member rubbing at my opening. He was getting ready to thrust inside and I closed my eyes tight, whimpering. Just then, I heard an angry growl and a large dark brown wolf appeared. The wolf emanated a strong aura and snarled at the rogue on top of me. It was Beta Max. The rogue shifted into his gray wolf and leaped at Max.

Max threw the rogue into a tree and jumped on top of him. In one swift move, he ripped out the rogue's throat and dropped his lifeless body to the ground.

Max shifted back and was standing naked a few feet away from me. I curled up on my side trying to cover up my naked body.

Ranger's big black wolf walked towards us and he growled. Max and Ranger stood still; their eyes glazed over as they spoke through the mind link. Max stepped over to the little wooden box that held clothes and put on some shorts. He handed me a shirt and turned his back so I could slip it on.

The Alpha's big black wolf come over to me and smelled me. I assumed he was checking to make sure I was okay. He took a few deep breaths before he turned and ran back towards the pack house letting out another howl. I slipped the shirt on and stood up. I was wasn't sure what to do, so I walked over to the basket I had left to pick it up, but Max grabbed it first.

"Lucy, are you okay? Would you like me to take you to the pack doctor?" Max's voice was laced with worry.

I shook my head, "no, I'm okay." I looked down at the ground and felt a bit embarrassed that Max had to save me again. I felt like such a weakling.

"Thank you for saving me again." My cheeks flushed red.

"Lucy, you don't have to thank me." He replied and rubbed the back of his neck. "Come on, I'll walk you back to the pack house."

When we came out of the tree line, we could see rogue bodies everywhere. We were one of the strongest packs in the country. I couldn't seem understand why fifty rogues would attack and feel like they stood a chance against Dark Moon. It was suicide.

As we reached the pack house, Max asked a question that surprised me. "Did you like the blueberry muffins I left you this morning?"

"That was you?" I whispered.

He nodded his head yes, with a sheepish grin on his face. "Lucy, I'm sorry, I know my Aunt Ursa could be really hard, but I had no idea it was so bad until I saw you last night." He saw me eating from the trash, oh no, my heart sank. I thought I sensed someone watching me last night. I'm sure my face was bright red with embarrassment.

"Please d-don't tell Ranger, I-I'm on punishment and am not allowed f-f-food until after tomorrow." I choked on my words as tears filled my eyes.

"I'm so sorry. That's a cruel punishment Lucy, I won't say anything. You can trust me." He pulled me into a hug. A hug that felt warm and safe. A hug that was truly meant to comfort. It was completely unexpected, and It felt so good to finally have a friend

CHAPTER 5 - FRIENDS

It's been two weeks since the rogue attack. Everyone has been busy with extra training and patrolling to bully me, including Miranda. My ribs have healed, and I've been feeling better than I have in a long time.

Max has been leaving food at my window ever since the blueberry muffins. Eating everyday has given me strengthen and energy. I'm able to complete my chores a little faster so I can get more sleep.
It's ten o'clock at night and I'm standing at the dryer folding the last stack of towels lost in my thoughts. Tomorrow is my eighteenth birthday. I'm not sure if I'm feeling scared or excited, maybe a little of both. I should be able to shift for the first time and get my wolf. I can't wait to meet my wolf; I hope she likes me.

Wolves are strong by nature and I'm worried that she will find me weak.

Once I get my wolf, I will be able to mind-link with the pack. I will also be stronger and heal quickly. My scent will become stronger and I will be able to find my mate, if he's in this pack. My mate! I sigh. The one person who is made for you and will protect you. I was daydreaming about my mate and having my first kiss, when I heard a tap-tap on my little window. It was Max.

I jumped up on the dryer and slid open the window. "How's the almost birthday girl?" Max asked with a big smile on his face. He was holding a box of pizza.

"PIZZA!" I squealed. I can't remember the last time I had pizza.

"I wasn't sure what you'd like so I got the meat lovers pizza." Max opened the box and slid it on the ground by the window.

"Perfect choice, all werewolves are meat lovers." I laughed.

"Dig in, we've got to get you healthy and strong for your first shift tomorrow." He sat down on the grass with his back against the house next to my tiny window. It's been years since anyone wished me a happy birthday and now, I was also getting pizza.

I slid my hand out the window and carefully lifted a heavy slice of pizza. It was loaded with Italian sausage, pepperoni, ham and bacon. It smelled so good; I was practically drooling.

I took a bite, "Mmmm, oh my Goddess Max, this is AMAZING."

He let out a laugh, picked up a slice. "It sure is," he said as he bit down on a slice.

I sat on top of the dryer and he sat outside under the stars. We both ate in comfortable silence. We had spent several nights eating like this and talking.

"Lucy, Ranger asked me to go with him to the Night Howlers Pack tomorrow to discuss important matters. We're leaving at dawn and should be back before sunset, so I can help you with your first shift."

"Sounds great. Thank you, Max."

"Would you like another slice?" He offered.

"I wish I could, I'm stuffed." I grinned up at him as I patted my full belly.

"Here, take this in case you wake up at night and need a snack." He wrapped up another big slice of pizza in the napkins and passed it through the window to me.

"Thanks Max, see you tomorrow night." I smiled back and closed the window as he left.

I set the slice of pizza down on top of my plastic tub and curled up in my dog bed. Max has officially become my favorite person at Dark Moon pack.

Max was twenty-three years old, two years younger than Ranger. He had found his mate when he was eighteen and they were expecting their first pup a year later. His mate, Olivia, was pregnant at the time and had been killed in the same rogue attack as my father and our Luna.

Max was the complete opposite of his younger sister Miranda. As I thought about Max, I laid my head down and prayed to the Moon Goddess that Max would have a second chance mate someday. If anyone deserved to be happy, it was Max. Whoever he ended up with, would be one lucky she wolf.

My eye lids became heavy and closed shut. Sleeping with a full stomach is amazing ... that pizza is amazing, I thought as I drifted off.

"Lucy."

"Lucy."

I was awakened from my slumber and opened my sleepy eyes. It was still dark. I thought I heard someone call my name.

"Hello Lucy."

I sat up in my bed. "Who's there?" I called out. I heard a female voice giggle, but I didn't see anyone.

"Lucy, it's me, Lia. I'm your wolf." The voice said.

It must be after midnight, technically making it my birthday already.

"Happy Birthday Lucy!" She said.

"Thank you." I said out loud.

"Lucy, you don't have to speak out loud, I can hear you

in your head."

"Oh right." I grinned. I closed my eyes and focused on Lia; I could see her in my head. She was beautiful. The color of sun and fire, with the same amber colored eyes as me. Her tail was wagging, and she looked like she was smiling, if that's even possible for a wolf.
"I'm so happy to finally have you with me." Feeling grateful to have someone to talk to all the time.

"Lucy, I've always been with you since the day we were born. I've just been dormant until your eighteenth birthday."

"When will I start to shift?" I asked excitedly.

"You can shift at will anytime. I'd like to stretch my legs out and go for a run soon please." She told me. "You should probably have something to eat first, the first shift will take lots of energy."
I grabbed the extra slice of pizza Max had given me and started to devour it. I heard Lia growl with pleasure at the pizza.

"Delicious!" She practically purred.

"We could go out tonight with Max for our first shift." I told her.

"Lucy, you're going to want to shift alone the first time." Lia said.

"Why?"

"It will be easier to explain when you've shifted, come on, we've got some time before sunrise."

"Okay, but we have to be really careful, I'm not allowed to leave the house, let alone at night."

"Don't worry, we'll be fine. Technically, it's early in the morning and not night." She sassed back.

I jumped up on the dryer and opened the tiny window to climb out. I ran towards the forest as quick as I can and seemed to be running faster than I ever have in my human form. When I reached my favorite fallen log, I stripped off my clothes so they wouldn't rip when I shifted and carefully hid them in a bush next to the log.

"Now what?" I asked Lia.
"Close your eyes and focus on what I look like." She told me. "Don't be afraid, it's going to hurt at first, but after a few times it will be quick and painless."

I was a little anxious about the pain part. I closed my eyes, took a deep breath, and focused on the beautiful wolf inside of me. I fell to my knees and heard the cracking of bones. The pain was white hot, and I tried not to scream because I didn't want to attract any of the patrols.

"Focus, focus Lucy, you've got this, almost there." Lia called out.
I was panting hard and drooling. I opened my eyes after ten minutes and saw my paws were digging in the wet earth beneath them. MY PAWS!! I was standing on all four legs! My fur was ... golden?

I don't think I've ever seen such a light colored wolf before, I thought to myself.

"You haven't Lucy. We're special." She said.

Of course, even in wolf form, I'm different. I hope the other pack members won't pick on me for it, I bitterly thought to myself, knowing they would.

"If they want to live, they won't!" Lia growled.
"Easy there girl, you want to go for a run?" I asked and she yipped back at me.

I felt Lia take over and start running faster than I could have ever imagined. We jumped over logs, bushes and rocks. We zipped through the trees feeling the wind in our fur. I felt so free.
We made our way over to the small creek up ahead, Lia bent down to lap up water. I saw our reflection; my eyes were the same color and our fur almost looked like it was on fire. I looked up to the sky and saw the beautiful moon hanging above me. I felt the urge to howl with joy but had to fight against it because I didn't want anyone to catch me.

This is amazing! I thought to myself as I looked around. I could see everything so much clearer with my wolf vision. Colors were somehow richer and tiny details had become sharp. My sense of smell and hearing seemed stronger too, like super senses.
We took off running again and rolling around in the forest. I could see the sky was getting lighter which meant that sunrise was coming. We made our way back towards the tree line to the fallen log where my clothes were hidden. I was unsure of how to shift back.

"Just imagine your human self." Lia told me.

I focused on my human self and heard the sound of bones cracking. I fell face first onto the forest floor and struggled to keep from screaming. My joints were burning, and my energy completely drained out of me. I wasn't sure if I actually passed out.

I was curled in the fetal position on the damp floor, naked. I couldn't move. I heard some fast approaching footsteps and closed my eyes. Lia was suddenly on edge and excited. A delicious smell of honey, cinnamon and apples hit me. The last thing I heard was a deep voice growl, "MINE."

CHAPTER 6 – MATE

It was dark and the only light in the room was coming from a warm crackling fire in the stone fireplace. I was sleeping in a real bed, with the most comfortable pillows and blankets. It's been years since I slept in a real bed. Lifting the covers, I looked down to see that I was wearing a large shirt.

The ceiling was high and made of logs, I was in a cabin. It was a large single room log cabin with two over-sized chairs sitting by the fireplace. A small kitchen and a door to what I believe is a bathroom.

It smelled delicious in here, like warm apple pie. I inhaled deeply, cinnamon, apples and honey. "MATE!" Lia jumped up and down.

"Are you sure?" I asked her.

"Yes, MATE brought us here." She wagged her tail.

I heard some movement coming from inside the bathroom and a moment later the door swung open. He was standing in the doorway with nothing, but a towel wrapped around his waist. I recognized those beautiful blue eyes and my breath hitched in my throat. "Alpha!" I gasped.

"You're awake." He stepped to the side of the bed.

My eyes trailed up his abs, to his chest, chiseled jaw and back to his eyes. I had never dared to really look at him like this before. He had a smirk on his face that told me that he knew I was checking him out.

"Mate is so handsome and he's an Alpha!" Lia gushed.

Ranger sat down on the bed and leaned into my neck. He inhaled deeply, "Mine." He growled in my ear as he peppered kisses on my neck. He pulled away and held my face in his hands staring deeply into my eyes. "Beautiful." He whispered. My skin was tingling under his touch.

I looked down at my hands to try and hide my blush. "Where are we?" I managed to ask.

"My cabin on the pack grounds. I found you after your shift and brought you here, you've been sleeping all day." He said.

"Oh, thank you." I whispered.

"Rex has been hounding me all day to hold you." He said as he moved closer.

"Who's Rex?" I asked.

"My wolf." He chuckled.

Lia purred at the mention of her mate.

"The old mutt wants to know your wolfs name."

"Lia, her name is Lia." I told him and Lia let out a joyous howl in my head.
Before I could say anything, Rangers eyes seemed to darken, and he kissed me. Sparks started tingling throughout my body under his touch. His lips were demanding and tasted oh so sweet. I wasn't sure exactly what to do but Lia kept pushing me. My hands made

their way to the top of his head and I ran my fingers through his hair, pulling him closer to me. Ranger let out a growl of approval.

He laid me back on the pillows and continued to deepen the kiss. His hand sent waves of tingles as he reached down my leg and trailed his way up. He moved to my neck, kissing and licking. A soft moan of pleasure slipped through my lips and my heart was pounding in my chest.

I stared up at the ceiling, the shadows and light from the fireplace were dancing on the beams. Ranger is my mate, I thought to myself. I won't be a slave anymore; he will take care of me and protect me. "Mate will take care of US and love US." Lia corrected me.

Ranger kissed my neck on the soft spot that would soon have his mark and I let out a loud moan. Oh Goddess, that felt so good. I could feel the heat pooling between my legs. He laid on top of me and I felt his member hard against my thigh. His hands grabbed the bottom of the shirt I was wearing, and he slipped it off me.

He looked down at my naked body with desire burning in his eyes. He kissed me again and his hand massaged my breast. I let my hands roam down his back feeling his muscles. His mouth kissed down my neck and to my other breast. He took my nipple in his mouth and sucked on it; his other hand moved down between my legs.
I gasped as he rubbed my lips feeling my wetness. The waves of electric tingles had my body screaming for more. The need to be with him was so strong, it was all I wanted.

"Someone is so wet and ready for me." Ranger grinned as he slipped a finger into my core. "So tight." He groaned.

I closed my eyes and threw my head back moaning with pleasure as his finger moved in and out of me. It felt so good. He added another finger and started moving faster. I let out another moan as his thumb circled on my clit. He grabbed my hair with one hand and worked his magic with the other hand. I felt my body tense up with a burning need to release.

"Look at me Lucy. I want you to look in my eyes when you cum." He ordered in a rough voice. His blue eyes were dark, and his wolf was close to the surface.

My mouth was slightly open, and I was breathing hard. I was squirming as I reached the brink of orgasm, ready to explode. My pussy clenched down hard on his fingers and wave after wave rocked through me as I cried out with pleasure. It felt amazing.

Ranger brought his fingers up to his mouth and licked them clean, tasting me. "You're mine Lucy." He said as he positioned himself on top of me removing his towel. Seconds later he was pushing the tip of his cock into me, he stopped at the barrier.

"It will only hurt for a few moments; I'll try to be gentle." I nodded my head.
With a quick thrust he was buried deep inside me. My nails dug into his back and a few tears escaped from the side of my eyes. He kissed the tears away and then began moving.

"You're so fucking tight." He groaned as he stretched

me out, stroke after stroke, to fit his cock perfectly. Pain was replaced with pleasure and the animal in me craved him. I was his and he was mine. I kissed his neck and he growled with pleasure. His thrusts became deeper and deeper and I felt myself clenching on his cock ready to release again.

"Cum for me baby." He said and I lost it. My body was in pure bliss as I rode the wave of my orgasm again.

"That's a good girl." Ranger continued to trail kisses and bites all over my body. He started thrusting deep and slow as he kissed me again. He slipped his tongue into my mouth and I eagerly kissed back.

My hands explored his chest and I remembered all the times I had daydreamed about rubbing his chest. The tattoo on his chest and arm was so sexy. I could hardly believe that he was all mine. I looked into his eyes again and there was such intensity as he was looking at me and thrusting with purpose. His own need to release was building. I wrapped my legs around his waist and felt him even deeper inside of me.

"Fuck, you feel so good!" With a few more thrusts and a growl, he released his seed deep inside me as another wave of orgasm hit me at the same time.

When I woke up in the morning, the sun was shining through the kitchen window and the fire in the fireplace had died down. Ranger was sitting at the foot of the bed staring at me.

"Mate is so handsome." Lia said to me.

I looked down and blushed. I felt the soreness between my legs from last night. What an amazing night it was.

I started wondering if I should get up and make him breakfast when he spoke.

"Lucy, I think the Moon Goddess made a mistake. I can't accept you as my mate. Dark Moon pack can't have a weak Luna and you've never been able to defend yourself. The pack won't accept you, the female Alpha needs to be strong and that takes years of training."

Tears swelled up in my eyes. Of course, this would be my luck I thought as I heard Lia howl out in pain. She was about to lose her mate because of me. Because I was weak. My father was going to let me start training when I was fourteen, to be a warrior like him, but I never got the chance.

"I can train, I can become stronger!" I said with tears running down my face.

"I've waited seven years to find my mate, now that I know you are unfit to be Luna, I need to select a strong she wolf for the pack. A weak Luna makes us all weak, and we can't risk that. I will not banish you Lucy, my wolf will not allow that."

"Please don't do this Ranger." I begged.

"I am your Alpha! You are to address me as Alpha at all times." He roared back at me as he stood up. "You will not tell anyone about us, and you will continue to stay in the pack and work as normal."
My heart felt like it was shattering into a million pieces.

Before I could say another word, he said the words I feared the most ... "I, Ranger LaRue, Alpha of Dark

Moon pack, reject you Lucy Michaels, as my mate and Luna."

Lia was howling in pain and my head was spinning. The pain from the mate bond breaking was unbearable, especially after mating. I tried to stand with the blanket wrapped around me, but the pain in my chest brought me to my knees as I screamed out loud. Trembling in pain, I crumbled to the ground, thankfully, the darkness consumed me.

CHAPTER 7 – WEAK

I opened my eyes, I was alone, on the floor right where he left me. The clothes I had left hidden in the bush when I shifted were sitting on a chair in front of the fireplace. I really wanted to shower, to wash away his scent from my body, but I didn't dare use his shower. I needed to get out of here.

I put my clothes on as fast as I could and left the cabin before Ranger came back. The cabin was by the lake on pack property and it was going to be about three miles back to the pack house. I started walking back along the path.

Alone with my thoughts, I wondered why the Moon Goddess cursed me. A mate is supposed to be the other half of your soul, made just for you, to love and protect you. Mine had just used me and threw me away, like I was garbage. Like I was nothing.

I heard Lia let out a low painful howl in my head. I could feel her pain. It wasn't her fault, it was all my fault, I was weak. She's probably going to leave me too. Everyone leaves me. Even my own mate didn't want me. I felt the tears fill my eyes.

"I'm sorry Lia, this is all my fault." I sobbed.

"We are not weak, we're stronger than they know." She told me.

I cried as I walked back absentmindedly through the

woods. Thinking about what happened last night and how I could have been so stupid. Did I actually believe he would want me, a pack slave? The pull of the mate bond really fooled me into believing he wanted me. I neared the tree line and walked across the grassy field towards the pack house. I entered through the back of the house at the kitchen so I could slip into the basement quickly and shower before anyone picked up Ranger's scent on me.

When I stepped inside, a dozen set of eyes stared at me. Alpha Ranger was having lunch at the huge kitchen island with Gamma Blake and Delta Cole. A few other warriors, including Beth, were also having lunch. Miranda was seated next to Ranger and ran her fingers through his hair as if he was her mate.

"Let me out, I'll kick her ass!" Lia snarled at me.

The silence was broken when Ursa came into the kitchen. "Where the hell have you been all night? Out whoring around?"

Miranda laughed watching her aunt abuse me. I froze, I couldn't tell them where I really was. "I'm sorry." I managed to say. I saw Ranger return to his sandwich as if he was disinterested.

"You have a lot of nerve standing here like that. If you're going to run wild and free all night long like a dog, then you will sleep outside in the dog kennel tonight." She grabbed my hair and yanked me to the back yard.

The kennel was a metal cage intended for large dogs but was kept in the back yard to punish naughty pups. It was too small to stand or shift in. Everyone followed us out the kitchen and to the kennel. They laughed as she shoved me into the kennel and kicked me before she locked the door.

"She's so pathetic." Beth laughed.

"Here doggy, doggy!" Someone whistled and they all burst out laughing.

"Did you get a whiff of her, she stinks." Miranda called out. "Enjoy your bath tonight when it rains."

Ranger just stood there stone faced. He was the Alpha and he did nothing. I was with him last night; he could have stepped in to keep Ursa from punishing me, but he didn't. I was trying not to cry in front of them as my eyes filled with unshed tears. I curled down in a tight ball and they started walking back to the pack house.

Ranger was the last to turn and walk away. I heard him utter "weak," as he left. I kept my head down and Lia growled in my head. He didn't care about me.

A few hours had passed and the smell of dinner cooking in the kitchen was floating in the wind, teasing my nostrils. My stomach grumbled; you'd think I'd get use to going without food after four years of torture. I spotted a large dark brown wolf running towards my kennel. It was Max, he stopped and sniffed the kennel, his wolf let out a whine.

"Lucy, I've been looking all over for you, where have you been?" I heard his voice in my head.

"M-Max? Can you hear me?" I wasn't sure exactly how to work the mind link.

"Yes, I can hear you. Remember, you just picture the person you want to link and then speak." He told me. "And don't forget to put up your wall when you want to keep your thoughts private."

"Right, thank you Max. I'm sorry I worried you. I got my wolf hours after you left, and she insisted on a run."

He sniffed the air again. "I can smell the Alpha on you Lucy, did something happen?"

"Please." I looked into his wolf's eyes, pleading. "I'm not supposed to tell anyone." The tears started falling from my eyes and the sting of rejection burned in my chest. The sky had turned gray and a storm was blowing our way. Max's wolf laid down on all fours in front of my kennel.

"He's your mate, isn't he?" Max asked but it was more of a statement to confirm what he already knew.

I nodded my head.

"Did he reject you?" His voice was laced with anger.

I nodded again.

"That stupid shit!" He growled. "I'm sorry Lucy, no one deserves that."

"Please don't tell anyone." I begged.

"I won't say a word." He sighed. "How did you end up in here?"

"Ursa!" I said.

"And he did nothing to help you?" He growled with disgust in his tone.

"No." I whispered. Not only did my mate reject me, but he left me out here to suffer. He just stood there and let Ursa give me a punishment I didn't deserve. He was the one that carried me back to his cabin, that made me believe he wanted me.

Max stood up and looked towards the pack house. "Alpha just mind linked me; he wants me in his office. I have patrol tonight, but I'll bring you something to eat." I nodded my head and Max made his way back to the pack house.

I curled back down trying to keep my body heat in as the first drops of rain started coming down. It was dark out and I was shivering. The cold night air whipped the rain around mercilessly. My clothes were soaked through and I really had to pee. I saw a flash of lightning in the distance and heard the crack of thunder.
I was curled up as tight as I could trying to stay warm. Lia had been quiet, except for an occasional whimper. She was hurting too, I felt terrible for her, she deserved her mate. I was the problem; I was not good enough for an Alpha. What the hell was the Moon Goddess thinking, of course Ranger would never accept me.

"How's it going Lucy, are you hanging in there?" I heard Max sneak up to my kennel in the dark.

"I'm hanging in there." I shivered.

"Here, I tried to find what would slip through the cage

holes." He opened up a ziplock bag and slipped me two big juicy looking sausages, a bread roll he had to break in half to fit through the openings in the cage and string cheese.

"Thank you so much." I said as I ate the delicious food.

"Anytime Lucy." He stood with a look of pity in his eyes. He waved goodbye and slipped away into the darkness, to return to patrolling.

The storm continued all night long. I could see the sky start to lighten up from the east, the sun would be rising soon behind the rain clouds. I couldn't catch a wink of sleep because it was so cold and wet.

I spent most of the night replaying what Ranger had said to me. That I was weak and had never been able to defend myself. That I was unfit to be Luna and the pack would never accept me. I was only fourteen when I was orphaned. I had no money and no one to help me.

HE was the Alpha. HE made me a pack slave. HE allowed the others to bully and beat me. HE never let me train. HE allowed them to starve me.

I heard the back door to the pack house open and close, HE stepped out on the back deck that had a covered patio to protect him from the rain. He was wearing a warm pair of sweatpants and a fitted shirt. He held a cup of coffee in his hand and stood there sipping it while staring me down.
My heart was aching, I couldn't stand to look at him. I did the only thing I could do; I turned my back to him and heard him growl. "You will not disrespect your Alpha."

Before I knew it, he had pulled me out of the kennel and held me up by my neck with my feet dangling. I tried to claw at his hand but had no energy. His touch was still sending tingles through my body and the heat felt good.

Max appeared from the woods. "Alpha." He called out. Ranger looked at him and then threw me into a puddle of mud. I could hardly move, and my body was shivering. Max knelt down by my side and felt my icy cold arm. I heard Ranger growl as Max rubbed my arm. "She's hypothermic and needs medical attention." He said.

"Weak, she's weak!" Ranger growled.

CHAPTER 8 – BLANKETS & TOWELS

Max picked me up from the mud puddle and started running to the clinic. He mind linked Dr. Baker so she could meet us there. Dr. Baker was waiting at the door and directed Max to take me to room three. No one was at the clinic this early so she worked alone to treat me.

"Is there anything I can do to help?" Max asked Dr. Baker.

"I need to get her out of these clothes, please grab an arm full of heated blankets from the warmer by the nurse's station."

I was stripped naked and under a sheet when Max came back with the blankets. They piled the blankets over me, and I stopped shivering after an hour. My wolf healing started to kick in and Dr. Baker brought me some hot chicken broth to sip.

Max came into the room holding some clothes. "I thought you could use some dry clothes when you're released, so I went to your room and picked some up." He removed the blankets from me and replaced them with new blankets from the warmer. Then, he pulled up a chair and sat beside my bed.

I felt a little embarrassed knowing he saw my small pile of clothes in the tub. As if he read my mind, he asked...

"Lucy, is that all you have, in the plastic tub?"

I couldn't even answer back, I just nodded.

"How could my aunt be so cruel?" He stood up and anger was radiating from him. "I couldn't even find an extra pair of shoes and yours are covered in mud."

Max paced the room, "I've asked my youngest sister Megan, to bring over a pair of shoes and a warm jacket. She's about your size."

His sister Megan was a year younger than me, shy and quiet. Unlike Miranda, Megan was very smart and tutored kids at school. It's hard to believe that Miranda is actually related to Max and Megan.

"That's very kind of her, thank you." My cheeks flushed.

"Are you ready for another cup of broth or would you like something to eat Lucy?" Dr. Baker came into the room.

My hand went to my heart and there was a burning feeling. It felt like someone stabbed me in the chest and I cried out in pain. The stabbing pain intensified, and I felt it in my stomach as well. I screamed in pain. It was like a vice grip on my heart. It started to spread and was complete agony.

Tears were streaming down my face and I could see Dr. Baker moving quickly to get a syringe. "What the hell is going on?" I cried.

"Mate," Lia said. "Mate is with someone else." She let out a loud sorrowful howl in my head.

Dr. Baker injected me with a sedative to help ease the pain. "Lucy did you find your mate?"

"He didn't want me." I panted.

"Did he speak the words of rejection to break the bond?" She asked.

"Yes."

"Did you accept the rejection yet?"

"No, not yet." I replied as tears continued to stream down my face. I was going to wait a few weeks to see if he would change his mind, for Lia's sake, I hoped he would.

I continued to lay there for the next hour trying hard to ignore the pain. Max sat silently next to my bed watching me and swapped the blankets again for heated ones as they cooled. When it was over, I felt exhausted.

I had shivered all night in the rain with no sleep. I fought back hypothermia and I experienced the cheating mate pains. What I needed now was some sleep, so I closed my eyes but was soon disrupted.

"Lucy... Lucy!" I heard Rangers voice come through the mind link.

"Yes Alpha?"

"I need my room cleaned and sheets changed within the hour." He ordered.

"Yes Alpha."

I looked at Max and sighed. "Breaks over, Alpha just mind linked me. He needs his room cleaned and sheets changed within the hour."

Max growled. "You have got to be kidding me! You're in no condition to do anything. You need rest."

"If I don't go, I will be punished again. This is the life of a rejected and unwanted pack slave." I sighed.

I got dressed and slipped on the shoes Megan had given Max. They were the nicest pair of shoes I've worn in years, they looked practically brand new. Dr. Baker handed me a turkey sandwich as I left and insisted I eat.

Max and I walked back to the pack house. The rain had ceased for the moment, so we walked slow to allow me to finish my sandwich. When we reached the door, I took the beautiful jacket off that Megan also gave Max and tried to hand it back to him.

"What are you doing?" He asked.

"Returning the jacket and shoes, please thank Megan for lending them to me."

"Lucy, she gave those to you. Please, keep them."

I didn't know what to say. It was the nicest thing anyone has done for me in a very long time. I threw my arms at him and hugged him.

Twenty minutes later, I was standing outside of Ranger's bedroom with clean sheets and all my cleaning supplies. My heart was racing, I knocked first and waited. No answer, so I went inside. The room was empty, thank Goddess!

I moved fast stripping the bed and putting new bedding on. I picked up the room, dusted, vacuumed and emptied the trash. I made my way to the bathroom and cleaned it. His shower gel scent was still lingering in the air and smelled nice.

I picked up his clothes hamper and walked out into the hallway. I drop the dirty clothes in the laundry shoot that brought them down to me in the basement. I returned to the room, put the hamper back in the bathroom and stocked the shelf with fresh towels. I was ready to leave when I noticed a pillow was crooked. I went to the bed and bent over to straighten it out.

Ranger's scent filled the room and I could feel his eyes on my ass as I was bent over the bed. I stood up and felt his arms snake around my waist, he buried his head in my neck and inhaled. I reminded myself to keep strong and fight against the mate bond.

"I'm done Alpha. Is there anything else you need?" I kept my voice even and cool.

"I have everything I need Lucy, but my wolf wants you."

"What's the matter? Didn't his wolf get enough of the slut he was fucking this morning?" Lia sneered in my head.

"Lia, that's not nice." He whispered in my ear and bit down on my earlobe.

Oh no, the mind link! He can hear my thoughts and

heard what Lia said. "I'm sorry Alpha, she's just upset, there's been a lot going on." I replied as I turned to face him. His blue eyes stared at me with such intensity.

"Get on your knees and show me how sorry you are!" He ordered.
He wants me to beg? I thought to myself. Hope he doesn't ask me to kiss his shoe. I got down on my knees and clasped my hands together, I was ready to apologize again when I heard his zipper open.

He reached into his pants and pulled his cock out. Stroking it a few times he looked down at me with lust in his eyes. He wants me to please him! I panicked and tried to scoot away.
"Bite him!" Lia said outraged.

"Lucy, you are mine and will do as I say." He demanded bringing his cock towards my mouth.

"I'm not your mate!" I shot back and ran to the bathroom. I tried to close the door and lock it, but Ranger grabbed the door and pushed me back. He was fast and strong.

He grabbed both my wrists and held them to the wall, above my head. His lips came crashing down on mine rough and demanding. I held my lips shut tight, even though the stupid mate bond was pulling me to kiss him.

"KISS ME BACK!" He growled and I could feel his wolf taking over.
I turned my head to the side, and he growled again. He began licking and sucking on my neck, the tingles were shooting throughout my body. His scent was de-

licious, I could feel the wetness between my legs. I squeezed my legs together as tight as possible.

He took another deep breath and a low growl rumbled in his chest. "I smell your arousal Lucy." His husky voice taunted next to my ear. "I know you want me."

"Let me go, I have work to do." I struggled back.

"What's the hurry? All the other she wolves would give anything to be able to spend quality time with their Alpha." He said and my wolf felt a jealous pain at the thought of her mate with other she wolves.

"WHAT THE HELL IS GOING ON HERE?" Miranda yelled from the door with her fists balled up and her face in rage.

"Babe, she walked in on me taking a piss and I was going to punish her." Ranger said as he zipped his pants back up.

"Maybe she should be punished in a dungeon!" She glared at me, still fuming. Surely, she didn't believe his lies, did she?

"Next time you deliver clean towels Lucy, you better fucking knock first, or you will end up in the hole. **NOW GET BACK TO THE BASEMENT!**" He roared.

CHAPTER 9 – FLAMES

I spent the rest of the afternoon and evening down in the laundry room washing, drying, folding and Ironing clothes for everyone who lived in the pack house. The storm continued to pour down, which means that most of the pack members were home all-day eating. There would be no scraps or leftovers for me today. They were having roasted chicken, potatoes and vegetables for dinner tonight, it smelled mouthwatering.

I heard the basement door open and close, perhaps I was wrong? Maybe Ursa put some food in my dog bowl by the stairs after all. She never gave me food on a plate or silverware, she just dumped whatever scraps I was lucky enough to get into a dog bowl by the stairs.

I looked towards the stairs and saw Ranger walking to the Laundry room in my direction. The closer he got the stronger his scent got. He's holding a duffle bag in his hand and I assume he's got laundry for me.

"You can leave the laundry on the ground Alpha, I'll get it." I called out and turned my attention back to the socks I was matching and rolling.

"I wanted to deliver this load of laundry personally." He stared intensely at me.

"No need to trouble yourself Alpha, you could have just dropped it in the Laundry shoot to me."

"Oh, but this is a special package Lucy."

"Then I'll be sure to take extra care when handling your special laundry Alpha." I said with a hint of sarcasm in my voice. What the hell did he have, a silk Armani shirt?

He opened the bag and pulled out a set of sheets. I caught a familiar scent from them and saw dried blood on the sheets. They were his sheets from the cabin, the loss of my virginity stained on them.

"Proof that you belong to me Lucy. That you willingly gave yourself to me." He threw the sheets at my feet.

I stared down at them for a moment and slowly lifted my eyes to meet his "You rejected me. I belong to no one."

"I need a strong Luna for the pack Lucy, but that doesn't mean I can't have you as a mistress."

I could hear Lia growling with anger.

"I'm nothing more than a weak slave to this pack, would the Alpha actually stoop so low and share my dog bed on the cold cement floor?"

"I will give you a bedroom upstairs."

"Your father gave me a bedroom upstairs. You let Ursa take it away. I will not whore myself for a bedroom!" I snapped.

A look of hurt flashed across his face as we stood staring at each other. A moment later we were standing in complete darkness, the power had gone out. There was a lot of commotion going on upstairs.

"The storm must have caused a power outage." He said.

I moved slowly out into the basement storage area and reached for a shelf. There was a box of glass jar candles on the top shelf. I stood on my tippy toes, but I was only five foot, three inches and couldn't reach them. Ranger pressed himself up against my back and reached up over me to bring the box down. I could feel the warmth of his body and the tingles shooting inside me as his arms brushed against mine.

"Thank you." I whispered.

I removed a big candle and a book of matches, then I lit the candle. "You should take the rest of the candles upstairs, there's another box on the shelf if you need more." I told him. He stared at me for a moment with a soft look in his eyes, then he nodded and left with the box of candles.

I went back into the laundry room with my candle and set it on top of the dryer machine. They had all stopped working when the power cut out, but they were dry, so I started hanging and folding them. I silently prayed the power would come back soon, so I could keep the room warm by running the dryers.

An hour later, I heard the basement door open again and thought it was Ranger. I looked at the figure approaching me and saw my favorite smile. It was Max.

"Are you okay Lucy?"

"I am now." I smiled back.

"The power is going to be out most of the night, a truck hit a major power line, everyone North of town is without power." He explained to me.

I sniffed the air, something smelled different about Max. I inhaled deeply, it was garlic, ginger and soy sauce. He smiled at me and removed a takeout carton of Chinese food hidden inside his jacket and some chop sticks.

"Chicken and vegetable chow mein." He grinned. And for dessert, he reached into his jacket pocket, pulled out an apple and a bag of M&M's.

My stomach growled. "Thank you." I hugged him.

"Enjoy, I'll see you in the morning." He said as he quickly slipped out of the basement before anyone caught him down here.

I hid the apple and M&Ms in my plastic tub under some clothes. I placed the candle on the floor and sat on my bed in the corner of the laundry room to eat my chow mein. The last time I used chop sticks was when my dad took me to have sushi for the first time in the city. My dad was amazing, he use to take me out for father daughter days. He was always, kind, patient and loving. I never understood how the Moon Goddess could pair him with Ursa after my mom passed.

I lifted a big piece of chicken from the chow mein and stuffed it into my mouth, this was delicious. I sat quietly enjoying the food by candlelight and listening to the rain outside. I don't think Max will ever understand how much he's done for me, I thought to myself. Too bad he wasn't my mate.

"Our mate doesn't deserve us." Lia said.

"Lia, do you think the Moon Goddess made a mistake?"

"I don't think she made a mistake Lucy. I think you do not understand how powerful and strong you really are."

"What do you mean, I never learned to fight, hunt or train." I told her as I chewed on a large piece of broccoli.

"There is more than what is at the surface Lucy."

I was chewing on long delicious noodles, lost in thought. I stared at the flame of the candle flickering before me feeling full and content. The flame attracted me to it, as if calling my name.
I moved my hand towards the candle and saw the flame grow six inches high. That's strange, I thought and pulled my hand back. Maybe I just imagined that? I tried it again and the flame rose ten inches high from the candle.

"Picture the flame in your hands Lucy." Lia called out to me.

"It will burn me." I told her.

"No, it won't, you have a golden wolf, Lucy." She said with great pride.

"Golden wolf? That's a myth!" I told her.

"Then you're talking to a myth." She pushed me again. "Imagine yourself holding the fire and controlling it."

I stared at the flame for a moment and set my food down. It was calling me. I held my hand out and pictured a flame in the palm of my hand. A small flame jumped up from the candle and grew into a big ball in my hand!

"How is this even possible?" I said out loud in shock.

It didn't burn or hurt me in anyway. It felt comfortable and warm and radiated power through my veins.

I imagined the flame moving to my other hand and suddenly I was holding two big balls of fire.

"What do I do with it now?"

"Imagine them burning out." Lia told me.

I did what she said and suddenly the flames were gone. I sat quietly in the dark for a while, with nothing but a single candle burning. I was wondering if this was dark magic or a curse. Maybe I was part witch? Both my parents were regular wolfs... I think.

"Lucy, you have been blessed by the Moon Goddess." Lia told me.

And to think, the only blessing I really wanted from the Moon Goddess was a loving mate. I wasn't sure what to do with this power or how to control it. If anyone finds out, I could be seen as a threat and possibly hunted down. Why would I be blessed with such a gift? Maybe I could sneak into the pack library and find a book on wolf legends to try and figure this out.

I wasn't sure what time it was, but I needed to take

a shower before going to sleep, so I took the candle into the bathroom with me. I turned on the water and stripped off my clothes. There was a comfort in the candlelight as the flame flickered. I washed my hair, then my face and finally my body.

I was deep in thought and taking a final rinse when the shower curtain was yanked off the shower rod. I was so startled I screamed. Ranger was standing there, holding the crumbled shower curtain in his hand. His eyes roamed my body as they turned darker.

I shut the water off and grabbed the towel to cover myself. Ranger let out a growl and lunged at me yanking the towel away. He started kissing my neck and trailing his hand on my body, he was still holding the shower curtain in his other hand. His roaming hand reached between my legs and forced two fingers inside me. My body wanted to betray me, it yearned for him and his touch. I did the only thing I could think of.

I imagined the flame from the candle catching the shower curtain on fire that he was still holding. In an instant he let me go and was trying to stomp out the fire on the burning curtain. I grabbed the towel and wrapped it around my body. "You should be more careful around candles Alpha."

He sighed and ran his fingers through his thick black hair. He stared at me and I could sense the internal struggle he was having with his wolf. "I came down for the other box of candles." He said as he walked away.

CHAPTER 10 – JEALOUS

It's been over a week since the night of the power outage, I haven't seen Ranger around much. He's been busy meeting with other Alpha's about the recent rogue problems. Several packs have had similar attacks and it seems as though the attacks are all related. Unfortunately, since Max is the Beta, he's been pretty busy with Ranger too, but he still finds the time to leave me food.

This morning he left me a zip lock bag against the window that had two hard boiled eggs, four slices of bacon and a banana.

"Mmmmmmm bacon, I love bacon." Lia said practically drooling.

I opened the bag and wolfed down the bacon. It was delicious. I cracked one of the hard boiled eggs, took a bite of it, and instantly felt nauseous. I spit out the egg in my mouth and couldn't even swallow it. Normally I loved eggs, but yesterday Ursa dumped some scrambled eggs and leftover French toast in my dog bowl, after I ate it, I threw up. I assumed it was probably the scrambled eggs that didn't agree with me or maybe I had eaten too fast.

Last night Max brought me fried chicken and potato wedges, I could hardly eat. I mean, who doesn't like fried chicken. Maybe I was coming down with a stomach bug? I set the eggs aside for now and hoped the bacon stayed down.

I went to the bathroom and brushed my teeth again. I stared in the mirror and noticed I was healthier and curvier looking thanks to Max. I was eating so much more and had gained a few pounds.

I clipped the front of my hair out of my face but left the rest down. During the fall and winter, I usually wore my long thick hair down because it helped to keep me warm. I put on black yoga pants with a dark blue, long sleeved, shirt.

I loaded all four washing machines with laundry and went upstairs to start cleaning rooms, making beds and swapping towels. Today was Saturday, lots of pack members went to town on Saturday, which means today would be a good day to try and slip into the library on the second floor. I wanted to look for anything about wolf myths, legends or curses to explain my new fire talent.

I was done with the second floor rooms and slipped into the big library at the end of the hallway. I moved fast looking for anything that could explain my ability to control fire and my golden wolf. After a half hour, I was still empty handed and needed to get to the third floor to start on those rooms.

It was nearly noon now and I had to move the laundry from the washers to the dryers so I could start four more loads. I headed downstairs but had to walk through the living room, dining room and kitchen to get to the basement door. When I walked through the dining room, I looked up to find six men I didn't recognize seated at the dining table with Ranger and Max. They were all staring at me. There was a lot of power and testosterone radiating off these men. Alpha's and

Beta's from other packs no doubt.

I froze for a moment wishing I could crawl into a hole. I nodded my head down to Ranger "Alpha," I said and turned to Max and nodded my head down again. "Beta."

"Please excuse my interruption." I moved to leave and the Alpha closest to me reached out and grabbed my arm.

"Who is this stunning little creature Alpha Ranger?" He asked. All eyes were on me and my eyes were on Ranger. I could see anger flash in his eyes.

"She is no one, Alpha Jordan. A mere servant in this house." Ranger told them and I looked down to the ground, feeling the sting in my heart and Lia's outrage at his words.

Alpha Jordan stood from his chair and lifted my chin up to look into my eyes. He was about thirty years old with light brown hair, green eyes and a beard. He wore a fitted suit without a tie and was very handsome.

"Do you mind if she joins us for lunch?" Alpha Jordan asked.

"My house manager runs a tight ship Alpha Jordan; Lucy needs to complete her work for the day."

"Surely you don't starve your servants, everyone needs to eat lunch Alpha. Indulge me, for it's not every day you meet such a beautiful she wolf." Alpha Jordan said with a grin on his face.

With irritation in his voice, Alpha Ranger caved into

his guest's request. "Lucy, join us for lunch." Ranger reluctantly said.

In one swift motion, Alpha Jordan pulled me onto his lap, and I could feel Ranger's fury as he struggled to control his wolf. I looked over at Max, who seemed to be amused and grinned at me.

Alpha Jordan brought a fork to my mouth with chicken on it.

"Please Lucy, eat." He fed me from his plate of chicken fettuccine alfredo. It was delicious.

"Alpha Ranger, please continue, you were telling us about your future Luna and the upcoming mating ceremony." Alpha Jordan said. Ranger's eyes shot to me for a moment and I felt my chest tighten up as Lia let out a low howl in my head.

"Yes, the next full moon in about three weeks. You may expect an invitation." Ranger said.

Alpha Jordan continued to feed me and himself with the same fork. "Lucy, you are unmarked, have you found your mate yet?" He asked me and my heart skipped a few beats. I couldn't bring myself to look at Ranger, I could feel his anger and frustration through the mate bond.

"I turned eighteen recently." I hesitated. "I-I do not have a mate... yet." I added.

He lifted his glass of water to my lips and I took a drink. Alpha Jordan was very attentive to me, kind and respectful throughout the entire lunch. He reminded me exactly of how our mate should have treated us and my heart ached.

The other Alpha was Alpha Liam, from our neighboring pack and his Beta and Gamma. Alpha Liam spoke, "perhaps Lucy would like to visit us next door to see if her mate is at our pack?" He smiled.

"Lucy isn't going anywhere!" Ranger growled. "She's loyal and dedicated to her pack."

"My Beta, Kline, found his mate at Alpha Jordan's pack last year when we visited his territory." Alpha Liam told us.

"Stephanie was the best cook at our pack house and so good with the pups." Alpha Jordan said as he brought another forkful to my mouth. "How is she doing Beta Kline?" He asked.

"Wonderful Alpha, thank you for asking. We're expecting our first pup next month, a boy." Beta Kline said with pride.

"Congratulations!" Alpha Jordan smiled. "I know just the gift to send to Stephanie for the baby."

"She's a wonderful addition to our pack and a great Beta female." Alpha Liam said.

"A mate is a blessing from the Moon Goddess, very few who truly deserve it are blessed a second time with a second chance mate. Only a fool would reject a true mate." Max said as the others agreed.

I was stunned, a pack cook that is now a Beta female, I thought to myself. Her mate is glowing with the mention of her name. He loved her, no matter what her status was. Had accepted her and wasn't ashamed.

My mate didn't want me. He wanted someone else. He used me and rejected me.

Why was I cursed by the Moon Goddess, I wondered? What exactly had I done to deserve such a miserable fate? I looked at Ranger and his eyes locked with mine. I realized he was reading my thoughts and I had forgotten to put my wall up.

When lunch was over, the Alpha's and Beta's stood up to return to their meeting. Alpha Jordan clasped my hand and kissed the top of it. "Lucy, it was an absolute pleasure, I look forward to seeing you at the mating ceremony in three weeks and dancing with you." He winked at me.

"Thank you, Alpha." I nodded and excused myself. I walked through the kitchen to the basement door and continued with the laundry. I moved the clothes into the dryer and started four more loads of towels in the wash.

I returned to the third and fourth floors to finish cleaning rooms. I was thinking about what had happened at lunch and replaying everything over and over in my head. Ranger was having his mating ceremony in three weeks; Miranda would become Luna.

"It doesn't look like Ranger will change his mind," I told Lia. "I think we need to accept the rejection and plan our escape."

"Any idea where you want to go?" Lia asked.

"Somewhere far away from Ranger and Miranda." I felt tears fill my eyes.

"I'm going to miss Max." She said.

"Me too." I told her and finished up the last room.

Ranger mind linked me, "Lucy, I want to see you in my office NOW!"

"Yes Alpha." I headed down to the first floor to his office. Before I could knock on the office door, Ranger yanked the door open and his eyes were livid. He grabbed a fist full of my hair, dragging me inside the office and locked the door.

He slammed my back to the wall and pinned me there with his hip. "HOW DARE YOU FLIRT WITH ALPHA JORDAN LIKE THAT YOU WHORE!" He slapped me so hard across the face my head whipped to the side.

"DO YOU WANT TO BE HIS WHORE LUCY? HE OFFERED TO TRADE THREE SERVANTS FOR YOU!" He roared.

"N-No." I shook my head, "p-p-please Alpha, you told m-me to stay for lunch." My face still stinging from his slap and the tears running down my face.

"YOU WILLINGLY SAT IN HIS FUCKING LAP, LUCY!" He struck my face hard again. "DID YOU ENJOY FEELING HIS DICK RUBBING AGAINST YOUR ASS!" I felt the warm blood running from my nose and my head was spinning.

"DID YOUR PUSSY GET WET FOR HIM LUCY?" He reached down and grabbed hard between my legs.

"P-please, you're hurting me." I cried.

Ranger buried his face in my neck, trying to regain control, breathing my scent deep. "FUCK! YOUR SCENT IS EVEN DIFFERENT. YOU SMELL LIKE THAT BASTARD." He growled as he flung me across the office. I lost my footing and crashed into the coffee table, headfirst. My world went dark.

CHAPTER 11 – PUP

My head felt heavy and I groaned as I attempted to open my eyes.
"Lucy, Lucy, can you hear me?" I heard A familiar voice call.

My eyes fluttered open and Max's worried face swam before me. "Mm-Max?"

"Easy Lucy." He helped me sit up. I was back in the laundry room, laying in my bed. The last thing I could remember was crashing into the coffee table. But, how did I get down here?

Max continued to look me over, "Lucy, what happened?"

I took a deep breath and recalled everything that happened earlier. "Ranger mind linked me after the meeting to come to his office, he was very angry about Alpha Jordan and lunch. He lost control, hit me and threw me into the coffee table."

"He rejected you, selected another Luna and is jealous when someone else looks at you." Max said shaking his head.

"How did I get back down here?"

"I don't know ... Ranger must have carried you back. I came to bring you dinner, but you've been out for hours."

"Mate just dumped us here, that jerk!" Lia huffed.

"What time is it?" I asked him.

"It's almost midnight, I'm on patrol tonight." He paused for a moment and then said "Lucy, I'm sorry you had to find out about the mating ceremony that way."

"I'm okay Max, I knew he would pick Miranda. I just didn't expect it to be so soon." I looked down at my hands, "I can feel his wolf still wants me. I hoped that maybe Ranger would change his mind and take back the rejection, but he's not going to do that."

"I thought for sure when he saw how Alpha Jordan wanted you and pulled you to his lap, that Ranger would lose it and claim you." He said. We both sat in silence for a few moments considering this.

"Does Alpha Jordan have a Luna?"

"She passed away giving birth to their twin pups six years ago. Alpha Jordan is a good man and has one of the strongest packs in the country." Max told me.

My stomach grumbled and Max chuckled. He held out a paper bag, "Steak and cheese sandwich, cookie and apple."

"You're a life saver Max." I smiled up at him.

"You'll always be my true Luna, Lucy." He smiled back. "I've got to get back to patrol, eat and then get some rest."

I ate my sandwich and couldn't fall asleep. I decided

to take a shower and wash the blood from my hair. I turned on the dryers to warm up the laundry room and headed to the bathroom. I stood in the shower and closed my eyes. The hot water felt soothing. I had three weeks until the mating ceremony to figure out what I was going to do. I wasn't sure where to go or how exactly to start somewhere new.

When my shower was done, I felt a wave of nausea come over me. I turned to the toilet just in time to throw up my sandwich. After I was sure my stomach was empty, I brushed my teeth and went back to bed. This time, I felt exhausted and fell asleep almost as soon as I curled up.

"GET UP YOU LAZY DOG!" Ursa yelled at me. I had slept in passed sun rise and knew I was late for my chores.

"The kitchen assistant is off today, and help is needed with the breakfast dishes upstairs." She barked at me.

"I'll be right up." I went to the bathroom first, brushed my teeth and then my hair. My stomach still felt queasy.

I stood at the kitchen sink and washed all the breakfast dishes, silverware and glassware. Then I moved to the pots and pans. Miranda and her minions came into the kitchen and sat at the island behind me. They were talking about the mating ceremony and the decorations. I continued to scrub away at the pots with my back turned to them and the cooks buzzing around the kitchen prepping food and vegetables for lunch and dinner.

The topic changed to dresses and Miranda was whining. "He wants me to wear his mother's ugly old dress, from twenty-six years ago, I'm going to look hideous!"

"I can't believe he still kept that old rag." One of them said.

"The last three Luna's in his family have worn that thing." Miranda pouted.

The back door swung open and a shirtless Ranger walked in. "What are you ladies talking about?" He asked as he walked over and kissed Miranda.

"How beautiful your mothers white Luna dress is." She lied.

"You will look stunning in it." Ranger told her and she giggled. "Did you send the invitations out already?" He asked.

"Yesterday." Miranda squealed.

"Did you send one to Alpha Jordan at Eclipse Pack?"

"I sure did." She said.

Ranger let out a low growl. "That prick."

I continued to scrub the pans trying to remain as unnoticed as possible. Ranger walked over to the coffee machine and reached for a mug. I saw him from the corner of my eye, he did a double take at me when he realized I was standing there washing dishes. He didn't acknowledge me, and I looked down at the pan I was scrubbing.

"Should we honeymoon after the ceremony or wait until summer?" Ranger called out as he walked back with his coffee to sit with them knowing I could hear him.

"Ohhh how about Hawaii?" Miranda said as she climbed up onto his lap.

"Hawaii sounds romantic, we can start working on making pups." He kissed her and the girls all giggled.

"Mate is trying to make us jealous!" Lia scoffed in my head and she was right. I could feel Ranger trying to read my thoughts, but my wall was up tight.

"How many pups do you want Alpha?" One of the girls asked.

"As many as my beautiful, *strong,* Luna is willing to give me." He said with an emphasis on strong.

"We're going to have strong and beautiful pups too." Miranda gushed and I felt the need to gag.

I tried to ignore them, but I couldn't. My heart was aching, and he was doing this on purpose. I've always wanted pups and a family, now I was destined to be alone, I thought bitterly to myself.

"I wouldn't be too sure about that last thought Lucy." Lia said to me.

"Why do you say that?" I asked her.

"I can hear our pup's heartbeat." She told me.

"Our pup?"

The pan I was scrubbing clanked into the sink loudly as it fell from my hands. I realized what Lia had said. My hands were shaking, and my heart was racing. That would explain the nausea I had the last few days, it's not a stomach bug. Oh Goddess! I'm pregnant!

"What the hell is she doing in the kitchen, stealing food?" Miranda said. "You're getting a fat ass Lucy, obviously you're stealing food." She scowled.

"Alpha Jordan didn't seem to mind her ass yesterday, isn't that right Lucy?" Ranger said with venom in his voice.

"Oh really, an Alpha? Setting your sights a little high don't you think?" Beth teased and they all laughed. "That's ambitious for a laundry maid."

I grabbed a kitchen towel and dried my hands. Then I nodded my head down to Ranger. "Please excuse me Alpha."

I headed down to the basement and could still hear them laughing. I searched through the big storage cabinet of pack house toiletries and found some pregnancy tests in the very back. I took one and made my way to the bathroom to confirm what Lia told me.

I got a positive plus sign before I could even finish washing my hands. I walked over to my bed and sat down trying to wrap my head around this. The tears started to flood my eyes My mate didn't want me, he rejected me. He wants to have his pups with Miranda, not me. I wondered if he would reject our pup or take it away from me. Lia was pacing, ready to attack.

What am I going to do? How would I take care of a pup? I can't even provide for myself. A pack is supposed to take care of each other, I've been abandoned, I thought to myself. I have nothing, I have no one.

"That's not true Lucy." Lia said. "You have me, and you have Max."

"Thank you, Lia, I'm so glad I have you." I told her.

"Now we have to figure out how to escape without the patrols catching us and where to go."

"We should go south; winter is coming, and it will be warmer south." Lia suggested.

"That's the first place they would expect us to go. The snow falls here and everywhere north of us, the further north you go, the heavier the snow gets." I told her. "Also, most rogues will be south for the warmer weather and easy hunting."

"Then we go east, Alpha Jordan's pack is east, maybe he will help us?"

"What if he doesn't and gives us back to Ranger? Our pup is technically the next Alpha, we have to be careful."

"We have the power of fire to keep us warm Lucy, we could go north into Canada." Lia said.

They would never suspect such a weak pack slave to head north I thought. "North it is!"

CHAPTER 12 – DISRESPECT

The pack was gathering this evening for a meeting. The Alpha had some important updates and announcements, so everyone was required to be there. The sun was setting, and I made my way outside. The stage was setup and most people were already gathered around. I stood quietly in the back of the crowd, wishing I didn't have to be here.

I looked over to the other side of the field and saw all the young pups running around playing. My hand involuntarily went to my still flat stomach and I wondered if my pup would look like Ranger or more like me. There was a young pup jumping around, he was about four years old, with jet black hair like Ranger's. I found myself smiling. It's been three days since I found out I was pregnant, and I already loved my baby.

"Testing, Testing." Ranger's voice pulled me out of my daydream. He was standing on the stage and his eyes scanned over the crowd.

"Good evening Dark Moon Pack."

"Good evening Alpha." The crowd called back.

Ranger went on to discuss the current rogue situation and our alliances with other packs. He went on to talk about the new patrol schedules of our territory for the winter and other pack business. Normally at mandatory meetings, I go unnoticed and ignored, but Ranger's eyes kept coming back to mine.

"Now before you are dismissed, I have one more very important announcement." His eyes found mine again. "On the next full moon, in less than three weeks, Dark Moon pack will welcome their new Luna." The crowd broke out in applause and howls.

"My mate, is none other than the strong and beautiful Miranda Taylor, from the Beta family." The applause and howls continued. I looked around at everyone and in this moment, I realized I didn't belong here. I don't belong in this pack. I don't know where I belong, or where my home is, but I know it's not here at Dark Moon.

Miranda stepped up on stage and gave Ranger a kiss, earning a few more howls. My heart was stinging as I tried to look unfazed. I was not going to let him see how much he was hurting me. Miranda stepped up to the microphone and waited for the applause to die down before addressing the crowd.

Just then, Ranger mind linked me. "My offer still stands to be my mistress Lucy." I could see a smirk on his face from where I stood.

"You have your Luna Sir; I'll wait for Alpha Jordan." I responded back through the mind link as I turned to walk back to the pack house. I've had enough of this.

Ranger let out a furious roar from the stage and everyone stood still. "How dare you disrespect your future Luna and turn your back while she is speaking, MAID." He yelled and jumped off the stage grabbing me by the back of my neck.

His eyes were dark with rage and there was a dangerous aura radiating off him. He shoved me to the ground before the stage and everyone stood back watching. **"Apologize to your Luna, MAID!"** He growled.

I knew this had nothing to do with Miranda and everything to do with my mention of Alpha Jordan. I glared up at him and reminded myself I would be gone soon. I turned to look at Miranda, who seemed to be enjoying this, "I-I'm sorry Luna, please forgive me."

"FIVE LASHES FOR YOUR DISRESPECT!" He called out. **"DELTA, BRING ME THE WHIP."**

Lia was growling in my head as I tried to take in what was about to happen. Please Moon Goddess, protect our pup. I looked down at the ground, my mind was racing. He was going to whip me in front of the whole pack, as I knelt here, carrying his pup.

I saw some tiki torches lit by the stage and considered burning this whole place down and escaping. There are at least four hundred wolves here and I'm pretty sure I wouldn't get far. Delta Cole appeared with the whip and handed it to Ranger.

Max stepped forward. "Alpha, I'm sure it was an innocent mistake and she apologized. Is this really necessary?"

"Stand down Beta!" Ranger used his Alpha voice and Max was compelled to step back. I looked at Max and saw the worried look on his face. The fear was building inside of me as I held back sobs.

"I will not tolerate any disrespect from anyone towards myself or your Luna, is that clear?" Ranger boomed.

"Yes Alpha!" Everyone said in unison.

If I tried to tell him about the pup now, he would probably deny it's his. Or worse, probably accuse me of trying to embarrass him and his chosen Luna. I felt Ranger's hand on my back, in one sharp yank, he ripped off my shirt and bra. I immediately crossed my arms over my exposed chest as the sobs escaped me, knowing what was coming.

"If you say yes to my offer now, I'll show you mercy Lucy." Ranger mind linked me again.

I felt my skin tingle when his hand brushed up against my back, he moved my hair to hang over the front of my shoulder.

"Last chance." He said.

I couldn't even answer back. I looked down at the ground, my eyes filled with tears and I fought to hold back sobs. I shook my head no and braced for impact.

He walked a circle around me with the whip dancing in his hand. "Count out loud after each lash, if you fail, you will earn another." He yelled.

CRACK! I felt the sting across my back as a scream left my lips. "One." My trembling voice said.

CRACK! This one caused me to fall forward on my hands as another scream rang out. "Two." I panted and crossed my arms back over my chest.

"Just like a whore, showing off your tits to everyone, you're going to feel the next one." He hissed through the mind link.

CRACK! I let out a blood curdling scream, my skin split open and the warmth of blood ran down my back. "Three." I sobbed and my head was spinning.

CRACK! I cried out as a wave of nausea struck me and I threw up the remnants of my lunch on the grass before me. "Four." I managed to say trying to catch my breath.

CRACK! I screamed again and my vision started to blur. I uttered a feeble "Five," before I collapsed and the last thing I saw was the stage catch fire.

I was laying on a cold hard surface face down. My face was on a towel and I felt a warm set of hands on my back. I opened my eyes and saw Max talking to someone, it was Dr. Baker.

"Try not to move Lucy, I'm placing stitches in one of the deep wounds that isn't healing fast enough." She said.

I was in the laundry room, laying on the folding table. "Lucy, when was the last time you let your wolf out?" Dr. Baker asked.

"I've only shifted once, about two weeks ago, on my birthday."

"That explains the slow healing. You need to let your wolf out at least once a week, to keep up your healing abilities." She told me.

"Lia are you okay?" I asked her.

"I'm here Lucy, I thought I was just getting weak because of our pup." She said.

Dr. Baker finished and covered the lash marks with ointment and gauze. I was debating telling her about the baby, to make sure everything was fine, but decided against it. She was Ranger's pack doctor, and this was his pup, her future Alpha. She would have to tell Ranger.

"How soon can her wolf run Doc?" Max asked.

"In a few days when the stitches heal." She said.

Once Dr. Baker left. Max went over to my tub of clothes, selected a baggy shirt and handed it to me. I sat up and slipped the shirt over my head.

"Lucy, the mark on the nape of your neck, when did it appear?" He asked me.

My hand instantly went to my nape and I didn't feel anything. "What mark?"

He took a cell phone out of his pocket, "Lift your hair back," he said. He snapped a picture and handed me the phone. I saw what looked like a crescent moon tattoo in a celestial design and gasped.

"I have no idea how that got there!" I stared in awe.

"I've seen that once before and if it's what I think it is, no one can see that." He said very seriously.

My head was spinning. "What do you mean?"

"You're an elemental wolf. Have you discovered your gift yet?" He asked.

I wasn't sure what to say, he knew!

"Lucy, you can trust me, I will help you." He gently placed his hand in mine.

"I trust him." Lia said to me.

I looked into his worried eyes staring back at me, "I thought it was a curse. I'm not sure how to control it and I'm afraid I'll hurt someone." I told him.

"It's okay, your gift is not a curse. It makes you very special and that scares others." He paused.

"There's a legend that some of the descendants of the Moon Goddess possess the powers to control the elements. Sometimes it skips generations and siblings, which has caused jealousy, fear and wars over the centuries. That's why it's important to keep it hidden Lucy."

I nodded my head. I knew I'd be hunted down if someone discovered my powers.

"The four elements are Earth, Wind, Fire and Water, which element can you control?"

"Fire."

Max paced the room for a few moments. "You're not safe here, we have to get you out of here. You have to make sure Ranger doesn't see the mark." His tone was laced with worry.

I hadn't told him that I was planning on leaving the pack soon. "Where should I go?" I asked.

"We need to get you north!"

CHAPTER 13 – PICNIC

It's been nearly a week and my wounds have finally healed. I've spent most of my time in the basement trying to stay away from Ranger and Miranda. Lia has been itching to go for a run and today is the perfect day.

Ranger has been away for a few days in the city managing the family's software and security company. Last night, I felt the cheating pains through the mate bond and knew that Ranger was sleeping with someone else in the city while Miranda was still here. Miranda, who is completely oblivious to his cheating, was happily shopping with her minions today. Ursa, was out running errands and I was going to enjoy a little freedom today. Max is going to meet me beyond the tree line to go for a run so that we can avoid the patrols.

"Coast is clear Lucy." Max mind linked me. I went up the basement stairs and slipped out the kitchen back door.

I walked into the woods and heard a rustling sound coming from behind a bush. A large dark brown wolf stepped out and I knew it was Max. "Lucy, hop on my back, you can shift when we're away from here."

I climbed on the back of Max's wolf and wrapped my arms around his neck. "Hold on tight." He mind linked me and we took off running towards a denser area of the forest. The forest looked beautiful this time of year. The trees and bushes that were scattered between the evergreen pine trees had turned to very vivid colors of fall. I admired the bright hues of orange, red and yellow, as Max ran faster and faster.

We reached a beautiful riverbed and I hopped off of Max. "I'll be right back." He said to me as he went behind a tree to shift back. A moment later, Max stepped out wearing a pair of shorts and a shirt.
Someone had placed a picnic basket and blanket under a tree near the riverbed. We walked to the tree next to the river. "I wasn't sure if you would be hungry now, or if you'd like to eat after our run?" Max asked me.

I was feeling a little anxious about shifting again and the pain involved. It might be a good thing if we eat after, in case I throw up. "Let's eat after our run."

"Sounds good. How about you go behind that tree and take off your clothes. Put on the large white shirt I left there for your shift, it's ok if it rips off when you shift. I'm here to help if you need anything."

Being naked was something that was normal in the wolf community, but I still wasn't used to it. I stepped out from behind the tree in the shirt and he walked over to me. I felt really anxious about shifting again and the pin involved.

"Lucy, take a deep breath and relax. Picture Lia in your mind and let her take control. Feel yourself merge into her and become one." His soothing voice guided me.

I heard the bones cracking and dropped to my knees, the pain was intense for a moment and then I heard the shirt rip off me. I opened my eyes and was standing on all fours. That was much faster than the first time I thought and much less painful.

I looked up at Max who was staring at me in complete shock. I wondered if I looked deformed or something. His mouth was hanging open and I stepped back feeling ashamed of myself. I let out a low whine and brought my head down.

"Lucy! You are the most beautiful wolf I have ever seen." He said in awe and continued to admire me. "Is it okay if I touch your wolf?"

I pressed my head into his abdomen, and he let out a chuckle. "Oh Lucy, do you have any idea how special and rare you are?" He said as he stroked my neck.

"I told you we were special." Lia chirped in my head. "Now can we pleaseee go for a run?" She asked.

"Lia's ready for her run now?" He asked.

"She sure is." I mind linked him.

"Okay let me shift and we'll go." He walked around behind me removing his shirt and slipped his shorts off, he shifted in a few seconds.

"Show off!" I rolled my eyes.

"I've been doing this for years; you'll get faster too." He laughed.

We took off running and racing through the woods. I let Max lead the way and enjoyed the fresh crisp air running through my fur. Running felt so good and Lia was happy.

Max mind linked me. "Lucy, let Lia take control and I'll let Milo out so they can run together too."

PAULINA VASQUEZ

I saw Max's green eyes darken as his wolf Milo took control. "All right Lia, it's all you girl." I told her and she eagerly barked and took over.

Lia ran fast and Milo was chasing after her. They yipped and playfully barked at each other as they jumped logs and big rocks. An hour later, we had circled back around to where we started, and Lia trotted over to the river to lap up water. Her golden fur was glistening in the sun light and in the water reflection.

Milo's tongue was hanging out and he jumped right into the water splashing us in the process. "Come on in, the water is refreshing."

"Don't you remember the swimming pool, I can't swim." I reminded him.

"You can't, but Lia can. It's a natural instinct for wolves." He told me and Milo barked happily.

"All right Lia, let's see what you can do." She jumped right in and paddled away with ease. Twenty minutes later, Milo was climbing out and Lia had spotted a big fish in the water she was stalking.
Milo shook out his fur and Max mind linked me. "If you're hungry, we can have our lunch now." He motioned towards the picnic basket with his head.

"I'll be right there." I linked back and Lia plunged her face into the water and came up with the fish in her mouth flapping around. I heard Max laughing as Milo yipped. Lia climbed out of the water and dropped the fish on the grass. She ate half and shared the other half of her catch with Milo.

"Are you ready to shift back?" Max asked me.

I nodded and headed back behind the tree where my clothes were. Five minutes later, I was naked on all fours breathing hard. I wondered if I would ever get use to that. I put my clothes on and headed over to Max, who was already dressed and getting our lunch out.

I sat down on the blanket and he handed me a ham and cheese sandwich. "Good thing I didn't pack tuna, we've already had fish," he jokingly said. He set out grapes, pretzels and some big chocolate chip cookies, then handed me a bottle of water.

It was wonderful being out here watching the river flow by. I haven't been on a picnic since I was little. Thanks to Lia, I even enjoyed a swim today. I couldn't help but think to myself that this was the best day I've had in years and I owed it all to the man sitting next to me.

We sat under the tree eating in silence before he spoke. "Lucy, you're a golden wolf. Did Ranger happen see your wolf the first night you shifted?"

"No, he found me after I had shifted back."

"A golden wolf is said to be the strongest wolf of all, even stronger than a pure white wolf. With some training, you could challenge any Alpha and win!" I couldn't help but laugh at what he just said.
He paused a moment, "I'm the fastest runner in the pack and I couldn't catch Lia." He said. "I'm sure that she wasn't even trying to run at her fastest pace either." He eyed me.

"He's right." Lia said.

"How could I be some super strong wolf; I've been weak my whole life. I can't even defend myself from bullies. My mate was so disgusted by my weakness that he rejected me." I said almost choking on the word rejected. It still stings.

"I don't know why the Moon Goddess does what she does, but I do know that you're very special. A golden wolf who's also elemental is rare, I'm not sure if we've ever had one."

"Max, do you think that Ranger will let me just leave after he has officially mated and marked Miranda?" I asked.

"I'm honestly not sure. If he marks her as his chosen mate, the mate bond will break completely, making it easier for you to escape. If you accept the rejection before, his wolf will weaken, and he might try to take it out on you."

"What happens if Miranda finds her real mate?"

"She already did. He rejected her last spring and she's been chasing Ranger ever since." He sighed.

"Do you think Ranger will hunt me down when I leave?"

"If he does, the north will be the last place he'll look. Trust me on this. The world's strongest pack and Alpha is north of us in Canada."

"What's the name of the pack?"

"Crescent Moon."

"Do I really want to go there? What if they kill me?" I asked.

"They won't."

"How do you know?"

"My good friend is the Alpha and he's got the same mark on the back of his neck as you."

CHAPTER 14 – BURN

The pack house has been absolute madness with only a week left until the mating ceremony. I was cleaning guest rooms today and preparing them for guests who will be occupying them later this week. The room I was currently cleaning was the same room Alpha Knox had given me after my father's death, when I came to live at the pack house. It serves as one of a dozen guest rooms now, while I sleep on a dog bed in the laundry room.

With a towel in one hand and glass cleaner in another, I wiped down the mirror in the bathroom. Then I moved to the closet door that also had a full-length body mirror on it. I cleaned the mirror and stopped to look at my own reflection.

I was wearing black stretch pants and a loose fitted brown sweater that complemented the amber colors in my eyes. I stared a moment later at my breasts which looked fuller and my hips that had slightly widened. I turned sideways and lifted my sweater up. A small bump was starting to show on my one month belly, werewolf pregnancies are shorter than humans. Alpha pups are born in three and a half months. I could just be bloated, I told myself.

"Or have eaten a really large meal." Lia chirped.

Ursa only gave me scraps, no way she'd give me a large meal. Thanks to Max, I was able to eat well and become stronger. Looking in the mirror, I noticed that my hair was shiny, and my skin had a glow. I looked healthy and well for the first time in a long time.

"We need to stay strong and prepare for our journey north." Lia reminded me and she was right. In a week from now, we would be making a run for it.

Max had helped me plan the best route of escape to get passed the patrols and any trackers that might come after me. I was going to run south to leave my scent and then get in the river to throw them off. They would naturally assume I floated south down river as an easy way of escape. No one would be strong enough to try and swim upriver, but Lia was strong and could easily swim back upriver against the current. I was going to run straight north for a few days until I reached Crescent Moon Pack.

I left the guest room and was finished with the others. I was on the second floor by the library door. I was thinking about sneaking in to see if I could find anything in there about elemental wolfs when the door was pulled open. I busied myself with the cart of cleaning supplies I was pushing and tried to act normal.

My nose filled with Ranger's scent and I could feel him behind me. "You've been trying to avoid me."

I turned around to face him and bowed my head. "Forgive me Alpha, I've been trying to avoid another lashing." A little passive aggressive of me I know, but knowing I was leaving soon gave me the courage.

"Something is different about you and I can't seem to place my finger on it." He looked quizzically at me. "Your scent is off." He inhaled again.

I knew it was the pup who had changed my scent and Ranger couldn't recognize it because it was a mixture of his scent as well. "Perhaps it's the new hair shampoo I've used."

He stared at me and I could see his eyes trail down my body. "Please excuse me Alpha, I have much to do before your mating ceremony." I bowed my head again, ready to leave.

He grabbed my wrist and turned me back to face him. "A little excited for the mating ceremony, are you? Hoping to see Alpha Jordan again?"

"I'm excited you have such a strong and caring Luna for our pack, Alpha." I replied with a hint of sarcasm in my voice.

"Look at me." He ordered.

"Do you not love your mate, Lucy? You refuse to let him be with you." I could see him struggling with his wolf. Rex was close to the surface and Lia was anxious. She could feel Rex's love for her and desire to be with her. It just made everything hurt more.

"I don't have a mate, I'm a rejected wolf."

He pulled me to his chest. "Lucy, you belong to me."

"If I belonged to you, Alpha, I would certainly be wearing your mark on my neck."

A growl rumbled in his chest; he obviously didn't like hearing me say that. He leaned down to try and smell my neck. At least, I think it was to smell me, no way he would bite me now. We heard a door open from one of the pack rooms and he instantly let me go.

He was standing there, still looking at me when I noticed Miranda and Beth had come out of Beth's room.

"What are you bothering the Alpha about, maid?" Miranda asked.

"I-I was just telling the Alpha how excited everyone is for the mating ceremony." I bowed my head down.

"There's still plenty to do, so get moving." She ordered.

I kept my bowed head down and pushed my cleaning supply cart down the hall to the broom closet. I could feel Ranger's eyes on my ass as I walked away. Stupid mate bond.

"Lucy, his wolf Rex was trying to connect we me." Lia told me. "I blocked him out."

"I'm so sorry Lia, I know this isn't fair to you. I'm sorry for the hurt this is causing, Rex doesn't deserve this either." I tried to comfort her.

"It's okay Lucy, we just need to keep our pup safe." She tried to assure me.

I went back down to the basement to finish the laundry. The weather was getting colder and made everything feel chilly down here. I turned on the dryers to fluff the clothes out and warm up the laundry room.

I had a basket of items that needed to be ironed, so I lowered the ironing board from the wall and plugged in the clothes iron. While I waited, I got my cup out and filled it with cold water from the laundry sink to drink. I really wish I had a cup of hot tea, but I wasn't allowed anything from the kitchen.

I went to my plastic tub and retrieved the old broken clock radio. I plugged it in the electrical outlet so that I could have some music while I ironed. After I set the dial to classical music, I started ironing and hanging clothes.

"Classical music is so soothing and I'm sure our pup is enjoying it too." Lia gushed.

I was so lost in thoughts about the pup, that I didn't even hear Miranda come down to the basement. She stood in front of the ironing board with an angry look on her face. Even though she had a strong family resemblance to Max, she was the polar opposite of him. She was a total and complete, self-centered, bitch!

"Luna, can I help you?" I asked.

"Yes Lucy, I am your Luna. As your Luna, I order you to stay away from MY MATE, unless you want to be whipped again?" She said with a nasty look on her face.

"I will do my best to avoid your mate, Luna." I replied and the word *Luna,* seemed to leave a bitter taste on my tongue. She was going to be a terrible Luna. She can have that cheating bastard, I thought to myself as I mentally rolled my eyes at her. Of course, since she's not his true mate, she couldn't feel the mate bond cheating pains. Joke's on her, he's even cheated on her.

"If I find out you tried anything with him, Goddess help you Lucy, I will rip out your throat." She threatened me.

"Yes Luna," I said.

"And don't even think about attending the mating ceremony. We don't want you embarrassing us in your rags." She growled.

Was she insecure or what? I thought to myself. I had no plans to attend the mating ceremony, the event was going to be catered by a professional company and I would not be needed. I would easily be forgotten in all the hustle and bustle of the event which would make it easy for me to slip away.

"Do I make myself clear?" She growled again and picked up my clothes iron, then set it on top of my right hand, burning it.

I whimpered in pain and Lia wanted to be let out to kick her ass. I had to struggle to hold Lia back and rushed to the sink to place my hand in cold water. "Now's not the time Lia, we only have a week left and we will be far away from here." I reminded Lia to calm her down.

Miranda grabbed my clock radio on the way out and smashed it on the basement stairs. I didn't own much, but that old clock radio meant a lot to me. It had helped me pass the time away these last four years. It helped soothe my soul and loneliness, like an old friend. I wanted to cry but kept reminding myself that I was leaving soon.

"How is Max related to that evil person?" Lia huffed.

"I don't know. But she can keep Ranger. He's no prize." I told Lia.

My hand was stinging and red, it would probably take a day or two for the burn to heal. I went to the bathroom and reached into my medicine cabinet for the burn cream. The mating ceremony couldn't get here fast enough.

CHAPTER 15 – THE HOLE

Two days to go, but who's counting! I can almost taste freedom from here. Or maybe it was an omelet I could almost taste. Ursa was on her cellphone talking to the florist and cooking herself a late breakfast. I glanced over at the omelet and it was filled with ham, sausage and vegetables. Just the way she used to make them for my father.

I was on dish duty again, washing the breakfast dishes. Ursa had been so busy preparing for the ceremony that she had not given me a scrap of food the last four days. If it hadn't been for Max, the pup and I would both be starving.

Ursa turned around to get a plate for her omelet and ended her phone call. "Awe, is the little mutt hungry?" She taunted me. Just two more days, I reminded myself. Two more days and I was done with her and her cruel behavior. I looked over at the flames on the stove and in an instant her omelet was on fire. Thick smoke billowed up in the kitchen. Bon Appétit, I thought to myself as people raced around grabbing the fire extinguishers and opening the windows.

"Serves her right." Lia told me.

"What is going on here?" Ranger asked as he entered the kitchen.

"Just a little stove fire." Ursa coughed.

"And who's fault was it?" He looked down at the mess on the stove.

"Lucy was supposed to be watching the stove while I was taking a call from the florist sir." She lied.

Ranger turned to me and his eyes were livid. "What the fuck are you trying to do, burn the house down?"

Little did he know, I could burn this whole damn house down in seconds if I really wanted to. "No Alpha." I responded.

Just then we heard screaming and it sounded like Miranda. A moment later, she stomped her way into the kitchen with Beth and Grace quick on her heels. We all turned to look at her and she threw herself into Ranger's arms crying. She was holding a white dress in her hands. Blake and Cole even came into the kitchen to see what the commotion was about. Did she break a nail? I wondered.

"Babe what happened?" Ranger kissed the top of her head and soothed her. I felt a pang of jealousy watching my mate soothe another when he hated me for being weak. Miranda buried her face in his chest, really turning up the waterworks.

"She ruined your mothers beautiful dress." Miranda sobbed.

Ranger took the dress from Miranda and held it up. **"WHAT THE FUCK DID YOU DO TO MY MOTHER'S DRESS, LUCY?"**

What? His mother's dress? I've never seen his mother's

dress. Was this the same dress that Miranda was calling hideous and didn't want to wear for the Luna ceremony? He turned the dress around and my mouth dropped open. Right in the middle of the dress was a hot iron burn!

I saw the smirk on Beth's face and knew this was a set up.

"YOU FUCKING BITCH!" He roared and, in a flash, held me up by my neck choking me.

The iron mark on the dress was much smaller than the one I used in the laundry room and the shape was different. I knew she had burned the dress on purpose so that she didn't have to wear it. She truly was evil.

"What am I going to do, the dress is ruined!" Miranda continued with her fake sobbing.

He threw me to the ground, "YOU'RE GOING TO PAY FOR THIS LUCY! A WEEK IN THE HOLE SHOULD TEACH YOU!"

Wait, What?! Did he just say the hole? I was supposed to be leaving in two days, I can't be in the hole.

"I didn't do anything. I've never even seen the dress." I pleaded, my eyes filling with tears. If he hadn't broken his side of the mate bond, he would have known I was telling the truth. He would have been able to feel the truth and my emotions.

"She's lying, I gave it to her to press a few days ago." Miranda screeched. Lia was ready to kick her ass.

Ranger let out a loud earth shaking growl and threw

me over his shoulder. He opened the back door and walked past the training grounds. I had heard stories of wolves who died in the hole or prisoners who went crazy in the hole. "Please, please don't do this Ranger." I begged.

"IT'S ALPHA TO YOU!" He growled and slapped my ass hard several times, I cried out in pain.

Everyone had followed us out the kitchen and other pack members joined behind us to watch. "Please Alpha, I won't survive this." I cried.

"My mother's dress didn't survive." He snapped back.

The guards were lifting a lid that covered a hole in the ground, it was about eight feet wide and twenty feet deep. He set me down next to the hole and I began to shake. I thought about trying to make a run for it. Lia could outrun all of them, but I knew I wouldn't be able to shift fast enough.

"Please just banish me and I'll leave." I begged.

"You're not getting away that easy Lucy." He roared. "Now take your clothes off!"

Take my clothes off? I had to be naked in the hole? The nights were freezing cold, this was a death sentence not a punishment. I was trying to gather the courage to tell him about the pup, maybe he would spare me. Or maybe he would take the pup and banish me after.

Lia was angry and saying something to me, but I couldn't hear a word she said. I was frozen in fear. I couldn't bring myself to move and Ranger became enraged. He started tearing my clothes off like I was a rag doll. "You will do as I say Lucy! If I tell you to strip, you will strip! If I tell you to spread your legs, you will spread your legs! If I tell you to bend over, you will bend over! I own you; YOU ARE MINE!!!" He growled sounding like a possessive mate.

I stood completely naked, arms folded across my chest, with the wind whipping my long hair around. Shocked faces stared back at us. Could they tell I was pregnant? Or were they shocked by what he said to me?

"You will regret this." I said to him. I looked down into the hole and my breath caught in my throat. Before I had time to register what had happened, I was falling. He had pushed me in.

I fell face down on the hard earth floor at the bottom of this cold dark pit. Pain seared through my body and I couldn't even scream. I tried to lift my head but couldn't, blood was running down my nose. I rolled to my side and turned my head to look up, the last thing I saw was Ranger. He was standing at the top looking down at me, his hands were clenched in fists as they closed the lid of the hole.

Darkness, it was complete darkness. I wasn't sure if my eyes were open or closed. If I had passed out or was just laying here. It had been a few hours or maybe days, I wasn't sure.

My baby! "Please be okay, please be okay." I cried as I placed my hand over my little bump. I felt the energy drain from me and my body was hurting all over.

"Lia are you okay?" I could hardly feel her.

Silence. There was nothing from Lia.

I tried to move but couldn't. I'm sure I had several broken ribs, a broken leg and a broken wrist from the fall. My face was throbbing, and my nose hurt. I felt my face and my nose was broken; the blood had dried on my face.

I drifted in and out of sleep, shivering in the cold, the earth was damp. My throat was burning for water but there was none. I could normally go days without food, but I was worried about my pup. I had lost track of all time.

"Lia are you there?" I called out to her. She was still silent. I wondered if she had left me.

I felt burning pain on my neck where my mates mark should have been. Then I remembered the mating ceremony. Ranger must have just marked Miranda at the ceremony. I realized that I had been down in this hell hole for two days. I was supposed to be making my escape today.

I thought about Max, he was my only friend, and would actually be worried for me. No one else would miss me or care that I was gone. After the pain subsided, I closed my eyes and listened to the faint heartbeat of my pup.

I woke up to feel the familiar cheating pains from my mate. My chest was burning, and the cramps were stronger than they've ever been. Ranger was having sex, but if he had marked Miranda as his mate, then why didn't our mate bond fully break?

Unless, maybe his wolf Rex, had not accepted her. The pain burned through me and I let out a scream. Withering in pain, I felt something wet between my legs and the smell of blood filled my nose. I placed my hand on my belly and could no longer feel my pup's heartbeat. The cramps grew stronger and I continued to scream.

I laid here alone in the darkness, naked and broken with nothing left to live for. There was nothing I could do; I was losing my pup.

CHAPTER 16 – BROKEN

CRACK! I let out a scream and tried to shield myself from the whip. I was panting hard and looked around for Ranger, but all I could see was darkness. There was nothing. No Ranger. No whip.

I heard the sound of the *CRACK* again and realized it was only thunder. I was still in the hole. The earth around me was cold and moist from the heavy rains. I was beyond hunger pains and dehydration. I had lost a lot of blood and felt so weak.

"Please Moon Goddess, bring me home." I prayed as I shivered from the cold. "End my suffering." Everyone I loved was gone, I had nothing, and I didn't belong here.

"I'm here Lucy." I heard Lia's broken voice.

"Lia? Where have you been? I thought you left me?" I cried, relieved I wasn't alone.

"I sent all my energy to our pup, trying to protect it. I'm sorry Lucy, I let you down." She whimpered with grief.

"Lia, it's not your fault. It's his. He never deserved us or the pup."

"I'm too weak to heal you, I think we're dying." Her voice was labored, and she was struggling.

"I feel it too. I love you Lia. You're the best wolf I

could have ever had. I'm sorry I wasn't stronger for you." I told her as I felt her fading.

I was ready, I wanted this to be over. I wanted to be with my parents. To leave this cruel world where no one loved me, and no one wanted me. Shivering, I thought about everything Ranger put me through, the abuse, neglect and punishments. He broke me because he wanted more power. He was too blind to see; the Moon Goddess had paired him with the strongest wolf known to our kind.

There was just one last thing I knew I needed to do. I needed to accept the rejection to set Rex free. It will weaken Ranger, but if Rex was still bound to us, our death would be much harder on him. I took a few more breaths to gather all of my strength.

"I, Lucy Michaels, accept the rejection of Ranger LaRue, Alpha of Dark Moon Pack, as his mate and Luna, I sever all connections through the mate bond."

My head fell back, and I heard the thunder roll again. In the distance an Alpha howled in pain and I knew Ranger felt the mate bond completely break. My eyes closed and I felt a gentle peace wash over me.

I saw a bright light shining through my eyelids and felt droplets of water on my skin. Someone was shaking me. "Lucy, Lucy, take it back Lucy. Wake up! You have to take it back! **LUCY!**" Ranger was frantic. He can't even let me die in peace I thought slipping unconscious again.

BEEP

BEEP

BEEP

I heard a beeping noise and my eyes fluttered open. I looked at the ceiling and white walls and recognized the pack clinic. There was a familiar scent in my room that was fading. The scent belonged to Ranger and it didn't have the same effect on me like it used to. I heard a voice outside my room door that I never wanted to hear again.

"How much longer until she wakes up?" Ranger asked.

"Her healing is very slow Alpha; she lost a lot of blood when she lost her pup. It could be a few more days." Dr. Baker was telling him.

"Is there any way to speed up her healing?"

"Unfortunately, not. We don't know the state of her wolf. She may have lost her wolf entirely, it's hard to tell. She's also been malnourished for so long; it could be attributing to her slow recovery."

"I want to know the moment she wakes up. The guards will remain at the door, no one visits her, not even the Luna."

"Yes Alpha." Dr. Baker responded.

He had some nerve, acting like he cared all of the sudden. I wasn't ready to face him yet and still felt exhausted. I closed my eyes and went back to sleep. A few hours later, I felt a warm heated blanket being placed on top of me and opened my eyes to find Max hovering over me.

"Lucy!" He leaned down to gently hug me.

"Hey Max." I croaked.

"Lucy, I've been so worried. I can't believe he threw you in the hole. I'm so sorry, we should have gotten you out of here sooner."

"How long have I been here?" I looked at the tubes connected to me.

"Three days."

"How long was I in the hole?"

"Six days." He said with a sorrowful look on his face.

"I thought I was going to die there."

"You almost did. When he went in to get you, I lowered the ladder to lift you out. You were covered in dirt and blood. You looked lifeless and your pulse was faint. Another hour and you would have been with the Moon Goddess."

"Why didn't he just let me die?"

"He needs you for his wolf. Rex has been demanding his true mate. I was in town when he took you to the hole. Gamma Blake told me what happened. Everyone knows you're his true mate and some thought you looked pregnant. Lucy, why didn't you tell me you were pregnant?" He sounded hurt.

"I'm sorry Max." I fought back my tears, as guilt flooded me. "I was scared. I thought because the pup was technically the next Alpha of Dark Moon pack, it might change things or compel you as the Beta, to tell him." I sheepishly admitted.

Max looked pensive and then he exhaled. "I understand. I'm just sorry I didn't get you out of here sooner. Now Ranger isn't going to let you out of his sight."

"Why not? He has his Luna and mate now, I felt it when he marked her" I said. "I've accepted the rejection and broke the bond completely."

"Lucy when you broke the bond, Ranger's wolf Rex, went crazy. When he pulled you out of the hole, he realized you were pregnant and that the pup had not survived. He completely lost it and Rex has shut him out. Ranger can't even shift."

"He deserves to lose his wolf." Lia said to me.

"Lia! You're okay. I thought I had lost you." I was so relieved tears rolled down my face.

"Lucy? Did I say something wrong?" Max asked.

"No, I'm sorry, Lia just spoke to me. I thought I had lost her."

"I'm glad Lia is okay." He smiled.

"I always did like Max." Lia said.

"Don't let anyone know that Lia is back yet, not even Dr. Baker, she might tell Ranger." Max said with a serious tone. "You need to heal and get your strength back, but you also need to drag it out. Pretend to still be weak, so we can work on the escape."

"What's going on?"

"Ranger is going to try and force you to take back your rejection because Rex needs you. He's weak and it makes the pack vulnerable. He might get desperate and try to forcefully mate with you."

"But he went through with the mating ceremony. The bond is completely broken, I don't think you can undo that."

"He's certainly going to try. He needs his wolf."

"I'm sorry Max. You're second in command of the pack and now there's going to be added stress to the pack because the Alpha can't shift. Hopefully Rex won't be upset too long and return to Ranger. I will not take back the rejection. I would rather die. I know it makes the pack more vulnerable, I'm sorry, but I can't. What he did, was unforgivable." I lowered my head.

"I understand. You don't need to apologize to me Lucy. The way you have been treated over the years, the abuse and neglect. It's unacceptable. This is going to be a hard, but necessary, lesson for Ranger to learn."

"Does Miranda know?"

"She's trying to figure out how to kill you. Half the pack and the elders are insisting on the true Luna."

"But, why would the elders care about a lowly slave?" I asked.

"They understand the significance of a gift from the Moon Goddess. They also understand consequences of disrespecting the Goddess, so the elders are worried. Lucy, the Moon Goddess chose you as the Luna and they have all turned a blind eye while you have been abused all these years." He replied.

"I have to get out of here!"

"Take it easy Lucy, you're safe here for now. There's a guard outside your door around the clock to make sure nothing happens to you and so you don't escape."

"Who's guarding the door now?"

He smiled. "You're looking at him."

"So, we secretly build my strength up, tell no one about Lia and I make a run for it before Ranger can torture me again." I recapped.

"Pretty much. Except there's also one more little detail." Max grinned at me and handed me a zippo lighter.

"What's this for?" I looked down at the zippo.

"Now you're armed! Anyone tries to hurt you again and you burn their ass!"

CHAPTER 17 – RUN

"WHY THE HELL WASN'T I NOTIFIED IMMEDIATELY WHEN SHE WOKE UP?" I heard Ranger roar outside my door.

"Sir, she just woke up twenty minutes ago." Delta Cole said. He was on guard duty outside my door and had switched places with Max. I had been awake last night, but Cole looked into the room this morning and caught me with my eyes open.

Dr. Baker was in the room examining me when Ranger swung the door open. His hands were clinched in fists and his piercing blue eyes trained on me. In a flash he was standing next to my bed. Feeling the tension in the room, Dr. Baker, excused herself. "I'll be outside if you need me."

Ranger stood silent for a moment looking me over before he spoke. "Why didn't you tell me about the pup? My pup?"

A lump formed in my throat thinking about my baby. "You rejected me because I was weak. I wasn't going to let you reject our pup too."

"You couldn't have hidden it much longer. You were planning on running away with my pup, weren't you?"

Hell yes, I was. "I-I hadn't thought that far yet. I was hoping you would have changed your mind about me before you marked Miranda." It was sort of true.

"I would have taken care of you Lucy. I would never have rejected my pup."

Yeah, I'm sure he would have taken care of me, in exchange for being his mistress, I mentally rolled my eyes. "You wanted your pups with Miranda. Shouldn't you be on your honeymoon in Hawaii, making all those pups you talked about?"

He seemed to be struggling for words and ran his fingers through his thick black hair. "You need to take it back Lucy, Rex needs you."
I wanted to scream *GO TO HELL*, but I said nothing.

His blue eyes softened, "Please Lucy, Rex has blocked me out and will not allow me to shift. The pack needs a strong Alpha, you have to take it back! The pack needs you."

"I thought you said the pack needs a strong Luna. Now you're telling me that you need me, so you can be a strong Alpha, because the pack needs a strong Alpha. The only thing this pack needs is their laundry done and rooms cleaned." He can go jump off a cliff at this point.

"I'm your Alpha and your mate, I need you, Rex needs Lia." I could hear the desperation in his voice.

"The last time I checked Miranda was your mate."

"Lucy—"

"You didn't need me when you rejected me. You didn't need me when you kenneled me like a dog. When you starved me for days, when you beat me, when you whipped me in front of the pack, when you pushed me in the hole and left me to die. And you sure as hell didn't need me when you marked and mated with your fake mate." I took a deep breath and wiped the tear that escaped from my eye. "All those things you did to me, you did to your pup too."

"Look, I made a mistake, a huge mistake. Rex has always wanted you and only you."

"But you didn't, YOU didn't want me! I'm sorry for Rex, but there's nothing I can do. My wolf left me when our pup died. I'm practically human. Maybe I should just go and live a human life in the city?" I tested the waters on the idea of leaving.

"You're not going anywhere Lucy. You belong with me and you will be with me." He took a deep breath; his eyes were livid.

"I would rather die than be with you." I shot back and saw hurt flash across his face. "You can't even be faithful to Miranda. You don't think I can't feel you cheating on her too? When you're in the city."

"It's different. Miranda is not my true mate."

"No, she's not and yet here you stand, marked and mated to her." I paused. "Please ... please just leave." I turned my head away from him. "I need to rest up so I can get better and return to the pile of laundry waiting for me, Alpha."

Ranger left the room and I could hear him in the hallway talking to Dr. Baker. "How long until I can move her?" I heard him ask, but where the hell did, he want to take me?

"We'll have to take x-rays again tomorrow, to see how fast she's healing without her wolf. It might be another day or two before she's stable enough to be moved, but she really needs bed rest for at least a week." She informed him.

"Can she have more pups?" He asked.

"Yes, but it's best to wait a few months."

"I'll be back tomorrow; mind link me if anything changes." He told her before he left.

I spent the day resting, eating and planning. When Dr. Baker runs the x-rays tomorrow, she will see my bones have healed and know that Lia is back. By the sound of it, Ranger was also planning to breed me as soon as possible. I have to get the hell out of here and I've made up my mind. I'm leaving at the break of dawn!

It was midnight and I heard the guards switching out. I was hoping for Max tonight, so I could discuss my escape, but ended up with Blake at my door. Blake had my door propped open and sat in the hallway guarding me or making sure I wasn't going to leave.
I was planning on slipping out of the tiny bathroom window at dawn, but to do that unnoticed, I needed Blake to close my room door.

"Gamma," I called out.

"Yes Luna."

What did he say? Luna? Did he just call me Luna? I must be hearing things, surely, he meant to say Lucy. "I'm a little hungry. Do you think you can find some food in the clinic kitchen?"

"Sure, I'll be right back." He walked down the hall to the kitchen. A few moments later he reappeared with prepackaged turkey sandwiches, muffins and milk for the both of us.

I figured since I was leaving in a few hours, I should eat what I could. We both ate in silence. When I was done, Blake took my trash and put it in the garbage.

"Thank you." I said.

"Sure thing. Is there anything else you need?"

"Umm, would it be ok if you closed my door and turned the lights off so I could sleep now?" I asked.

"No problem, good night." He said.

"Good night." I yawned. Mission accomplished! With the door closed, I should be able to sneak into the bathroom and slip out. I laid on the bed snoozing, waiting for the hours to pass. The patrols were heaviest at night and my golden fur color would make me much easier to spot at night, so I had to wait for the break of dawn to make a run for it.

I had the zippo lighter in my hand, and I was tip toeing to the bathroom. I could see the sky getting lighter as the sun started rising. This is it! I was suddenly scared and excited all at once.

"It's show time!" Lia chimed. She was just as anxious to get the hell away from here as I was.

I slid the window open quietly and wiggle out. I ran to the tree line and dropped on my hands and knees. I closed my eyes and pictured my wolf, praying my shift would be quicker than it had been as my bones started cracking.

Two minutes later, my torn gown was on the ground and I was picking up the zippo in my mouth. I ran south and stopped occasionally to rub myself on some trees and rocks so my scent could be followed south. When I reached the flowing river, I hesitated.

"I've got this!" Lia reassured me and waded into the water. I gave full control to her and she started swimming upriver to the north. She was swimming with great ease and kept her head above water with the zippo still in her mouth.

"Lucy? Lucy are you there?" It was a mind link from Max.

"Yes Max."

"Blake just mind linked us that you're gone. Ranger is sending out the trackers, keep running and stick to the plan." His voice was urgent.

"I will. I'm sorry I didn't get a chance to say goodbye."

"Be safe Lucy and trust in Lia."

"Max, there's a tote bag in my tub, pictures of my parents—"

"Don't worry about it. I'll keep it safe for you until I see you again.

Now run Lucy and don't forget to break the pack bond before you step out of the territory."

"Thanks Max, I owe you my life."

We reached the most northern point of the pack territory and Lia got out of the water and shook out her fur.

"LUCY!" Ranger called through the mind link.

"LUCY, PLEASE, I NEED YOU!" He called again.

I stood with one paw in the pack boarder and the other paw over the border. I spoke the words through the mind link, "I, Lucy Michaels, break all ties and connections with Dark Moon Pack and am no longer a member."

The pack felt the breaking of the bond and several howls could be heard in the distance. The hunt was on and I need to move quick. After years of neglect and abuse at this pack, I was finally free. I turned tail and ran north, in the direction of the most powerful and deadliest pack in the world.

Let's hope they don't try to kill me too!

CHAPTER 18 – CAUGHT

The wind had a chill that promised flurries of snow this evening. Lia was in control and running through the dense mountain woods heading north. She only stopped twice for water.

There's no way Ranger's trackers could find us now; Lia was so fast compared to other wolves. Her super speed made the scenery blur by fast. The further north we went, the colder it got. A few more hours of running and the sun was setting.

"We should find a place to sleep for the night." I told Lia.

"I can keep running Lucy, I'm picking up a faint smell of rogues and want to make sure we're safe."

I didn't think there would be many rogues this far north because winter is coming. The snow tends to move rogues further south, towards warmer weather and more resources. We continued to run for a few more hours and the snow flurries started to come down. Lia had thick fur to keep us warm, but I could feel her getting tired after running all day and we both needed sleep.

We stopped at the opening of a small cave and sniffed around. "There's a hint of mountain lion, but I think it's long gone." Lia told me.

Lia had great night vision, but we still needed a fire to

light our way into the cave and warm it up, so I shifted back to my naked self. I flipped the zippo lighter on and was mesmerized by the flame. There was a deep connection that radiated through me. I imagined the ball of fire in the palm of my hand and suddenly it was there, sending a warmth through my body. I closed the lighter shut and the flame in my hand remained.

I looked in the rock cave and it was vacant. I went back out and stood at the opening of the cave. I imagined the flame in my hand burning the inside of the cave walls to heat it up. In a matter of seconds, the cave had become a burning inferno radiating heat.
I willed the fire gone and it disappeared. I slowly entered the cave again and it was warm and cozy, the rock walls would retain heat for a few hours. I shifted back into my wolf to stay warm and curled up to sleep on the soft dirt floor. I felt Lia purr as we drifted off.

A low angry growl pulled me from my sleep. I looked around and heard another growl at the entrance of our cave. Lia bared her teeth back and returned the growl. Before I knew it, we were dashing out of the cave and chased a mountain lion up a tree.
The big tawny cat was perched on a branch, it spit and hissed down at us while Lia considered kitty tartare for breakfast. "Maybe we should try and hunt something a little smaller, that won't gouge out an eye." I suggested to her because we had zero experience hunting.

"I'm good at catching fish." She reminded me.

"Let's run a bit more and stop to fish when we get through the mountains." I told Lia and she agreed.

She picked up the zippo in her mouth and started running again. Dawn was breaking and the ground was dusted with a little snow. I could see the white puffs of our warm breath in the air. I was so thankful to have Lia and her warm fur coat.

A few hours later and Lia was stalking fish in the ice cold river. She stood on the riverbank with large rocks and boulders, her eyes locked on the fish below. In a flash she plunged her head into the water and came up with a fish flapping in her mouth. Before we could even move, there was a howl ripping through the air, and we heard a stampede of wolves heading towards us from all directions.

We dropped the fish and looked for a place to hide. I couldn't let Lia be seen and she was too big to hide somewhere out here. I shifted back and crouched my small frame down between two big boulders in the riverbed. My legs were still in the water and I suddenly remembered that I couldn't swim in human form.

I peeked out between the boulders and saw wolves with red eyes. Rogues! They were met with fierce looking pack wolves who pounced on them. Did I cross over to pack lands? I wondered. I held my breath and stood as still as possible watching things unfold.

The fighting continued as rogue after rogue was torn to shreds. Maybe I could slip away before anyone noticed me. "Grab the zippo." Lia reminded me. She had set it down on top of the rock next to the bolder I was hiding behind when she was fishing.
I reached for the zippo with my shaking hand and

could hardly move. My legs had gone numb from the icy water I was standing in. The fighting was almost over, and I stood frozen behind the boulder, clinging to the zippo. I peeked out again from the crack between the boulders, I saw a huge black Alpha. He had the same silky shine to his coat as Ranger's wolf. The sheer power radiating from him could be felt from where I was hiding. He ripped the head off one of the rogues as if it was a sport. There must have been at least a hundred warriors and they all looked formidable.

"I don't think we could slip away from them without being noticed now." I told Lia.

"If you shift, I could outrun them." She suggested.

"They would all know you're a golden wolf. Even if we are strong, we don't have any training or fighting skills. I don't think we could take them."

"Maybe we could torch our way out of here?" She said.

I don't like the idea of killing innocent people, but I was running out of options. I was standing in a river naked; my legs are numb; my hands are shaking and I'm sure my lips are turning blue.
I don't belong to a pack anymore, so technically I'm a rogue now. Any rogue who trespassed on pack lands is usually killed with no questions asked. I've heard of female rogues being captured and turned to pack slaves or sex slaves for unmated males. What if they tried to send me back to Ranger?

One of the warriors grabbed a rogue who was still alive and shifted back to human form. He threw the rogue on the ground before the Alpha, who was still in wolf form. "Why have you trespassed on our land rogue?" The warrior demanded.

"Someone thought they saw a golden wolf yesterday and we've been tracking it." The rogue told them.

"Sure, and I'm a unicorn!" The outraged warrior growled. "Take him to a cell," he ordered, and the rogue was dragged away into the woods.

"Someone must have spotted us yesterday and moved all night to catch up with us." Lia whispered to me.

"Alpha, I'll send the crew over to dispose of the bodies." Someone said.

"RATS! Now what are we going to do? It's going to take a while for them to dispose of the dead bodies. I'll die of hypothermia before I can climb out of this river." I told Lia.

"You missed one." A deep husky Alpha voice said as he shifted. "A female rogue, and she's hiding behind those rocks."

They all turned towards my hiding place. "Come out now and I'll make your death quick. Stay in that water and you'll be dead soon enough." The warrior called out to me.

He was right, I was going to freeze to death. I flipped open the zippo and imagined the ball of fire in my hand. As it grew bigger, I felt the warmth radiate through my body, thank the Goddess. I could feel my legs again.

I stood for a moment unsure of what to do. If I could

create a distraction long enough with fire to shift, I might be able to run before they could catch me. A few warriors started walking towards my hiding spot and I willed the fire to create a ten foot wall of flames between us.

The river was only about thirty feet wide. I started wading to the other side of the river to make a run for it. I looked over my shoulder and saw my wall of fire was extinguished already. In a panic, I hadn't realized how deep the river was. I was being swept away by the current as my bare feet slipped out from under me.

My arms started flapping around and I couldn't swim. My body crashed with a big boulder under water and I was sure my shoulder just broke. I dropped my zippo lighter in the water and was completely defenseless. I was thinking about shifting and letting Lia swim us to safety. Suddenly, I was lifted in a big bubble of water out of the river. I was levitated over the river and dropped on land with the water bubble splashing all around me.

I was naked on the ground, choking and coughing up water. My head was spinning, and I was struggling to breath. I was surrounded by naked male wolves with no way to escape. My shoulder was burning with pain and my eyes seemed to be leaking tears. I looked up and to my surprise a familiar face with beautiful blue eyes was staring down at me.

"Ranger!" I uttered as I slipped into darkness.

CHAPTER 19 – MATE AGAIN

I opened my eyes and saw a dark blue bed canopy with gold trim overhead. I was in a huge bed under warm blankets that had amazingly fluffy pillows. The ceilings were high with beautiful inlays, the windows were grandiose, and the furniture looked fit for a castle. Where the hell are we? I thought as I sat up in the bed and scanned the impressive room I was in.

The big wooden door creaked open and a she wolf poked her head in. Her jet black hair was in a cute pixie cut and her blue eyes sparkled. She smiled and stepped into the room completely. She may have been a little bigger in size than me and a few inches taller, but she had a powerful aura.

"Ah, Lucy you're awake."

How did she know my name? She looked a little familiar, but I couldn't place her. She stood silent for a moment with her eyes glazed over mind linking someone. A moment later her focus retuned back to me.

"Your shoulder had to be reset, but Dr. Ross said you should be healed in a few days."

"Why am I here? Shouldn't I be locked in a cell?" I asked.

"A cell is no place for our Luna." She smiled.

My heart sank. I'm pretty sure I've seen her before at Dark Moon pack. She was probably guarding the room to make sure I don't escape again. Ranger was going to drag me back as soon as possible, if he doesn't try to mate with me in this big bed first.

"Knock, knock." Said an old familiar voice walking through the door.

"Alpha Knox?" I questioned as I recognized the former Alpha of Dark Moon pack and Rangers father.

"Lucy my dear, it's so good to see you." He smiled warmly at me.
Alpha Knox was in his late forties, he was a handsome, older version of Ranger with a touch of gray hair and a few distinguished crow's feet around his blue eyes. It had been a long time since we've seen him at Dark Moon pack. I wondered where we were and what he was doing here.

"Please, please Alpha, I need to get out of here." I begged and tears swelled in my eyes.

Alpha Knox was friends with my father and was a great Alpha. He wouldn't approve of the cruelty Ursa or Ranger showed me. His mate, Luna Clair, was also killed in the same rogue attack as my father and we've hardly seen him around Dark Moon since.

He looked at me with sympathetic eyes. "Lucy, you're my son's mate and the Luna of this pack. This is where you belong."

Sobs rippled through me and I couldn't control my cries. No one was going to help me, and Ranger would punish me. The door pushed open and through my tears, I saw Ranger's figure move towards me. Those blue eyes trained on me and his hands clenched in fists. His Alpha aura was stronger than I've ever felt and filled the entire room. Was Rex back I wondered?

As he walked closer, something looked different about him. He was slightly fuller and about two inches taller. His hair is shorter, and he looked like he hasn't shaved in over a week. When did he get that small scar through his right eyebrow?

"Lucy, this is my youngest son, Diesel LaRue, Alpha of Crescent Moon pack." Alpha Knox introduced him.

"Crescent Moon Pack?" I said in shock. "We're in Canada?"

"Yes, and yes. This is Crescent Castle." Said the familiar looking female. "You probably don't remember me, but I'm Payton LaRue. I'm the Beta of Crescent Moon." She smiled at me.

I was alone in a room with three blood Alpha's, Ranger's father, brother and sister. My head was spinning, and I felt nauseous. I'm in big trouble now.

"Can I get you something, you must be starving?" Payton asked me.
I shook my head no. "Please, I can't go back to Dark Moon Pack. I'm not the Luna and I don't belong with Ranger." I cried and looked down at my trembling hands.

Diesel let out a low growl. They all stood silent, eyes glazed, mind linking each other.

Alpha Knox spoke first, "Lucy, when did you leave Dark Moon?"

I looked at the window and it was dark out. "About two days ago."

"That was fast!" Payton said. "It's typically a three to four day trek."

"She has no idea how fast it was!" Lia whispered to me.

Diesel was pacing the floor back and forth with his fists still clenched. I wasn't sure if he was angry or annoyed. I vaguely remember Alpha Knox having other children. I was only fourteen when the rogue attack happened and went to live at the pack house. I had assumed they had just left for College or found mates. I had no idea they were running the world's strongest and deadliest pack.

"You're no longer a pack member of Dark Moon Lucy. Do you have any idea how dangerous it is to be a rogue? Why did you leave the pack?" Alpha Knox asked.

I hesitated for a moment. "A-After you left Sir, Ursa moved me out of the room you gave me and into the laundry room. I've lived down there for four years, sleeping on a dog bed next to the laundry sink and doing everyone's laundry. I became the pack slave and wasn't even allowed to train."

"RANGER ALLOWED IT?" Payton growled outraged.

I was starting to like her more and more, I thought to myself. "So am I." Lia chimed back in my head.

I continued telling them what had happened. "After four years of being starved and beaten, I finally turned eighteen and shifted, so I decided to leave."

They all remained silent taking in what I had just said.

"Who beat you?" Diesel's husky voice demanded. He was still pacing and not looking at me.

"A few other pack members, Miranda, Beth, Grace, Steven and of course Ursa. Alpha Ranger thought I was weak; he beat me and threw me in the hole for six days."

Diesel let out an angry growl, then he turned his back to us and ran his fingers through his jet black hair. He took a few deep breaths, as if trying to control his self and that's when I saw it! The same Crescent Moon tattoo on the back of his neck.

"Beta Max was nice to me and became my only friend. He started sneaking me food daily because Ursa only gave me table scraps a few times a week. One night, after Alpha whipped me in front of the pack—"

I was interrupted by another angry growl coming from Diesel.

"— after the whipping, Dr. Baker had to stitch up some wounds on my back. Max had carried me back and stayed with me while she treated me. He noticed a mark on the nape of my neck in the Crescent Moon shape. He was the only one that figured out I was an elemental wolf."

"Which element do you have Lucy?" Payton asked.

"FIRE!" Diesel responded.

I nodded my head. "I don't know much about it or how to really control it. I had been planning on leaving Dark Moon anyway and Max suggested I head north to Crescent Moon. He said he trusted the Alpha of Crescent Moon to help me." I paused.

"Max told me that he had only seen the mark once before and that the Alpha of Crescent Moon was a good friend of his. He told me to keep the mark hidden and head north to Canada. We planned my escape to make it look like I had headed south. No one in their right mind would head north with winter coming." I finished.

"Does Ranger know about your element, Lucy?" Alpha Knox asked me.

"No Sir." I answered.

"Do you believe Ranger will be looking for you?" Payton asked.

Tears started filling my eyes and I wasn't sure what to say, if they called Ranger they would know. "P-please, please don't s-send me back," my shaky voice begged. The three of them stood looking at each other again.

"Lucy, what happened?" Payton pressed.

"Ranger is going to punish me. He can't shift, Rex has blocked him out, an-and it's all my fault." I was crying uncontrollably.

"Why is it your fault Lucy?" Alpha Knox asked.

"Be-because he rejected me for being weak and I accepted his r-rejection." I was shaking and the tears were flowing. There was no way they would help me now, knowing that Ranger needed me. I was going to suffer at Dark Moon for the rest of my life.

"NO! YOU ARE NOT HIS MATE LUCY! HE DOESN'T DESERVE YOU!" Diesels husky voice sent ripples through me and he moved next to my bed.

I looked up and locked eyes with Diesel, he looked so much like Ranger and yet so different. I was instantly pulled into a warm hug; the smell of woodsy pine and fresh musk filled my nose and engulfed my senses. My stomach fluttered with butterflies and my skin tingled under his touch. What the hell is happening?

"MINE!" Diesel growled.

"MATE!" Lia howled.

CHAPTER 20 – MINE

Diesel's POV

I pulled her out of the water and dropped her before me using a water bubble. She looked up at me with the most unique amber colored eyes that ignited a fire within me. Her face held fear and she uttered "Ranger," before she fainted.

Did she think I was Ranger? How did she know Ranger? I wondered if she was from Dark Moon, and why she would be so far north.

"Turn around!" I growled at the warriors. She was naked and I didn't want anyone looking at her. I mind linked my Gamma, Zeke, to bring me some clothes.

I walked over to her and held her to my chest to keep her warm and so I could inhale her scent, it was sweet lavender and vanilla. The most amazing thing I've ever smelled. Her skin was sending tingling sparks through mine and Duke immediately recognized her as our mate.

I brushed her long wet hair away from her face, she was a beautiful little thing. Zeke's wolf appeared behind me and had some clothes in his mouth. "Thanks Zeke." I said as I took the clothes.

I slipped a long shirt over her head and some shorts on myself. She was elemental and had used a fire wall. I moved her long dark brown hair to the side and saw the same Crescent Moon tattoo I had on the back of my neck. She was light as a feather, I held her tight to me and ran back to the castle. I mind linked Dr. Ross to expect me with a patient. I then linked my father to meet me in the infirmary. If she knows Ranger, my father might recognize her.

I ran up the stone stairs and through the double wooden doors of the castle. I raced to the back of the south wing and into the infirmary. I placed her on a bed and Dr. Ross started examining her. Duke was possessive and didn't want anyone touching his mate. I stood at the foot of the bed closely watching everything Dr. Ross did. Even though he was a mated male, Duke wanted to rip his throat out for touching our mate.

My father arrived and instantly recognized her. "Lucy! That's Lucy Michaels, Peter's daughter. What's she doing so far from home?" He asked with concern in his eyes.

Dr. Ross was lifting her shirt off and bringing out the x-ray equipment, I let out a growl and Duke was on edge.

"Son, what's wrong?" My father asked.

"She's my mate." I told him.

"That's wonderful! About time you found your Luna." He smiled and gave me a proud congratulatory hug. "What happened to her?"

I explained what happened with the rogues her use of elemental fire and her fear of Ranger when she saw me. I know my older brother and I have a close resemblance but I'm nothing like him. He's always been a self-absorbed ass.

"She used elemental fire? Her mother, Alice, also had the gift." He said with surprise in his voice.

"Dad, why didn't you tell me?"

"It was so long ago, and she passed away shortly after Lucy was born." He told me. "Peter later found his second chance mate and married Ursa."

"Her shoulder is broken and has started healing; I need to reset it and then you can take her Alpha. She's going to need rest for a few days and food." Dr. Ross instructed.

My dad placed his hand on my shoulder. "It's a good thing you found her today, there's one hell of a snowstorm coming in tonight."

"Let's make sure Ranger doesn't find out she's here yet, there's a reason she was running and afraid." I told my dad and he nodded his head.

An hour later, I was carrying Lucy up the stairs of the north wing to my room. "Mate is so beautiful." Duke sounded like a lovesick puppy.

I gently placed her in my bed and covered her up. I considered lighting a fire in the fireplace to make sure she was warm, but decided against it, in case she freaks out and can't control her element. I added an extra blanket on top of her and sat a while studying her beautiful face. She had long thick eyelashes, a cute little nose and full cherry lips. I could hardly wait to taste those lips.

She would probably sleep for a few hours, so I went down to my office to do a little research. I filled Payton in on the news and she was beyond thrilled to finally have a Luna and sister. I asked Payton to check in on Lucy frequently and let me know when she was awake.

I was back in the library looking for a particular book and thinking about Lucy. I was getting ready to return upstairs to my room and check on her. She must have been exhausted because she's been sleeping for six hours now. Duke was also getting anxious to see her again.

Payton mind linked my dad and I. "She's awake."

When I reached the door, I realized my sister and father were already in there with her. Her eyes glistened with tears and she looked me over. She is the most beautiful thing I have ever set my eyes on. I could feel Duke pushing me to hold and comfort her.

"Lucy, this is my youngest son, Diesel LaRue, Alpha of Crescent Moon pack." My father told her.

"Crescent Moon Pack? We're in Canada?" She asked.

"Yes, and yes. This is Crescent Castle." My sister told her and introduced herself, then she offered her something to eat.

"Mate looks so distressed." Duke was pacing in my mind.

"Please, I can't go back to Dark Moon pack. I'm not the Luna and I don't belong with Ranger." She cried.

136

I let out a low growl. Why the fuck would she belong with Ranger? She's MINE, I thought to myself.

"Calm down son, don't scare her. We need to find out what happened to her." My father said through the mind linked. "Lucy, when did you leave Dark Moon?" He asked her.

"About two days ago." She said.

I linked the others, "There's no way to run that in under three days even in the best of weather." I started pacing, my mind was racing.

"That was fast." Payton said. "It's typically a three to four day trek."

"Maybe she's confused or lost track of time." My dad linked us back.

"Why would she leave the pack with winter in the air to be a rogue?" Payton asked through the mind link.

"You're no longer a pack member of Dark Moon Lucy. Do you have any idea how dangerous it is to be a rogue? Why did you leave the pack?" Dad asked.

"A-After you left Sir, Ursa moved me out of the room you gave me and into the laundry room. I've lived down there for four years, sleeping on a dog bed next to the laundry sink and doing everyone's laundry. I became the pack slave and wasn't even allowed to train."

"RANGER ALLOWED IT?" Payton growled and mind linked us. "I'm going to put him in a cell and make him sleep on a damn dog bed!"

Lucy's voice was shaking. "After four years of being starved and beaten, I finally turned eighteen and shifted, so I decided to leave."

"SHE WAS BEATEN AND STARVED! WHAT KIND OF SHIT IS GOING ON AT DARK MOON?" I linked the others. I swear to the Goddess, I'm going to punish everyone who laid a finger on her.

"Who beat you?" I wanted to know, trying to control my anger.

"A few other pack members, Miranda, Beth, Grace, Steven and of course Ursa. Alpha Ranger thought I was weak; he beat me and threw me in the hole for six days." She let out a few more sobs.

I let out a growl, **"HE PUT HER IN *THE HOLE!* IM GOING TO FUCKING PUT HIM IN A HOLE!"** I linked the others.

"Son control yourself; you're scaring her. We'll deal with Ranger later." My dad linked me back. Duke was snarling and raging, I tried to calm him down as well.

Then I heard her say, "Beta Max was nice to me and became my only friend. He started sneaking me food daily because Ursa only gave me table scraps a few times a week. One night, after Alpha whipped me in front of the pack—"

Another growl escaped me, I was livid and wanted to whip Ranger myself. He was a sorry excuse for an Alpha! My father built that pack up and all he did was bring it down. My friend had to sneak her food for crying out loud.

"— after the whipping, Dr. Baker had to stitch up some wounds on my back. Max had carried me back and stayed with me while she treated me. He noticed a mark on the nape of my neck in the Crescent Moon shape. He was the only one that figured out I was an elemental wolf."

"Which element do you have Lucy?" Payton asked.

"FIRE!" I said. She's the opposite of my element and a perfect balance for me.

She told us how Max helped her plan the escape and sent her north for my help.

"Does Ranger know about your element Lucy?" My dad asked her.

"No Sir."

"Do you believe Ranger will be looking for you?" Payton asked.

"P-please, please don't s-send me back." She cried.

"Lucy, what happened?" Payton tried to get more. I had a feeling there was a whole lot more going on here.

"Ranger is going to punish me. He can't shift, Rex has blocked him out, an-and it's all my fault."

"Well there's some karma for you." Payton linked me.

"Why is it your fault Lucy?" Dad asked.

"Be-because he rejected me for being weak and I accepted his r-rejection." She was sobbing and struggling to breathe.

"She was his mate and he rejected her for being weak? Is he stupid?" Payton said through the link.

"NO! YOU ARE NOT HIS MATE LUCY! HE DOESN'T DE-SERVE YOU!" I told her and moved closer to the bed.

She looked up at me with those beautiful amber eyes, tears streaming down her face. I wanted to kiss her, hold her and never let her go. Ranger was an idiot and now she's mine. Mine to love, mine to protect and mine to cherish. I was her second chance mate and I will not let her down.

Duke couldn't stand it anymore and we sat on the bed to hold our mate. She took a deep breath and relaxed in my arms, sobbing into my chest. The Moon Goddess had given her to me, and I was going to protect her and love her.

"MINE!" I instinctively growled. She was MINE.

CHAPTER 21 – COMFORT

"Lucy, no one is telling Ranger anything. You're safe here. There's still a lot more we need to talk about and sort out but it's getting late. You need to eat something and get some rest; I know you're exhausted. I'll have Helga bring you some dinner from the kitchen." Alpha Knox assured me as he stood to leave.

"My bedroom is at the opposite end of this hall Lucy, if you need anything, please don't hesitate to come over." Payton said and left.

"I'll leave you two to talk." Alpha Knox closed the door behind him.

"Sounds good to me," Lia purred in my head. I did a mental eye roll.

Diesel was still sitting on the bed, facing me. "I don't know everything that happened at Dark Moon, but I know there's more. I'm not going to force you to tell me everything, but I do want to know. When you're ready, I'm here to listen." Diesel told me.

I nodded my head. I felt anxiety growing, if he finds out I was used and tainted he wouldn't want me. I was too weak to protect a pup.
He interrupted my thoughts, "how's your shoulder feeling?"

"It's getting better," I said.

My heart was racing, I wasn't sure what to think or say

to him. This is what they call a second chance mate, I was given a second chance mate.

He placed his hand below my chin and lifted my head, his blue eyes softened. "Lucy, please try to relax, no one is going to hurt you here. I will never let Ranger hurt you again. Max sent you here because he trusted me, I need you to trust me too."

"Max never told me you were Ranger's brother."

"He probably understood if Ranger was treating you badly, that you would be too afraid to seek help from his brother. He may be my brother, but we are nothing alike." He said to me. This much I knew was true. Ranger always made me feel nervous and Diesel had a calming effect.

I looked down at the beautiful blanket and wondered if this was his room. His scent filled the air and it was so comforting. When he held me and stroked my hair moments ago, it was the safest I've ever felt. His Alpha aura was pure power and I wasn't even afraid.
There was a knock at the door and Diesel answered it, he returned with a tray of food and set it on the table next to the bed. He leaned over and reached across my body for another pillow, Goddess he smelled wonderful.

"He sure does!" Lia purred in my head.

"Lean forward a bit," he requested, and I complied. He propped the pillow behind me so that I could sit up with ease.

He sat on the left side of the bed facing me and brought the food plate over from the tray. It smelled delicious, carved turkey, mashed potatoes with gravy, mixed vegetables and a bread roll. He gave me a heart fluttering smile and brought a fork full of food to my mouth. I didn't even bother to resist; my right shoulder was still healing, and my arm was still in a sling. I was right-handed and would surely have embarrassed myself trying to eat with my left hand.

"How's your wolf doing?" Diesel asked me.

"Lia is doing good, just resting up." I answered and Lia howled with joy in my head because her mate was worried about her.

"Lia," he grinned at me. "Duke is looking forward to spending some time with her."

I smiled back and took another delicious bite from the fork in front of me. If he meets Lia, he's going to know she's a golden wolf. I wasn't sure I was ready to tell anyone about Lia yet. Besides, what kind of golden wolf am I? I can't even fight.

Diesel is the Alpha of the strongest pack in the world and I'm, well, I'm a rejected weakling. The only thing I can do well is his laundry. As soon as he figures this out, he's going to reject me too.

"I'd give anything to know what you're thinking right now." His husky voice broke my thoughts.

I smiled for a moment before I responded. "There's just so much going on, it's a bit overwhelming." I took another bite of food.

"If there's anything you need or want, I will move heaven and earth for you little one," he said.

"How about that bread roll? I want that delicious looking roll."

"This roll?" He laughed and brought the roll to my mouth; I took a bite. "I will get you a mountain of rolls my queen," he joked.

I didn't know exactly what to say, I had so many questions. "Is this an actual castle?" I asked and took another bite of the roll; it was so warm and soft.

"It is. It was built in the early eighteen hundreds by my great ancestors and it's surrounded by beautiful mountains. Our family comes from Crescent Moon. My father was the second son of my grandparents, which meant that my uncle Titus was the heir of this pack. Dark Moon had a bad reputation and a cruel Alpha, so my father challenged him to the death and won. He became Alpha of that pack and built it up to one of the strongest in the states."

"How did you end up back at Crescent Moon?" I asked and drank the water he held to my lips.

"Just after the rogue attack that killed my mother Luna Clair and your father, we discovered that my uncle Titus was behind the attack. Ranger became Alpha of Dark Moon on his twenty first birthday and had no interest in confronting my powerful uncle. I had the water element on my side and a hunger to punish my uncle. I came back to Crescent Moon at nineteen to challenge him and avenge my mother. I won and became Alpha of the largest and strongest pack."

"Why did your uncle attack the pack?"

"I'll let my father explain that, if that's okay with you?"

I nodded, "okay."

"Would you like me to run you a hot bath?" He asked. "Your legs must be sore from all that running."

"Yes please! Mate is so thoughtful." Lia chimed.

"That sounds wonderful, thank you." I told him.

He disappeared behind a door and I heard water filling up a tub.
"Lucy, the fireplace is double sided between the bedroom and bathroom by the tub. Would you like me to light a fire in it to keep both rooms warm?"

There was a little chill in the air, and I nodded, "Yes please."

He moved quick and placed a stack of wood in the fireplace. Then he reached for a match and lit the small kindling to start the fire. "The fire should be full in just a bit."

I reached my hand out and felt the power of the small flame. I imagined a full crackling fire and the flames grew instantly filling the room with warmth. Diesel smiled proudly at me and said, "Thank you."

He walked back to the bed and carried me bridal style into the bathroom. Talk about a grand chamber. Wow! It had a massive rock shower, double sink vanity, a water closet for the toilet, a lounge chaise in the corner by the huge claw foot bathtub and of course the beautiful double sided fireplace protruding from the stone wall.

He set me down on the chaise and turned off the water. "I added bath salts and bubbles to help relax your muscles."

"Thank you." I smiled; he really was so thoughtful.

He stood for a moment as if debating on what to do next. "Stand up, I'll help you get in."

My breath hitched in my throat and the butterflies in my stomach took flight. I hesitated.

"I've seen you naked already." He flashed me a sheepish grin. "Besides, you've only got the use of one arm and the tub is really big. I don't want my mate drowning again." His smile widened.

"Fine." I rolled my eyes and stood up.

He chuckled and started to carefully remove my sling. Then he slowly lifted the large shirt up over my head. The glow from the fireplace was the only light in the chamber and I saw his eyes darken. His hands moved slowly down my sides and trailed tingles in their wake. He gently lifted me up and slowly lowered me in the water.

His arms and shirt got soaked from the bubbles and water when he set me in the tub. The warmth from the water instantly soothed and relaxed me. Diesel pulled his wet shirt off and knelt beside the tub.

"Oh, sweet Moon Goddess!" Lia panted in my head and I almost laughed out loud at her. "Down girl," I told her. I turned to look at the fireplace on the other side hoping he didn't see the blush creeping up my face.

I tried to lean back on the tub to relax, but my body floated up and I got a mouth full of water trying to sit up again. "Oops, too much water, I suppose." Diesel chuckled again. "I could come in and be your lifeguard."

"The pool is big enough," I jokingly said. Before I realized what I had actually said, he was naked and sliding in behind me.
Diesel pulled my back into his chest and the sparks were flying. He put his head in my shoulder and inhaled. "Relax, I won't do anything you don't want me to do, except maybe wash your hair."
I let out a nervous giggle and took a deep breath. His scent washed over me, and I laid back into him. I felt a low purr in his chest, and I knew his wolf was happy to have us close. I couldn't believe how comfortable I was around him. How natural this felt.

I looked towards the other side of the chamber at the window and watched the snow falling. Diesel started massaging the shampoo into my hair and then on my scalp. Everything seems so surreal. A week ago, I was in the hole, cold and starving. Now, I'm in a castle with prince charming, warm, fed and safe.

The crackling sounds from the fire were relaxing, the warm water was soothing, and Diesel's touch lulled me. I continued to watch the snow fall and my eyes became heavy. I was so relaxed and comfortable, I drifted to sleep.

CHAPTER 22 – TITUS

I opened my eyes and thought I had dreamed the whole thing. But here I was, laying on my back in the big comfortable bed, wearing a bath robe with my hair wrapped in a towel. Diesel must have carried me out of the tub and put me to bed. I looked down at my waist and found Diesel. He was sleeping on his stomach with his arm draped around my midsection. He was topless and wearing dark gray sweatpants.

I had a great view of his sexy back and shoulders. He had the same tribal tattoos covering his left chest, shoulder and arm as Ranger. Even though they had so many mom similarities, I couldn't help but admire Diesel for their differences. Diesel even made the small scar in his eyebrow look sexy.

"Are you done checking me out yet?" His gruff voice said as he squeezed his arm tighter around my waist, drawing a giggle from me.

There was a knock on the door and Diesel groaned. "Come in Payton."

She came into the room and smiled wide. "Good morning Lucy. I brought you some clothes and boots for today, in case you want to get out of bed and explore the castle."

"Thank you, Payton." I smiled.

"Don't mention it. Maybe if you're feeling up to it tomorrow, I could take you shopping. That is, if your gracious mate will spare you and give us his black card." She gave Diesel a grin with her eyebrows raised.

"It just so happens, that I've got business in the city tomorrow. So, if you ladies would like, you can both come with me and shop while I attend to business at the office."

"YAY!" Payton clapped her hands and jumped on the bed with us. Then she grabbed a pillow and bopped Diesel with it. I couldn't help but laugh.

"How's your shoulder feeling Lucy?" She asked.

"Much better, I think it's almost healed."

"Lucy, my father just mind linked me. He wants to know if you're up to having breakfast downstairs?" Diesel asked.

"Sure, let me get dressed."

"Come on, I'll help you." Payton picked up the clothes and headed for the bathroom. When I stepped out, I was wearing blue jeans with a black sweater and black boots. Diesel came over and secured the sling on my arm.

We headed down a beautiful staircase to make our way to breakfast. We passed a few pack members who stared at me curiously and greeted the Alpha and Beta. My eyes tried to take in as much of the castle's beauty and craftsmanship. It was stunning.

We were approached by an older gentleman who appeared to be a butler. "Good morning Alpha, Beta, Miss." He bowed his head to us. "Alpha Knox is in the family dining room this morning waiting for you." He raised his arm and motioned towards a big wooden door.

"Good morning Lucy. How did you sleep?" Alpha Knox asked me.

"Wonderful, thank you."

Diesel sat at the head of the table and pulled me onto his lap. Payton sat to the right of us and Alpha Knox was seated on the left. They both had big smiles on their faces and my cheeks flushed red. Platters of food were brought in and set before us, eggs, sausages, bacon, potatoes and toast with three different jams. A young lady poured coffee and set a decanter down of juice next to a pitcher of water.

"Thank you, that is all." Diesel dismissed them.

"Lucy, do you like coffee?" He asked.

I shook my head no. "I prefer the juice please."

He poured a glass of juice and started to fork food on his plate. I remembered when Alpha Jordan pulled me to his lap and fed me, it seemed a little awkward at the time, but sitting in Diesel's lap felt so natural. His desire to protect and take care of me drove his behavior. He began feeding the both of us and Alpha Knox broke the silence.

"Lucy, I'm sure your mind is swimming with questions, and I'll do my best to answer them."

I thought for a moment, I did have a lot of questions. Where do I start? "Are there others out there, who are elemental?"

He considered the question for a moment. "Possibly, but most have been hunted down and killed." He paused a moment. "I guess I'll need to start at the beginning."

Payton had stopped chewing and was listening to her father intently as well.

"Your father Peter and I were friends since we were pups, he was originally from Crescent Moon and became the best warrior we had. When my brother Titus became Alpha, Peter and I headed south with a few others and eventually took over Dark Moon pack. A few years later, we were in northern Alaska for pack business. We stumbled on a small pack no one had ever heard about. Your father and I both met our mates there. Clair came back and became my Luna. Your mother Alice, was her best friend and came back to be with her mate, Peter." He stopped to sip his coffee.

"There's an old legend that says, the direct descendants of the Moon Goddess shall possess the powers to control the elements. Over the centuries the special gifts have skipped generations and siblings. While Clair did not possess any powers herself, Diesel was blessed with the elemental gift of water. It skipped Ranger and Payton, but it doesn't necessarily mean their children or grandchildren won't have the gift. Your mother on the other hand, also had the gift of elemental fire. I didn't expect it would pass to you, because it often skips generations." He said.

Diesel gently squeezed my hand and gave me a reassuring smile.

"My brother Titus was the Alpha of Crescent Moon and became obsessed with trying to find an elemental wolf to mate with and create stronger offspring. When he failed to secure one, he set his eyes on your mother. She refused and a war broke out. He shot her with a silver bullet through the heart. We lost a third of the pack in that attack."

I tried to process what he had just told me. Diesel looked up at me with concern in his eyes. He wiped the tear that escaped from the corner of my eye.

"I'm sorry Lucy. Crescent Moon had nearly fifteen hundred pack members and we had four hundred, half were women and pups. Titus left us alone after that and we continued to build the pack up and forge alliances with other packs. When Diesel turned eighteen, his wolf was stronger than any Alpha I'd ever met, and he discovered his power to control water. He trained relentlessly and as Diesel grew stronger, Ranger became more insecure. Their relationship has never been the same.

A year later my brother paid rogues to attack us looking for Diesel, but he was in the city that day on pack business. That was the day I lost Clair and my best friend. And I believe you know the rest." He finished with sadness on his face.

We ate breakfast in silence, thinking about what we had just heard. Someone knocked on the door before opening it and two men walked in, they radiated power. The first was tall with dark brown hair styled in a faux hawk, brown eyes and a serious look on his face. The other was a little shorter, about six foot with sandy blond hair, brown eyes and a goofy smile on his face.

The serious one nodded his head to us. "Alpha, the warriors and pack are training at the indoor arena today. Will you be joining us or inspecting?" He asked.

"Lucy, you know my Beta, Payton, already. This is my Gamma, Ezekiel and Delta, Elliot."

"Please, call me Zeke." The tall serious one said.

"I will not be at training today." Diesel told them. "Payton will be there for inspections shortly. I will be helping our Luna settle in." He winked at me.

Both of their eyes widened in surprise. "Welcome Luna." Zeke bowed his head again.

"I'm so glad he's finally found you! If you need any-thing, Luna, do not hesitate to come to me, your trusty Delta." Elliot flashed me a toothy smile and bowed his head. Diesel growled possessively and Alpha Knox tried to hide a chuckle.

"Come Lucy, Dr. Ross wants to look at your shoulder again and then I'll give you a tour." Diesel set me on my feet, and I waved goodbye to the others. After Dr. Ross examined me and verified my shoulder had fully healed, we went on the castle tour.

The castle had four wings, the east and west wings were pack rooms. The northern tower was the family wing and the southern wing was the largest central wing of the castle. It was complete with a grand ball-room, dining hall, library, movie theater, billiard and game room, main kitchen, formal sitting room, offices, pack lounge and the infirmary.

The basement had a massive, well stocked, supply room for food and necessities, in case of severe weather. There was a full gym and indoor heated swimming pool, as well as an underground parking garage. We reached the last big room in the basement and I heard the familiar sound of washer machines and dryers tumbling. I opened the door and looked at the laundry room. I stood frozen and panic bubbled inside of me. Was he going to lock me down here?

My head was spinning, and my chest was tight. Tears streamed down my face and Diesel pulled me into his chest. "It's okay baby, you're okay." He cooed in my ear. "Look at me Lucy, baby look at me." He cupped my face and looked into my eyes. "We hire and pay all the wolves who work in this castle. I would never enslave anyone, that is not who we are."

He studied my face for a moment. "What Ursa and Ranger did was cruel. No one deserves that. Please, please baby, do not let that define you. That part of your life is over. You are so much more than that, you are strong, smart and beautiful." He took my hand and placed it over his heart, it was beating wildly. "You are the other half of me and my Luna, little one."

I looked deep into his beautiful blue eyes and I saw so much raw emotion swimming around. "You are MINE." He said.

"Yours." I nodded and his lips came crashing onto

mine with such passion and desire.

CHAPTER 23 – LIGHTS

After the castle tour, I asked Diesel if I could spend some time alone in the library and he walked me back over to it. I stepped inside and admired the general splendor of this beautifully crafted Library. The room was round, with dark wooden shelfs that were lined with books three stories high. It had two large sliding wooden ladders and a beautiful fireplace. There were two large study tables in the middle, with computers and several deep armchairs around the room.

I found the section on werewolf history and pulled several books down. The fireplace was already stacked with wood, so I lit a match and brought the fire to full. I sank into a cozy armchair by the fireplace flipping through books and reading page after page. I had just finished reading about the rare white wolf. I turned the page to read about a wolf even more rare than a white wolf—

"The Golden Wolf." Diesel's voice came from over my shoulder. I had been so engrossed with the book that I didn't sense him entering the Library. "Are you reading up on myths?" He asked sounding amused.

"Lots of fascinating things to read up on. I was hoping to find more information on elemental wolfs." I said.

"There's very little you'll find in books. My father helped me train and expand my power. I'm sure he would be happy to help work with you as well."

"That would be wonderful." I smiled.

"Come, we're having dinner at a special spot. Leave the books on the chair, no one will touch them." He grabbed my hand and led the way.

We were on the top floor of the northern tower, where our room was. Diesel stopped and pulled a small door open that went further up into the tower. We climbed the dark circular stairs and reached another door. Diesel smiled and held the door open for me. It was the pointy cone shaped room at the top of the northern tower. There were several telescopes in the corner and star charts on one side of the wall. In the center of the room was a table with the glow of a single candle and dinner plates set up.

"This is the astronomy observatory." He flipped a switch on the wall and the metal roof started to retract back. Moments later, we stood in a glass top room with a beautiful view of a crescent moon and stars. There wasn't a cloud in sight.

"Do you like it?" He asked as he took my hand and seated me at the table.

"It's amazing, I can see the stars so clearly."

"If you look towards the north on clear nights like this, you'll be able to see the Aurora Borealis."

My breath hitched. "The Northern Lights!"

He gave me a wide smile. "This is the best view in the house!"

He uncovered our plates and we had Lasagna, Tuscan vegetables and garlic bread knots for dinner. He poured me a glass of water and also offered me wine.

"I've never had wine before." I blushed.

"Would you like to try some of mine?" He offered his glass. I took it and had a small sip. It tingled my tongue before I swallowed it.

"It's not bad." I smiled and he poured me a small glass.

We ate our dinner and pointed out stars and constellations in the sky. He tried to convince me that the Sirius constellation was actually a great Alpha wolf and not a dog. I gawked and awed at the light show the northern lights put on.

We finished with dinner and Diesel uncovered chocolate cannoli for dessert. I've seen cannoli's before but have never had them. "That looks delicious!" I practically drooled and Diesel brought a fork full across the table to feed me.

"A girl could get used to this." Lia said to me.

I smiled wide and Diesel brought another fork full to my mouth. It was so good, I let out a low moan and Diesel gave me a low growl in response. "I'll be sure to give your complements to Helga." He laughed.

"This is just so amazing." I looked out and the view was breathtaking.

"When my father was a pup, he would often have sleepovers in this room, it was his favorite room in the castle."

"Ohh that sounds wonderful, I would love to sleep up here!" I said dreamingly.

I stood up and went to the glass edge. I wondered, since my father and Alpha Knox grew up together, how many times he slept up here under the same glass walls. Now I was destined to be Luna of Crescent Moon and this castle felt like home. Diesel stood behind me and wrapped his arms around my waist. I leaned my head back on his chest. I looked out and saw the lights from pack houses and family homes scattered across the land. The mountains were snowcapped, and everything looked picturesque.

I looked to the West and saw what looked like a small town. "That's the village over there." He told me. "It's completely owned by the pack; we rarely get humans this far in the mountains. My favorite Chinese food restaurant is there." He smiled.

"I love Chinese food!"

"We'll have to take you there soon."

Someone knocked on the door. "Come in." Diesel called out and a woman entered to take the plates away. She was followed in by two butlers, one who carried a mattress and the other who carried bedding and pillows. They moved the table out of the center of the room and placed the mattress down. I looked over at Diesel and he grinned at me. "Your wish is my command."

He took my hand and brought me to the mattress in the middle of the room. "It can get cold up here at night, but we've got thick blankets." He pulled me into his chest, he smelled intoxicating.

"Since it was your idea to sleep in the astronomy tower Lucy, I'm willing to share my body heat with you." He laughed. "Body heat works best without clothes and I want to make sure my little mate is snug and warm." He said and pulled his shirt off.

This man was panty dropping, chiseled perfection, I thought to myself.

"He sure is!" Lia purred in my head.

He reached for the bottom of my sweater and started lifting it up.

"I promise not to bite, unless you want me to."

"I DO, I DO!" Lia panted in my head.

"Control yourself Lia." I told her.

He took another step closer to me and inhaled my scent, I could feel the heat radiating off his body. I lifted my arms up giving him permission to undress me. My sweater was gone, and he pulled me into a hug reaching for my bra hooks. He planted a kiss between my neck and shoulder where his mark was supposed to go. I swear my knees almost buckled under me.

My bra fell to the ground and I felt so exposed in the glass room. He sat me down on the mattress and pulled off my boots and socks slowly. Then he stood up and kicked off his shoes and socks. I don't know where I found the courage, but I reached up and un-buckled his jeans and slid them to the floor. I heard another growl from deep within his chest. He stepped out of the jeans and knelt down in front of me, wearing nothing but his boxer briefs.

He laid me back on the mattress and unbuckled my jeans. He pulled them off slowly and sat back on his heals to take me in. My arms instinctively crossed over my chest.

"Don't hide from me Lucy, you are absolutely beautiful." He positioned himself over me and looked deep into my eyes, as if looking into my soul. His lips softly kissed mine and he placed a few more kisses on my neck and down my shoulder.

He reached down and peeled off the last shred of clothing I had on. He pulled the blankets back and I crawled in. When he removed his boxers, I found myself desperately wanting to look at him but kept my eyes on the moon.

"Little one, this is all yours. You're free to look as much as you want and have anything, anytime you want." His husky voice teased me and I felt heat pulsing through my body.

He lifted the covers up and I felt my ass exposed when he climbed in next to me. I wanted him in every way, right here, right now. But, I knew I needed to wait, I was broken, and he deserved to know what he was getting. I have to find the courage to tell him what happened at Dark Moon and pray he doesn't reject me.

Diesel reached for me and closed the gap, his arm snaked around my waist. My back was pressed into his chest and we were buried under heavy blankets together, naked. Everything felt so right with him. Like two pieces of a puzzle finally coming together. We laid quiet for a while and watched the northern lights dance beautifully across the sky before drifting off to sleep.

CHAPTER 24 – TRUTH

I was falling, falling into a cold dark pit. I crashed to the bottom of the hole laying in my own personal hell surrounded by darkness. My heart was racing, and I could taste the blood running from my nose. There was a stabbing pain in my stomach, and I reached for my baby. Cradling my little bump, I cried frantically. "Please be okay, please be okay."

"Lucy, Lucy, wake up." Someone was shaking me.

A scream escaped my lips and I sat up in bed, sweat was beading on my face and my heart was racing. I felt strong arms pulling me into the comfort of a warm chest. I was struggling to breath and couldn't control my sobs. A familiar woodsy and musk scent hit my nose and started calming me.

"I've got you, you're safe." Diesel cooed as he rubbed circles on my back for a few minutes until I was calm enough.

"It was just a bad dream."

"No." I sobbed. "It wasn't. It really happened; it was real."

He looked down at me with pain in his eyes. "I want to know."

I wanted to tell him everything, but I didn't know how. I didn't want to lose him. I looked into his searching eyes and my heart ached. I knew I had to tell

him, he deserved to know.
"The night of my first shift, Ranger found me and dis-covered I was his mate. H-He took me to the cabin an-and mated with me. Then he rejected me."

Diesel let out a low growl.

"H-He said I was weak and couldn't defend myself. He said I was unfit to be L-Luna and he needed to pick someone who was strong for the pack, so he picked Mi-randa." The tears streamed down my face.

Diesel pulled me back into his chest. "Ranger is a self-centered fool."

"That's not all." I pulled back and looked down sob-bing.

"You can tell me." He said.

I hesitated, took a deep breath. "After he rejected me, he tried to sleep with me again, but I refused. He wanted to keep me as a mistress for Rex, so the pun-ishments continued because I wouldn't give in. I had already planned my escape, but then Miranda burned an iron mark through your mother's Luna dress and blamed me. Before I knew it, Ranger had carried me out to the hole, he ripped my clothes off and pushed me in."

I looked up into Diesels eyes and could see he was struggling to control his wolf. He didn't say anything.

"When he pu-pushed me in, he didn't know that I was pregnant. I-I lost the pup—" I sobbed.

He pulled me into his chest and kissed the top of my

head. I could feel his strong heartbeat drumming and anger pulsing through his aura. He placed his head down into my neck and inhaled deeply, trying to calm himself.

After what seemed like an eternity, he looked into my eyes. "I don't know anyone who could endure what you've been through and still survive. You're the strongest she wolf I have ever met and I'm lucky the Moon Goddess sent you to me." He lifted my chin and placed a kiss on my lips. "You were born to be a Luna Lucy. My Luna."

Lia happily yipped. "Mate still wants us."

I threw my arms around his neck and cried tears of relief, tears of joy and tears for my pup. He pulled me back down under the blankets and I laid my head on his chest. We laid in silence for the next hour just breathing in each other's scent. The sky started to lighten with the break of dawn on the horizon.

"I have to attend to business at the office today. Are you still feeling up to shopping? There's a large mall by the office and a closet that needs to be filled with clothes." Diesel kissed the top of my head again.

"I don't want to disappoint Payton." I looked up at him and smiled, my eyes felt swollen from crying.

An hour later, Payton, Elliot, Diesel and I, were all standing on the roof top of the west wing at the helicopter. Elliot and Payton sat in the pilot seats and placed large headphones over their ears. Diesel sat in the back and pulled me on his lap.

He put large headphones on both of our heads, and I heard his husky voice come through. "The headphones are so we can hear each other. If you get scared, you can hold tight to me little one." He winked at me.

He was wearing a tailored, dark charcoal, suit and blue tie that complemented his smoking hot body. His muscled arms wrapped around my waist and he planted a kiss on my neck.

"We're all cleared for takeoff Sir. We should arrive in Vancouver in forty-five minutes." Elliot's voice came through the headphones and he started the take off. Diesel instinctively rubbed circles on my back to ease the flight jitters. During the flight he pointed out landmarks, bodies of water and other interesting points below. The city came into view and we descended on the helipad that topped a tall building which read, LaRue Enterprises.

Diesel linked his fingers through mine and walked us towards the elevator. The office building was sleek and modern. We walked past his secretary, who was an older she wolf in her fifties. "Good Morning Sir, the files are all on your desk and your coffee is ready." She smiled.

"Thank you. Pearl, this is my beautiful mate, Lucy." He introduced us and she beamed back a smile.

"Welcome Luna! Is there anything I can get for you?"

"The keys to the Escalade please, Elliot is taking the ladies shopping." Diesel said.

"Yes sir, I'll be right back."

We stepped into Diesel's office, it had floor to ceiling windows with stunning views of the city. I walked over to them and looked out. Diesel sat down in his large leather chair. He pulled out his black card and handed it over to Payton.

"Come here." He motioned for me to come over to him. When I was close enough, he pulled me onto his lap. "Now, I want you to go with my sister and do me a favor."

"A favor?" I repeated.

"I want you to try and max out my black card." He placed a kiss on my neck. "Buy anything you want, little one."

"Don't worry, I'll help her." Payton gave him a wide smile.

Three hours later and Elliot was making another trip to the mall parking garage to unload our bags. I can't remember the last time I had anything new from the store and was nervous when Payton stacked arm loads of clothes for me at the register. We continued to shop and went into a boutique dress shop, where she forced me to try on casual dresses and formal gowns. "Diesel will love all of them on you." She smiled and walked all of them over to the register.

We met Elliot back at the food court and ordered some burgers. I chewed on my burger and looked around, the mall was filled with humans shopping and the occasional wolf. I couldn't seem to shake the feeling that we were being watched.

"Is there another pack in this city? I asked.

"The city is neutral territory, there are wolves who work in the city from other small packs. There are also lone wolfs who choose to live human lives here." Elliot said.

Maybe I was just sensing other wolfs nearby and Lia was on edge being in a new environment. She was missing the comfort of her mate. We continued eating our lunch and Payton filled me in on LaRue Enterprises.

The company developed security software and systems. Ranger managed the U.S. branch and Diesel managed the Canadian branch. Diesel had expanded his branch internationally a few years ago and held eighty percent of the shares in LaRue Enterprises as a result. He came into the city every Monday for meetings and handled all other business from home.

We continued shopping for two more hours and had bags full of shoes, coats, jackets, makeup, toiletries, accessories, and underwear. Payton bought herself a few items as well, including a new designer handbag.

It was late afternoon and Diesel was done for the day. Elliot had just finished cramming all the packages into the helicopter. Diesel lifted me up and placed me on his lap. A pink lingerie bag tipped over next to us and some panties rolled out. "Have anything special in there for me?" His eyebrows wiggled up and down and I let out a nervous giggle.

All the shopping was exhausting, I turned into Diesel and laid my head down between his neck and shoulder. I planted a gentle kiss on his neck and felt his chest purr and relax. He smelled delicious.

"Everyone all set?" Elliot asked and Diesel nodded his head.

"How was the shopping Delta? Did they give you any trouble?"
Diesel asked.

"No Alpha, but they did threaten to have my eyebrows waxed at one point." He said and Diesel let out a laugh.

"Oh, but I did run into Alpha Jordan at the mall when I was carrying bags out to the car, he sent you his regards."

"Jordan Monroe? Did he say what he was doing so far north?" Diesel asked.

"No, he didn't." Elliot answered.

Alpha Jordan was nice to me when he visited Dark Moon, but he was also the cause of jealousy for Ranger. I was glad I didn't run into him. I'd really hate for him to tell Ranger where I was. I wasn't ready to be discovered yet.

Lia was on edge. "What's the likelihood he would be in Vancouver, at the mall, at the same time as us?" She asked me.

CHAPTER 25 – DATE

"Hello sleeping beauty." Diesel's sexy voice said when I opened my eyes. He was carrying me down the stairs into the Castle. I had fallen asleep on the flight back.

"I have a meeting in my office with my chief warriors that should have started ten minutes ago. I was going to take you to the room to sleep, but since you're awake we'll head on over."

"Okay, but can you put me down first?" I smiled.

We reached his office door and he set me down. He held my hand and opened the door. "My apologies for the delay."

We walked to the conference table and everyone was already seated. Diesel sat at the head of the table and pulled a seat for me on his right side. Payton was the Beta and sat at his left side, across the table from me.

"Lucy, you already know my father, Alpha Knox, Beta Payton, Gamma Zeke, and Delta Elliot. My chief warriors and trainers over here are Danny, Paul, Lance, Athena and Nolan. And this is Sam, our chief tracker." I smiled and nodded hello at them.

Diesel proudly smiled, "This is my mate and Luna, Lucy Michaels." I seemed to receive warm smiles from around the table except for Athena, who kept her eyes on Diesel.

"Report." Diesel said in Alpha mode.

Sam, the tracker, spoke first, "Alpha, the snowstorm dumped over two feet of snow. The trackers have not picked up any scent of rogues in or around the territory with the exception of the recent attack."

"We burned all the rogue bodies before the storm hit, so there's no trace of the attack left at the river." Nolan, the warrior informed us.

"Still, it's highly unusual for any rogue to be so far north during the snow season," Sam added.

"Alpha, we questioned the rogue in the dungeon again. He said there's a large bounty on a runaway she wolf they were hunting. He still swears a few of them saw a golden wolf and they ventured off course trying to track it." Paul informed us.

"Any idea who the runaway was or who put a bounty on her?" Diesel asked, trying to hold back his anger.

"Ranger is looking for us!" Lia whispered in my head and I tried to keep a straight face.

"No, but it was someone with a lot of disposable income. The bounty was a million dollars to bring her back alive."

"Anything else?" Diesel asked.

"That's it Sir. We'll try questioning him again in a few days." Paul added.

"Will the Luna start training with us soon?" Athena asked with a smug look on her face that seemed to say she wanted to get her hands on me.

"She could try, but I will claw that look right off her face." Lia snarled to me.

"I will be personally working with the Luna for a while on her special combat skills Athena." Payton answered to my relief.

Diesel looked stone faced as he spoke. "I will look for all of your training evaluations this week and review them. If there's nothing else, you are dismissed." Everyone left except for Alpha Knox and Payton.

"Do you think it's Ranger?" Payton asked Diesel.

"He certainly has the disposable cash and a reason. Without his wolf, he wouldn't be able to lead a hunt." Diesel said trying to control his anger.

"Lucy, I know you've never trained before, but everyone between the ages of fourteen and fifty trains in this pack. It will raise suspicion if the Luna doesn't train." Alpha Knox said.

"Technically, she's not the Luna yet until after the mating ceremony and she is marked." Payton said. "I will train in private with her until then."

"I'd also like to work with you on your elemental training." Alpha Knox said.

"Lucy how do you feel about that?" Diesel asked.

"I think it's a great idea! It will help make me stronger." I smiled, though I felt uncertain about how they would react when they see Lia.

"Son, we're five weeks away from the December full moon, we should start planning the Luna and mating ceremony." Alpha Knox was eager to move forward.

"Lucy you don't have to hide here, you're the rightful Luna of Crescent Moon and you belong here with us. No one will take you away." Payton said with a re-assuring smile.

"Thank you." My heart felt so warm.

After the meeting, we headed down to the kitchen. "Anything special you'd like for dinner tonight?" Diesel asked.

"Whatever sounds good to you." I said.

"YOU sound good to me." He grinned causing me to blush. "Go put on a warm coat and meet me at the entrance hall."

"Okay." I replied and walked towards the north tower stairs to fetch one of my new coats. I saw Athena heading towards the dining hall and smiled at her. She gave me a cold glare and walked off. Yep, she definitely doesn't like me.

Fifteen minutes later, I was standing in the entrance hall wearing my coat. Diesel came through the front doors wearing his snow parka, hat and gloves. His blues eyes were sparkling and made my heart flutter.

"Where are we going?"

"Date night!" He smiled and placed a beanie on my head. He leaned down and scooped me up, carrying me outside into the cool night air.

"Your chariot awaits my lady." He set me down on a large black snowmobile. He straddled the driver's seat in front of me and started the engine. He reached back for my hands and placed them around his waist and into his coat pockets. "Hold on tight little one." He called back to me.

"Don't mind if I do." Lia purred back and I let out a giggle as I leaned into his back and held on tight. The snowmobile glided smoothly across the top of the snow. We entered the woods and Diesel zipped through the trees easily.

Twenty minutes later, we pulled into the village and there was a soft glow from the old fashioned street-lamps that lined the streets. Diesel helped me off the snowmobile and we walked towards a wooden building with a sign that said, 'Chinese Chopsticks'.

He held open the door and placed his hand on the small of my back. "I hope you're hungry."

"Good evening Alpha." An older she wolf said. "Table for two?"

Diesel nodded his head and she led us to a quiet booth in the corner. "Do you have any favorites you'd like to try Lucy?" He asked me.

"I'll have whatever you're having." I smiled.

"The usual." He ordered and she bowed her head.

"Did you enjoy the snowmobile ride?"

"It was pretty awesome. The forest looks so beautiful with the fluffy blanket of fresh snow."

"If you're up to it, I'd like to drive you to Crescent point after dinner."

"Sounds great, what is it?" I asked.

"You'll see." He smiled.

Several large bowls were placed on the table, egg flower soup, dumplings, fried Rice, chow mein noodles, garlic chicken, vegetable shrimp, and kung pao beef. We ate dinner and Diesel told me more about the pack, talked about his parents and discussed places he couldn't wait to take me. He traveled a few times a year internationally for business. I thought about how I was rarely allowed passed the tree line at Dark Moon and now I was sitting here talking about traveling overseas. If this was a dream, I hope I never wake up.

As we finished up dinner, our fortune cookies were served. I took one and opened it. "What does yours say?" I asked Diesel.

He looked down and laughed when he read the little paper in his hand. "It says, the fortune you seek is in another cookie."

"What? No, it doesn't!" I laughed and reached for his fortune. "It really does say that!"

"How about yours?" He asked me.

"Big journeys begin with single steps." I read mine out loud.

"I guess that means you're ready to take the journey to Crescent Point tonight." He smiled.

We were back on the snowmobile and my nose was getting cold, so I buried my face in Diesel's back for warmth. He smelled so good, I thought to myself. My life, my journey, had taken me someplace special. One Alpha broke me, and another is putting me back together. The world with Diesel was so different and I loved it. We arrived at Crescent Point; the moon had illuminated a beautiful light on the snow. It was a look out point to view a magnificent waterfall.

"This place is amazing!" I said.

"You should see it in the warmer months, under a full moon, green grass and wildflowers." His husky voice said as he pulled me into a hungry kiss. His tongue slipped into my mouth to deepen the kiss and sparks shot through my body. I kissed back, desperately wanting more. We broke apart to catch our breath and he rested his forehead on mine.

"Duke can hardly wait to run with Lia. He's been a lovesick puppy ever since we found you." He smiled.

I reached my hand up and placed it on his cheek, I looked into the eyes of my mate. My mate who had loved and accepted me just the way I was. I knew in that moment that I wanted to take another step in this journey.

I took a few steps back and continued to look into his eyes. "I have something I need to show you." I started removing my clothes.

CHAPTER 26 – LIA

Diesel's POV

Having her straddled behind me and squeezing me tight feels so good. She is right where she was meant to be, with me. I needed her like a fish needs water.

"I need mate too!" Duke barked at me. "We need to mark and mate already!" He howled in my head. If it was up to him, he would have done it the moment we set eyes on her. Holding him back hasn't been easy.

"Duke, I've told you before, we need to go slow. Our mate isn't ready yet, you can't rush these things." I told him.

"You won't be able to stop her heat; she will be ours soon!" He reminded me.

"Let's hope she's ready and that she wants us." I told him.

"I want to see my mate and run with her." He demanded.

"Soon Duke, soon." I assured him and he whimpered in my head longing for his mate.

So much for a ferocious Alpha wolf, Duke was turning soft on me.
"Speak for yourself pup." He snickered back at me.

We made it to Crescent Point, this place was beautiful no matter what time of year. The waterfall had a strong connection to my element and pulsed power through my body. I watched as Lucy took in the view of the waterfall with wonder in her eyes. "This place is amazing." She smiled.

"You should see it in the warmer months, under a full moon, green grass and wildflowers." I imagined bringing her here for a picnic in the spring and spending hours mating with her on this exact spot. I pulled her to me and kissed her. I struggled to control my need and bent down to rest my forehead onto hers. I looked into those enchanting eyes of hers and my heart was on fire. I wanted her, every inch of her.

"Duke can hardly wait to run with Lia." I told her and he barked in my head, jumping with joy. "He's been a lovesick puppy ever since we found you."

She was quiet for a moment contemplating what I had just told her. I wish I could read her thoughts, but since she wasn't marked yet or officially a member of the pack until the Luna ceremony, I couldn't mind link her or feel her emotions. She took a few steps back from me and continued to gaze at me. "I have something I need to show you." She started taking off her clothes.

I wasn't sure what to say or do, I watched her undress and set her clothes down on the snowmobile. She crouched down in the snow and I heard the sound of bones cracking. My shift took only a few seconds, but hers was longer. She's still new to shifting, I realized. Duke was howling in my head, begging to be released, he was about to gaze on his mate for the first time.

Then, I saw her! My breath caught in my throat, my mouth fell open and I blinked my eyes several times in disbelief. She looked up at me with those same amber colored eyes and her fur - Sweet Moon Goddess, could it be?

I fell to my knees in complete shock. I couldn't find any words. How is this possible? How did I not know? This is incredible!

She walked over to me and licked me on the cheek. My voice came out nearly breathless, "Lucy, you are amazing!" I rubbed my head on her wolf head and she cuddled back, rubbing her head back against me. "Lia is so beautiful."

Duke started barking at me. "Mate! I want mate! MATE, MATE, MATE!"

"Lucy, I wish I could mind link you and hear what you're thinking. Duke is begging to be let out. Is Lia ready to meet him?"

She nodded her head and barked.

"Okay boy, that's a yes, be gentle with her." I told him and quickly took my clothes off to shift.

A second later Lia pounced on my big black Alpha wolf. Duke barked with joy and Lia yipped back at him. They started rubbing their bodies up against each other, exchanging scents. Duke gave Lia a slobbery lick across the face and she did the same. They were soon chasing each other in the snow and rolling around. Lia let out a low howl and motioned at us to follow her and took off running, she was fast! We couldn't catch her.

"Mate is so amazing and beautiful." Duke proudly told me.

"She sure is!" I agreed. I looked around for her, where did she go?

She pounced on us from behind a big fallen tree and we rolled around. Duke desperately wanted to mount and claim her, I had to hold him back. We ran back to the snowmobile and when we stopped, Duke stuck his muzzle under Lia's tail and sniffed her.
"DUKE, STOP ACTING LIKE A HORNY OLD DOG!" I scolded him.

She started to shift back, and it took her almost a full minute. My shift was about three seconds. When she was done, she stood up and I pulled her naked body to mine.

"Still think I'm a myth?" She smiled up at me. All I could do was kiss her and I felt her hands roaming on my back and down to my butt. Her touch was magic on my skin.

"Let's get home and get you warm before I take you right here, right now, little one." I managed to say. I wanted her as much as Duke did.

"Now who's acting like a horny old dog?" Duke snickered at me.

We zipped back on the snowmobile and my mind was racing. She was a golden wolf with elemental power. Has this ever happened before? A golden wolf is the strongest of our kind. What was it that we learned about them in school? I struggled to remember. I couldn't believe she was my mate!!

We came to a stop at the front of the castle. "Is it okay with you if we show my father and Payton, I think explaining it might be difficult for them to understand. My father will have more knowledge than I do, and we will want to consider all of this before anyone see's Lia."

"Okay." She responded.

I mind linked my father and Payton to meet me in the library. It should be empty this late in the evening and we will have plenty of space for Lucy to shift. I also want to look at that book she had in the library yesterday on golden wolves. We made our way to the library; my father and Payton were already there. I turned and locked the door, then I pulled the shades closed on the windows.

"What's going on son?" My father asked.

"There's something you need to see, please turn around." I told him and they both gave us questioning looks as they turned around.

"You ready to do it again?" I asked Lucy and she nodded.

A minute later Duke was howling in my head and full of pride gazing at his magnificent mate. I couldn't take my eyes off of her. She lifted her head up and looked at me, I bent down and kissed the top of her head.

"You can turn around now." I told my father and Payton. Both of their eyes practically jumped out of their heads.

"OH. MY. GODDESS." Was all Payton was able to say as her mouth hung open.

"Is she what I think she is?" My father asked.

They continued to stare completely astonished. My father reached his hand out wanting to touch her. "Lucy, may I?" he asked.
She nodded her head yes. Duke didn't like the idea of anyone touching our mate and I had to calm him. My father ran his hand over the top of her head. "Amazing!" He managed to utter lost in thoughts.

They turned around and Lucy shifted back. When she was dressed, we sat down in the armchairs. I picked up the book that Lucy had yesterday and turned to the page about golden wolves.

I read out loud, "The golden wolf is the rarest werewolf of all, born once every century. The golden wolf possesses great strength, speed and agility beyond any other wolf. Legend says that the golden wolf is a descendant of the God Apollo and his mortal lover Cyrene, who was a strong and beautiful huntress. Apollo was the son of Zeus and Leto. His mother Leto, had the ability to turn herself into a she wolf."

We sat quiet for a long moment before my father spoke to Lucy. "We know your mother was a descendant of the Moon Goddess, Selene, and possessed the gift of elemental fire which she passed to you." He paused for another moment. "Your father was unusually strong and fast, he could have easily challenged any Alpha and would have won. He wasn't a golden wolf, he was a dark charcoal gray color. It took nearly a dozen rogues to bring him down that day. I believe he was a descendant from Apollo, and you are the golden wolf of the century."

"And to think, I always believed the golden wolf was just a children's story." Payton said in astonishment.

CHAPTER 27 – EMOTIONS

"Come on Lucy dig deep and find that anger to fuel the fire circle." Alpha Knox said. I was currently at the north end of the territory with Alpha Knox and Diesel, practicing my element training. I kept putting up a fire circle around them and Diesel kept extinguishing it with water and snow. I actually managed to singe his arm hairs yesterday.

It's been a week since Diesel first saw Lia and I've been training every day. Payton trains in human form with me, teaching me how to spar, strike and defend while Diesel coaches. Then I spend an hour with Alpha Knox on my elemental training and Diesel helps. After lunch, Diesel and I train in our wolf forms, with Payton coaching, because I can't mind link with Diesel yet, so she calls out the instructions from him.

We've discovered that my fire power is linked to my emotions. While elemental wolves can only control the element, they cannot produce the element. Diesel must have a water source to manipulate and control the element and I need a fire source or spark.

We wrapped up training for the day and shifted back, my shifting was getting faster with each shift. "Lucy, you're learning so fast no one would believe you're new to it. I can't wait to see you spar with the warriors. They won't know what hit them!" Payton laughed.

My golden wolf also made me strong and fast in human

form. The training was teaching me techniques but the power of my strikes and speed came from the wolf within me.

"I wonder if your pups will inherit your super strength and both elements?" She said out loud and I started wondering the same.

"Just a reminder, you actually have to mate first in order to make pups." Lia teased me.

"Lucy, I was thinking about going into the village this afternoon for a manicure and pedicure, was hoping your mate could spare you for a few hours?" Payton smiled at her brother.

"Lucy?" Diesel asked.

"Sounds great." I replied, I've never had a manicure or pedicure.

"Be back by dinner, we're joining the pack at the dining hall tonight." Diesel gave me a kiss and we went to our rooms first, to change and freshen up. I actually took a quick shower and made it back downstairs at the entrance with my jacket before Payton.

"And where is our lovely Luna heading to?" Delta Elliot had just come through the front door.

"We're off to the village for Mani and Pedi's, want to join us?" Payton had just appeared behind me and answered Elliot, I burst out laughing.

"No thank you." He laughed and tossed Payton the car keys.

We parked in front of the spa and Payton insisted we go to the village coffee shop a few doors down, before we go to the day spa. We walked into the coffee shop and stood in line to place our orders. I felt someone watching me and turned around to find Athena and Sam having coffee. Athena just glared at me.

"Pay no attention to her, she's just jealous." Payton said.

"Next please!" The cashier called out, then she recognized Payton.
"Oh, hello Beta. What can I get for you?" Asked the woman whose name badge said Riki.

"I'll have a large iced mocha latte and the Luna would like to try the large iced pumpkin spiced latte." Payton ordered.

"Luna is it?" Came a voice from behind us, we turned to find Athena standing there. "I wasn't aware that she had been marked and claimed yet. The Alpha isn't having second thoughts about a rogue, is he?" She faked concern.

"Not at all." Payton smiled back. "Diesel is a little old fashioned when it comes to true love, as opposed to superficial relationships." Athena gave Payton a sour look before she turned and left.

"Let me out! I will rearrange her face." Lia snarled.

"Order for Beta Payton." A voice called out and Payton picked up our drinks. "Thank you, Riki." Payton thanked the woman behind the counter, and we made our way to the spa.

We were seated in pedicure chairs next to each other, sipping our lattes. I don't care for coffee, but this pumpkin spice thing was more like a dessert and tasted nothing like coffee.

"Is Athena always this pleasant?" I sarcastically asked.

"No, she's been bitter ever since Diesel dumped her last year." Payton said.

I let out a little gasp and Payton turned to me, "I'm so sorry, I probably shouldn't have said anything." She looked uneasy.

"No, it's fine. Really. No one would expect him to make it to twenty-three and still be a virgin." I said trying to sound as lighthearted as possible.

"He's going to be twenty-four next week." Payton smiled at me.

"I guess I have a lot to learn about my mate." I said with a smile, trying to hide what I was really feeling.

I tried to enjoy the rest of the pedicure and manicure and didn't even notice when the lady mixed up the colors I had selected for my toes and hands. I ended up with a silvery gray on my hands and a dark red on my toes. My mind kept drifting back to Athena and Diesel, she was beautiful and his strongest female warrior. Of course, she had intrigued him. She was perfect Luna material, but knowing that he had slept with her made my heart ache.

"I can't wait to kick her ass in training!" Lia huffed. "She'll be lucky if I don't set her hair on fire." She added.

"Come on Lucy, we've got some time before dinner, I'll do your hair and makeup." Payton smiled at me.

An hour later and I was wearing a form fitting, gray, sweater dress, with black tights and heeled boots. Payton put big rollers in my hair for a little more wave and did my makeup. "You don't even need makeup, you're a natural beauty." She told me and I blushed.

We walked through the big double doors of the dining hall, heads turned, and whispers buzzed. We made our way to the big table in the front, Diesel stood up and pulled me to him. He kissed my lips and whispered in my ear. "You look absolutely delicious."

"Let the woman breath for a moment." Gamma Zeke said as he smiled at me. "Luna, I don't believe you've met my mate yet, this is Vannica." He introduced me to a beautiful, young, exotic looking woman with shoulder length brown hair and big brown eyes. She stood to greet me, and I noticed her swollen belly, she was expecting a pup. I congratulated them. It was their first pup and Zeke was a nervous, overprotective, wreck trying to tend to Vannica. It made my heart warm and I felt a longing deep inside.

"How's the Luna ceremony planning coming along?" Vannica asked.

"We were hoping to start that this weekend. We've got less than four weeks until the December full moon." Payton said.

"Count me in!" Vannica said, "I need a little excitement, Zeke won't let me do anything!" She laughed.

Dinner was served and we had roasted chicken and pork tenderloin. I felt Lia on edge. "Are you okay?" I asked her in my head.

"I'm fine, but if the mutt over there keeps it up, I'm going to singe her eyebrows off with the candle on the table." Lia huffed. I looked over to see Athena staring daggers at me and whispering with the other she wolves around her.

Dessert was being served and I selected an apple tart. I quietly ate my tart and started wondering how long Diesel and Athena had dated. Diesel was laughing at something Elliot had said and I looked up at his handsome face. I was struggling with my emotions, knowing he had been with Athena and she clearly still wants him.

"Are you okay?" he asked.

"I'm fine." I lied.

"Lucy, the flames on all the candles keep rising up a few inches." He whispered.

"I'm sorry, Lia is just a little tired, I'm going to go upstairs and get to bed early." I said and left the dining hall. When I reached our bedroom door, I wasn't really ready for bed yet. I wanted to be alone with myself and clear my head. I headed for the astronomy observatory.

The bed on the floor we slept in from the first night was still here. I flipped the switch and retracked the roof top to reveal the glass top and a flurry of snow gently falling. I took my boots off and laid back on the bed watching the snow. It reminded me of a snow globe.

A little while later, I heard the door creek open, and the room was filled with his scent. "Are you going to tell me what's wrong or should I mark you right now and read your thoughts?" Diesel said as he sat down on the bed next to me.

"How long were you with her?" I asked.

"With who?" He sounded confused.

"What do you mean with who? With Athena of course, why else would she be giving me jealous glares!"

He paused for a moment and spoke. "Lucy, that was a long time ago, before I even knew you existed. When I was dating her, she found her mate and rejected him, so she could be with me. I told her I wanted to wait and see if destiny would bring me a second chance mate and couldn't be with her, so I broke it off."

"What do you mean second chance mate? You had a first mate? Why didn't you say anything?" I demanded.

"Lucy, I wasn't sure that it even counted. We'd never even kissed." He ran his fingers through his hair and took a deep breath.

"It was my eighteenth birthday and I was still at Dark Moon. I caught the scent of my mate and made my way over to her. I wanted a mate more than anything. When I set eyes on her, it was the Delta's daughter, Fatima. She had her eyes set on the next Alpha, and the next Alpha of Dark Moon was Ranger. She rejected me on the spot."

"I don't remember anyone by the name of Fatima living at the pack house, what happened to her?"

"After my father passed the pack over to Ranger, a new Beta, Gamma and Delta were selected. Max was my best friend and Ranger tried to drive a wedge between us by making Max the Beta, instead of me. The twins, Blake and Cole, became the new Gamma and Delta. Blake was a few minutes older than Cole, so he got the higher ranking. Fatima and her parents moved to the city so she could attend college. After I became Alpha of the largest and strongest pack in the world, she tried contacting me, but I've never responded."

"What about Athena?"

"Lucy, I wasn't even sure I was destined for a second chance mate or that I even deserved one. Athena means nothing to me. You're all that matters to me, little one."

He pulled me to his chest as the tears ran down my face. "There's so much I don't even know, next week is your birthday and no one told me." I sobbed.

"I don't even know what to get you for your birthday."

He kissed my lips softly. "You're all I want." His eyes darkened.
My emotions were all flooding through me at once, relief, jealousy, desire, possessiveness, longing and heat. "Then have me." I whispered back.

CHAPTER 28 – CLAIMED

His lips came crashing down on mine. I kissed back just as hard and just as hungry. I wanted him more than anything. I wanted to feel him deep inside of me, claiming me, possessing me. There was a fire raging inside of me and it needed him. I reached down and pulled his shirt over his head and kissed his neck. He growled with pleasure. "Lucy, you're going to drive me crazy."

"Good." I said and locked lips with him again, our tongues dancing with each other. He pulled my dress up and threw it on the floor. Then he trailed kisses down my chin, throat and chest before removing my new black lace bra and tossing it over his head. He kissed and caressed my breasts gently biting and sucking on my hardened nipples.

Slowly he kissed down my stomach and hooked his fingers in the waistband of my tights and panties, sliding them off together. I laid completely naked before him. His eyes darkened and his aura radiated heat and desire.

My heart was racing, and I felt the heat pulsing through my core. He stood in front of me and unbuckled his pants, pulling down his pants with his boxers. His huge cock sprang free and was fully erect. The sight of him standing above me naked made my juices flow.

"Little one, are you sure?" His husky voice sent waves

of heat through me.

"I've never been more sure!" My voice quivered with excitement.

He kissed my knees and spread my legs as he licked and kissed his way up my inner thighs. He paused at my sex and inhaled the scent of my arousal. He licked his lips and started kissing and licking my pussy slowly, teasing me. I let out a whimper and he plowed his tongue deep into my pussy.

My head was spinning, and I lost control of my senses. I grabbed fist fulls of his hair and pulled him closer into me. He growled with pleasure and repeatedly thrusted his tongue in and out of me, tasting me. He then focused his attention on my clit and pumped two fingers in me. My legs began to quake as he sucked harder devouring me. A loud moan ripped through me and my orgasm exploded. Diesel growled and continued to enjoy every last bit.

He trailed kisses back up my stomach and to my neck. His teeth grazed over the soft spot on my neck and I moaned as sparks traveled through my body. I reached down and stroked him, feeling his girth in my hand and he let out a loud lust filled growl.
He kissed me deeply once again. I felt his cock pressed at the entrance of my wet and ready core. "Tell me if it hurts or if you need me to stop." He said and I nodded my head.

He pressed in slowly and I felt the sting of being stretched. He began rocking in and out, filling me, the more he gave, the more I wanted. My nails scratched at his back as his trusts moved deeper and faster. The pleasure was so intense and raw, it tingled throughout my body. His scent engulfed me, the sensation of his body pressed against me, I was on the edge of orgasm again. I wrapped my legs around him and he dug deeper into me. I was half panting and half moaning, completely lost in pleasure.

Diesel was sucking hard on my marking spot when I felt the sting of my skin being pierced. A wave of pleasure sent an earth shattering orgasm through my body as he marked me. He licked the spot on my neck and continued to thrust deeper inside of me. His blue eyes locked with mine and nothing else seemed to matter. We were lost in our own world. He was mine and I wanted to claim him.

My teeth extended and I licked his neck. He let out a moan and thrusted harder and harder. I felt another orgasm building, my walls clenched down around his cock. "Ohhh Lucy!" He managed to utter, and I plunged my teeth into his neck. He roared and I felt his orgasm explode deep within me triggering my own at the same time.

Lia was proudly howling with joy, having mated and marked our mate. We laid there panting, trying to catch our breath before we started again. I was sore and tired, but I wanted more. There was going to be little sleep tonight, I wanted him deep in me, right where he belonged.

It was lunch the following day before Diesel and I emerged and went downstairs to eat. We walked into the kitchen and Payton shrieked when she saw us come in. I was engulfed in a hug immediately. "It's about time!" She said as she took in the marks on both of our necks. Now that we had mated, my scent was different, Diesel's scent was strong on me.

The main kitchen had a large wooden table where we casually ate sometimes. There was a platter of sandwiches and fruit set in the middle of the table, as well as a tureen of chicken noodle soup. We sat at the table with Payton, Vannica and Zeke and started eating. We talked about the upcoming Luna and mating ceremony. Technically, since we had already mated and marked each other, we would not be marking each other at the ceremony. This will be the equivalent to a wedding and becoming one with the pack as the Luna.

The ceremony will take place outside, beneath the December full moon. The celebration dinner and dancing will be held in the grand ballroom. We selected invitations, Payton was in charge of sending them out and managing the guest list. Helga was going to work with the caterer on the menu and set up the refreshment team that would be serving drinks. Vannica was going to oversee the decorators and the set-up team.

Elliot had just walked in and joined us at the table, he ladled a large bowl of soup and sat down to eat. "I'll be in charge of looking after all the unmated females, you know, in case I find my mate." He grinned and we all burst out laughing. Elliot was a year younger than Diesel and was still waiting for his mate. I hope he finds her soon, he's really a fun loving guy.

Now Payton, was a completely different story. Diesel had told me that when he took over Crescent Moon, there was a small group of warriors still loyal to his uncle. After Titus lost, Payton discovered one of the warriors in that group was her mate. He decided to turn rogue and reject her. She was heartbroken. Both

Diesel and Payton, shared the same pain of being rejected immediately by their mates and this brought them closer together.

"Are you going to buy a dress or have one made?" Vannica asked me, pulling me from my thoughts.

"Oh, I hadn't really given it much thought actually." I said.

"We have just enough time to have one made! I can schedule the dressmaker from the village to come to the castle and get started." Payton clapped excitedly.

"That's perfect." Diesel smiled.

"There's a dressmaker in the village?" I asked.

"Oh yes! Ms. Hall, she owns *Shari's Designs,* in the village. She has impeccable taste and can craft a beautiful gown in less than two weeks." Payton told me. "We'll schedule an appointment as soon as possible."

"What kind of cake are you going to have?" Elliot asked. "Red velvet is my favorite!"

"Oh, I love red velvet too! Max once snuck me a red velvet cupcake, it was amazing." I said and then realized what I had actually said.

"Maximus Taylor? The Beta at Dark Moon?" Zeke questioned.

"Yes, he was my only friend at Dark Moon." I said and felt a bit of jealous emotion pulse through Diesel. "Like my big brother actually." I quickly added. "He saved my life on more than one occasion." I felt Diesel's jealous emotion die down after I referenced Max as a brother. I reached over and placed my hand in his and he was completely at ease after that. He lifted my hand to his mouth and kissed it.

"How are you feeling little one?" Diesel asked me through the mind link. Now that he had marked me, we could mind link with each other and feel each other's emotions. I would be able to mind link with the rest of the pack once the Luna ceremony took place.

"I'm doing great, just a little sore." I told him through the link with a smile on my face.

"Good." His husky voice came through my mind. "I want you to feel me and miss me."

Lia let out a happy yip and Diesel laughed, "Lia are you ready for a run with Duke?" He asked her.

She yipped again. "You bet I am."

"Please excuse my mate and I, we need to let the wolves run." He took my hand and we headed to the woods.

We quickly undressed and shifted. Lia and Duke took control and ran towards the north end of the territory. Duke spotted a large snow bunny and soon enough both Lia and Duke had it trapped. Duke was teaching Lia how to hunt, and she adored her Alpha. Duke sank his teeth into the rabbit's head and killed it. He then picked it up and dropped it in front of Lia. She ripped it open and took the first bite, they shared the rest of the rabbit.

After the snack, they ran a bit longer and started

wrestling with each other. Duke nuzzled Lia's neck and softly started biting on it. Lia submitted and laid down, lifting her tail. Duke mounted her from behind, they both started growling and panting as they mated. When they were done, Duke let out a proud thundering howl that let the entire pack know he had claimed his mate.

CHAPTER 29 – MYSTERY SCENT

Diesel's POV

If it was up to me, I'd spend all weekend wrapped up in bed with her. But she insisted we get cleaned up and head downstairs for breakfast. I could hear her in the shower and decided it might be faster if I joined her. I stepped into the large rock shower and stood under the rain fall water head with her. I quickly washed my hair and Lucy started soaping me up with her loofa.

When she reached my rod, she spent extra time washing and stroking it. The beast stirred inside of me; she was teasing me. I instantly hardened and she smiled, pleased with her handy work. She rinsed me off and dropped to her knees taking me into her mouth. She sent my world spinning in less than ten minutes and swallowed every last drop. "Happy Birthday Baby!" She smiled up at me.

"Happy Birthday indeed." Duke purred at me.

I was about to scoop Lucy up and take her back to the bed when Payton mind linked me. She had been on patrol early this morning. "Alpha, we've picked up some unusual scents at the southern border. Some rogue and some not."

"What do you mean some not?" I asked.

"I could be wrong, but I'm picking up a strong scent, like an Alpha." She said.

"Is it Ranger?" I questioned. Brother or not, I will rip his throat out if he touches my mate.

"I'm not sure, he's mated with someone else, so his scent might be different. I don't know what Miranda's scent is like. Do you think Lucy might recognize it?"

I hated the idea of asking Lucy to possibly scent that Bastard. If rouges were close this time of year, there was a reason for it, especially if an Alpha may be working with them or paying a bounty. I mind linked Zeke and Elliot to meet me at the tree line behind the castle. Then I linked Paul, to have him assemble fifty warriors just in case. I asked my father to stay here and make sure no one breeched the castle.

I explained to Lucy what was going on and she agreed to come to the boarder with me to see if any scents were familiar to her. We stepped outside and met with Zeke and Elliot at the edge of the forest.

We were ready to shift, and I mind linked Lucy, "Don't shift, no one has seen Lia yet." We didn't want anyone to see her golden wolf yet. We were going to wait until after the Luna ceremony, when she would be accepted into the pack and lead in the traditional moonlight run.

"Should I run in human form?" She asked me.

"No, you can climb on Duke and ride over, it will be much faster."

Moments later, she had her hands wrapped around Duke's neck and he ran with great pride carrying his Luna on his back. My gamma and delta ran behind us, and the warriors ran in formation behind them. We reached the southern border and Lucy walked around inhaling. She stopped and sniffed again.

"What is it?" I asked.

"The stench of rogues for sure. It smells like the rogues that last attacked Dark Moon pack." She told us.

"Are you sure? Did you get close enough to them to scent them well?" I asked. Surely, she didn't fight them off when they attacked.

"Oh, I got close enough." She said to me. What did she mean by that? Close enough? Her wall was down so I read her thoughts - *if Max hadn't saved me, that rogue would have raped me.*

I let out an angry growl and everyone looked at me. Lucy had not realized I read her thoughts. Then I heard Athena mind linking Kayla, "Did you see how she had to ride on his back. Is her wolf too weak for that run? He should have left her at the castle, we don't have time to babysit."

"How dare she!" Duke snarled to me. He was pissed off and ready to snap her jealous neck. Athena will be the first person I put in the ring with Lucy at the training arena, I thought to myself. Athena won't stand a chance. Lucy might be little, but she can shred even the toughest Alpha.

"Is everything Okay?" Lucy asked me through the mind link.

"Yes, but you're going to start training with the pack

soon. I want you ready for any threat."

She looked over where Athena was standing and smiled. "Sounds like fun." She mind linked me back.

"Beta, Gamma." I called out to Payton and Zeke. "I want a revised patrol schedule this afternoon, double the patrols and overlap the runs. I don't want any un-expected surprises."

"Yes Alpha." They said in unison.

"Diesel, I'm picking up the Alpha scent. It vaguely feels familiar, but it's not Ranger." Lucy said.

"Are you sure?"

"Yes. Ranger was more apples and cinnamon. Miranda is strong roses and coffee. This scent is none of those, it's fresh cut grass and oak."

I dismissed everyone and they went back to the cas-tle or patrol. Lucy climbed back up on Duke and we walked back taking our time. There was something eating at me, so I mind linked with Lucy.
"Lucy, last week you said that Max had saved your life on more than one occasion. I was hoping you could elaborate on that for me." I asked.

She hesitated. "Well, you already know that Ursa starved me. One night after not eating for almost a whole week, Max saw me eating out of a garbage can in the middle of the night. That's when he started sneak-ing me food every day."

If I ever see Ursa again, I'm going to rip out her heart, I thought to myself.

"There was the time Blake and Cole threw me in the deep end of the swimming pool and I almost drowned. Max pulled me out. Another time, I had hypothermia from being locked in a kennel all night during a freezing storm, Max saved me."

I hated thinking about how much those assholes tortured her. "Anything else?"

"When the rogues attacked, I was at the tree line, I had been sent to stock the shift clothes. I tried to hide in a tree, but a rogue scented me and chased me down. He tried to rape me, but Max saved me, and he killed the rogue."

"Ranger doesn't deserve Max." I growled back.

"He was a very good friend. The only thing I actually miss from Dark Moon." She said with a hint of sadness.

I missed Max too, he was my best friend since we were pups. Now I'm discovering how he protected Lucy when she had no one. How he saved her life. I could feel how much he means to her. "Payton?" I mind linked my sister.

"Yes Alpha." she said.

"Let's be sure to send an invitation to Beta Maximus Taylor, at Dark Moon. But, don't tell Lucy, it's a surprise."

"Then Ranger will find out." She said.

"When the Alpha of the largest pack in the world is having a Luna ceremony, news travels fast. I'm sure he already knows." I informed her.

"You're right. He's got to be foolish to try anything at this point." She said. "Please remind Lucy, that Ms. Hall will be here for the dress measurements any minute now."

We arrived at the tree line and Lucy jumped off so I could shift back. She held out my shorts and then yanked them away teasing me. I would have bent her over a fallen tree right here, right now and taken her, but she needed to get to her dress fitting. I also had to take care of pack business before the birthday celebration this evening. Payton always planned a big birthday party for me every year and this year, I was looking forward to dancing with my mate.
We walked back towards the castle and another detail was bothering me. "Lucy, you can't swim?" I asked.

"No, I've never learned, but Lia is an excellent strong swimmer." She smiled up at me.

"We have an indoor heated swimming pool; I'd like to teach you."
"That would be great! You are my personal lifeguard after all." She kissed me and went off to meet Payton. She was right, there isn't anything I wouldn't do to guard her life.

I was lost deep in thought when I walked into my office. A fading scent that was still lingering in the air hit my nose. Duke snarled angrily and I walked around the room sniffing harder. It can't be? I inhaled again, fresh cut grass and oak. Duke was on edge.

There was no way another Alpha could set foot on this territory and not be noticed. I mind linked my father to meet me at my office, maybe he would recognize the scent. I sat in my chair and saw the note taped to my computer screen. I pulled it off and smelled it, fresh cut grass and oak. There was just one sentence hastily scribbled —

"She is mine and I will have her soon."

CHAPTER 30 – SURPRISE

With three days left until the Luna ceremony, Diesel and Payton had stepped up their training sessions. I was ready to join the warriors in training. I was currently walking towards the east end of our territory, to the training grounds and arena. The indoor arena was used during the snow season for trainings. Diesel and Payton were already at the arena and Alpha Knox walked with me.

There was something so warm and comforting when I was with him. He had worked hard to help me train and control my element. When he wasn't working hard, he spent time cooking for us and telling me stories about the mischief he and my father got themselves into when they were young. Being here at Crescent Moon, with him, felt like home.

Most Alpha's lose their sanity, become cruel killing machines or withdraw completely when they lose their Luna. Some even kill themselves. When Alpha Knox lost Luna, Clair, he focused his energy on helping his children. His children that Clair had given him, who were also a part of her.

Ranger was a new Alpha and neither wanted or asked for Alpha Knox to stay and help at Dark Moon, so he left. He returned back to his childhood home at Crescent Moon when Diesel became Alpha. He had been instrumental in the success that Diesel and Payton had with this pack. The pack that my father grew up in.

We reached the arena and before we walked in, Alpha Knox stopped me. "Lucy, I want you to know how proud I am of you and am honored to have you as the Luna of my family pack. I wish I could go back in time and change what happened to you at Dark Moon, but I can't. I'm glad that the Moon Goddess sent you to us because you are exactly what this pack and my son needs." He paused for a moment.

"When you go in there, hold your head up high. Be the strong Luna you were born to be and the descendent of Gods I know you are. Always remember, it's not how you started, it's how you finish." I wrapped my arms around him and received a warm embrace, he had become a second father to me.

When we stepped inside, everyone stopped what they were doing and stared at me. Some were exercising and lifting weights, others were sparring in human form and there was even a special area for combat in wolf form; but in this moment, they all stood frozen. Diesel was standing with the chief warriors assessing the fighting going on in front of them. They had been reviewing the defensive and offensive strike techniques as well as the strike power and take down. They also stopped and watched me make my way towards Diesel.

"To what do we owe the pleasure of this visit to the arena, Luna? I wasn't aware you'd be touring today." Athena said with a half assed bowed of her head to me.

"Oh, I'm not here for a tour. I'm here to assess the talent of this pack and perhaps give a few pointers." I said with confidence.

"I had no idea we were in the presence of such a skilled warrior." Her voice laced with sarcasm.

Lia was ready to chew her up and spit her out. "Oh, this is going to be fun!" Lia sneered in my head and I saw Diesel's lip twitch in a smile.

"Time to show her who she's dealing with." Diesel mind linked me.
"I understand you're rather a skilled warrior yourself Athena. Should we put our human to human combat skills to the test?" I asked.

"If it's okay with the Alpha." She said.

"The Luna will be training with the pack and assisting just as I do. If you would like to test your skills against her, please feel free to form a single line. Athena will go first. This will be human to human combat." He said.

No one else stepped up to the line, but everyone started to gather to watch. Payton smiled widely at me and mind linked me. "You've got this!"

I looked out to the faces and Alpha Knox nodded his reassuring head at me. Athena was hopping around getting loosened up. I stood in the middle of the fight arena and assumed my fight stance with my fists clenched.

She lunged at me and I quickly moved out of the way and stuck my foot out to trip her. She landed on the ground and some laughter could be heard from the crowd. Athena growled and came running back at me with a flying fist aimed at my face. I gave her a side kick and she was launched in the air, landing twenty feet back.

She came at me a few more times and I blocked her, landing strikes of my own. She was not able to land a single strike on me. I was very fast thanks to Lia. I almost felt guilty, but since Athena was a bitch to me, I didn't mind checking her. The crowd was cheering like crazy for their Luna. I could feel Athena's frustration and rage as she lunged at me again. This time, I cartwheeled over her back and kicked her from behind. She landed with a rough thud on the ground and the crowd went wild.

I heard a growl and the sound of bones cracking, before I knew it, Athens gray wolf lunged at me with bared teeth. In a split second, I had moved out of the way and felt my own bones cracking. I let out a thunderous angry growl that shook the whole arena. HOW DARE SHE TRY TO CHEAT AND USE HER WOLF.

I stood snarling and ready to rip her throat out right here. My wolf was twice the size of hers and wanted blood. Athena's eyes were wide open with shock and she dropped down on the ground exposing her neck in submission. Lia wanted to sink her teeth into this bullying bitch. I've seen her type before, the shitty Miranda types who preyed on the weakness of others. NO MORE. I was going to put a stop to this and make an example out of her.

The arena had gone silent and everyone looked shocked, except for Diesel. Diesel looked proud. Everyone started dropping to their knees and bowing their heads as I looked around. I realized that I had shifted. Three hundred of our elite fighters were kneeling in awe of Lia. She stood tall and proud daring anyone else to challenge her.

"As you can see, Crescent Moon has been blessed by the Moon Goddess with the strongest wolf known to our kind as our Luna. Dukes mate, Lia, is a golden wolf. We would like to keep this as a pack secret so that we may keep the element of surprise in a battle." Diesel said.

"YES ALPHA!" Rang in unison through the arena. Followed by, "LONG LIVE LUNA LUCY. LONG LIVE LUNA LIA." Howls rang out through the arena.

I looked around the arena at all the kneeling wolves and caught a familiar scent in the air. One I would recognize anywhere! My eyes looked around again and I saw Gamma Zeke standing by the door in shock. He dropped to his knees and behind him stood a young she wolf and the other wolf I was looking for.

Big smile, sandy blonde hair, green eyes, very thick muscular build. Warm honey and citrus sweet orange, it could only be MAX! We locked eyes and I let out a joyous howl.

"LUCY!" He yelled as he ran over to me. I was still in wolf form and could not shift because my clothes were torn to shreds when I shifted unexpectedly.

"Did you know?" I asked Diesel through the mind link.

"Surprise!" he linked back with a smile on his face.

I dug my wolf head into Max's abdomen, and he wrapped his arms around my wolf neck and gave me a hug. Lia was also happy to see our friend. Then he stood up and gave Diesel a hug.

"Thanks for everything you did for Lucy, I really appreciate it." I heard Diesel say as they hugged.

"I wish it had been more. I was so surprised and happy to hear you were second chance mates." Max said as they pulled apart. "I hope you don't mind; I brought my youngest sister Megan with me as my date for the ceremony." He added.

I yipped happily and Megan giggled. I remembered the time she had sent clothes and shoes over with Max for me. Speaking of clothes, I needed some right now.

"I need some clothes." I mind linked Diesel.

"Payton went to get you some clothes, hang tight babe." Diesel said as he stroked my head.

"Lucy, I brought you the tote bag with your special belongings." Max said as he held out the old bag that contained pictures of my parents, my father's old hat and my mother's necklace. I could also see the stuffed beige wolf poking out that my father gave me when I was little.

Ironic isn't it? Of all the colored wolves my father gave me, he gave me the one closest to my golden wolf. I wonder if he actually knew what I would become. I can't believe Max kept my things safe for me and remembered to bring them all this way. He truly was a wonderful person and friend. I tried to hold back my happy tears and could feel Diesel's happiness for me through the mate bond.

I put my head on Max's shoulder to thank him and he rubbed the top of my head. I heard an angry possessive growl coming from behind me and turned around to look for my mate to calm him. Diesel stood there with a knowing smile on his face, looking at Payton. She was the source of the growl and stood with clothes in her hand as if she had been stuck in a trance.

Max stared back at Payton with a look of surprise and I heard them both call out, "MATE."

CHAPTER 31 – NEW ADDITIONS

After training, Kayla helped an embarrassed Athena to the infirmary, and we made our way to the family dining room for lunch with our newly arrived guests. I was seated on Diesel's lap and looked over at a smiling Payton who was happily seated on Max's lap grinning at all of us. Max was over the moon and Alpha Knox was also beaming with pride.

Megan was seated next to Max and we waited for the arrival of the Gamma couple and our Delta to join us. Megan had a quiet and thoughtful look on her face. Platters of food were being brought in and placed in the middle of the table. It smelled delicious; grilled chicken Caesar salads, panini toasted sandwiches and a lovely tomato basil soup.

"Maximus, it's so good to have you with us again, tell me, how are your parents doing these days?" Alpha Knox asked.

"They're doing well Sir, thank you. They've been traveling throughout Europe a great deal." Max responded.

"That's wonderful to hear." Alpha Knox smiled. "Megan my dear, you've grown so quickly. You should be almost ready for college soon, yes?"

"Yes Alpha." She said. "I've been looking at a few universities, as a matter of fact, we're supposed to be touring a few campuses after we leave."

"Is that where Ranger thinks you're at, looking at universities?" Alpha Knox asked.

"Yes Sir. We didn't share the invitation with him, but the news of the new Luna has reached the pack." Max said.

Gamma Zeke and a heavily pregnant Vannica stepped into the room. Their pup was due in two weeks. "Please excuse our tardiness Alpha." Zeke said.

"No worries, Elliot is still making his way over." Diesel said.

"How wonderful to hear all the excitement of the morning."
Vannica said as she lowered herself in the chair Zeke pulled out for her. "Does this mean that Maximus will be leaving Dark Moon?" She asked.

Max may be a beta, but Payton was Alpha born and therefore had a higher rank. This means that Max would join our pack to be with his mate. Diesel spoke, "Max you've always been a brother to me and later to my mate also. We would be honored to have a second beta at Crescent Moon."

"Thank you, Alpha, the honor would be mine!" Max smiled. Payton's eyes glistened with tears of joy and she kissed Max.

I would not only get to keep my favorite sister-in-law at Crescent Moon with us, but I would also have Max join the family. Can this day possibly get any better?

I mind linked Diesel. "Everyone seems thrilled expect

for Megan, I wonder if she's upset about losing Max at Dark Moon?"

"I noticed that as well." Diesel said.

The door swung open and Elliot walked in. "I was on patrol this morning and missed all the excitement. Why didn't anyone tell me about Lucy's wolf being —" he paused mid-sentence. His eyes darkened and he sniffed the air. He turned to look at a doe eyed Megan staring back at him. She whispered a faint "MATE" and Elliot was suddenly beside her pulling her from her chair into a hug to bury his nose in her neck.

"Guess that solves that problem." Diesel laughed back through the mind link to me.

Congratulations were delivered from around the table to the newly found mates and the new additions to our pack. We started eating and I gazed at all the happy faces in the room, I felt as if my world was finally complete. I went from being all alone, to having a family and being surrounded by people who loved and cared for me.

"It's truly a blessing when the Moon Goddess gives you the opportunity to find a second chance mate." Alpha Knox said.

I thought for a moment about what he said and my father. "I'll never understand why she paired my father with Ursa." I said.

Alpha Knox looked at me for a moment before he spoke. "Ursa wasn't your father's real second chance mate, she was a chosen mate. After your mother passed, word traveled quickly about her special gift.

We kept you hidden for a while until your father secured a new chosen mate and people outside the pack might assume that you were the product of his second relationship. He was worried that someone might try to take you if they thought you might have the same gift."

"You mean, he mated with her to help protect me?" I said in disbelief.

"I don't think anyone suspected how truly awful she was until after your father passed. When you moved to the pack house, I asked Ranger to ensure your well-being. I suppose he was so consumed with his new-found power to worry about an orphaned child." He added with a hint of sadness in his voice.

"She threw me out of my home." I said.

"Your grandmother, Peter's mother, was originally from Dark Moon pack. When your grandfather found her, he was a warrior at Crescent Moon, and she joined Crescent Moon. The family home at Dark Moon, belonged to her and your father inherited it. It is rightfully yours Lucy and will pass to you after Ursa's death." Alpha Knox said to me.

I had no interest in it, I was in a much better place than I could have ever imagined with a wonderful mate. I had everything I wanted right here in this room. Diesel squeezed his arm around me and kissed my neck.

"Are you reading my thoughts again?" I mind linked him.

"Not at all." He lied. "I was just admiring my mate."

216

We finished eating and discussed details of the up-coming ceremony. Guest rooms in the west wing had been prepared to receive some of our guests travel-ing from afar to attend the ceremony and we expected most to arrive at the castle the morning of the event.

"Your parents are more than welcome anytime they wish." Diesel told both Max and Megan.

There was a knock on the door and Tonia, the house manager stepped in. "Luna, Ms. Shari and her assistant are here for your final gown fitting."

With all the excitement today, I had completely for-gotten all about that. "Please show her to the front parlor Tonia, we'll meet her there momentarily."

Vannica let out a squeal of excitement. "This is going to be so exciting, come Megan, you have to see this stunning dress. Don't worry Delta, we'll return your new mate to you shortly." She winked at Elliot.

"You ladies make your way over there; we have some pack business to attend to." Diesel said and placed a kiss on my lips.

We walked into the front parlor and closed the doors behind us. Ms. Hall was already setting up and a young lady, I presumed was her assistant, held the garment bag that contained my dress.
"Ms. Hall, it's a pleasure to see you again. Thank you for coming to the castle." I extended my hand.

"Thank you, Luna, and please, it's just Shari, call me Shari. This is my assistant Rashi. She was able to pull some strings and find the finest mulberry silk that Asia has to offer for your dress." She said.

"Mulberry silk!" Vannica clapped her hands with excitement.

Rashi opened the garment bag and lifted the gown up. The bodice had intricate hand sewn beading and the sleeves were off the shoulders. It was breathtaking! Payton helped me put on the under dress, which will fill the bottom of the dress out in a prefect A-Line shape. Considering it was December, I was thankful for the additional fluffy layer underneath the dress. I stepped in the middle of the room and Shari slipped the dress over my head. It was a perfect fit.

"You look amazing." Megan said.

"Luna, can you twirl around? I'd like to see how the dress moves when you dance." Shari asked.

Payton grabbed my hand, "I will be Diesel and dance with you." She giggled as we tried to waltz.

"Oh, Goddess Lucy, we need to teach you to dance in the next forty-eight hours." Vannica said and we all burst out laughing. She was right, I never learned to dance, and I've never really danced with anyone before. I need dance lessons quick.

"Marvelous! You look marvelous." Shari gave us her approval and no other alterations needed to be made to the dress.

"I was worried the bust might be a tad loose, but you've filled it out beautifully." Shari said.

"Allow me to help you slip off the dress Luna." Rashi said and lifted the dress up.

I slipped off the under dress as well and headed for the bathroom. My head was spinning from all the dancing and twirling Payton put me through. I sat on the toilet with the seat down for a moment and still felt a bit lightheaded. I stood up and looked in the mirror.

I looked exhausted and needed a nap. I splashed my face with cold water and felt a wave of nausea sweep through me. I lifted the toilet seat and emptied the contents of my stomach.
Damn Payton and all of her twirling!

CHAPTER 32 – LESSONS

Diesel's POV

It was just before dawn and the flames in the fireplace flickered. I sat quietly in the armchair in our bedroom while Lucy was still sleeping. She seemed a little tired last night, so we went to bed early after dinner to give the newly mated couples alone time.

I couldn't have selected a better mate for my sister and was happy to have Max with us. They were the perfect fit for each other. I can't help but wonder what Ranger's reaction will be when he finds out. We haven't always been like this. Growing up Ranger and I were close; we did everything together. On his eighteenth birthday, we got the same chest and arm tattoos, I was only sixteen at the time. After Ranger got his wolf, we grew apart and he became obsessed with the Alpha role he would soon inherit from our father.

Once I turned eighteen and finally had Duke, everything changed. I was not only stronger than Ranger, but also discovered my elemental gift. Instead of seeing me as a strong asset to the pack, Ranger became more and more insecure. My father helped me train my element and Ranger's resentment continued to grow.

Obsessed with strength and power, Ranger pushed me away, just as he did our father and Lucy. I replayed the information over and over in my head that Max shared with us yesterday when the ladies went to the dress fitting.

Ranger was still not able to shift, and Rex had cut him off after losing his mate. I've heard of this happening before, but it's rare, when a human and wolf do not feel the same about a mate. He was so desperate for more power that he wanted a strong Luna. What he failed to see was that the Moon Goddess had already given him a mate even stronger than he was and he broke her. Ranger never deserved Lucy. Hell, I'm not even sure I do!

His loss of Rex has consumed him so much he hardly leaves his office. Max confirmed that Ranger sent patrols out to look for her at other packs and as far south as California, but had no luck tracking her. Max had no knowledge of a million dollar bounty placed on Lucy and rogues hunting her. But it certainly doesn't clear Ranger, he could have still been behind it and not told Max.

I filled him in on the unusual rogue activity in the area and the note left in my office. Security had been beefed up and even though I'm sure Lucy could defend herself; she was always with either my father, Payton or myself. I was not going to risk anything happening to my mate. Max had also given me greater details of how Lucy was abused and treated at Dark Moon. Most people treat dogs with more care than Lucy was given. I was personally going to pay Ursa a visit, she was not going to live beyond the new year!

I also considered challenging Ranger and overthrowing him. He does not deserve to be Alpha and with Rex gone, he would soon have others challenging him.

It might even be fun to watch Lucy challenge him for Alpha and take the pack. I decided to give this more thought after the new year.

I heard Lucy turning and tossing, she was mumbling in her sleep again. I walked over to the bed and she had her hand over her stomach. "Please be okay, please be okay." She cried. She was having another nightmare about being in the hole. I laid next to her and held her to my chest, and she calmed right down. I stroked her beautiful long hair and inhaled her scent. Strange, the vanilla scent seemed to be much sweeter, not that I minded.

Two hours later, we were seated at the breakfast table in the dining hall and Lucy sat on my lap. She hardly ate breakfast. Max was excited to see how far Lucy had come along in her elemental training, so she invited him to her lesson today with my father.

After breakfast we met my father at the northern end of our territory with Payton and Max. My father would light a match and with the single flame, she practiced her basic warmups. She casted tall flaming walls, large circle rings of fire and throwing large balls of fire. Her fire was hot enough to incinerate metal.

Her lesson today was on targeted control, such as burning a single leaf on a branch without burning the whole branch. My father was instructing her on target focus when Max asked a good question. "If Lucy is also a descendent from Apollo, who is the sun God, could she possibly create a flame from within herself?"

"Excellent question Max, I've been considering the same!" My father said. "Lucy's element is linked to her emotions, the stronger her emotions, the stronger her fire becomes."

What an interesting idea I thought. I wonder how we could test the theory?

After the morning lesson, we walked back to the castle. Max and Lucy were talking about her escape the day she left Dark Moon. She was telling us about a mountain lion that Lia wanted to eat, and we all laughed at her first ambitious attempt to hunt.

"Laugh now, but my mate could char anything without even lifting a paw to hunt." Duke reminded me.

"Lia is great at catching fish." Max told us.

Lia could swim well but I remembered that Lucy couldn't. "Lucy, we're going to skip training at the arena today and have a swimming lesson this afternoon instead." I said.

"The only lesson Lucy really needs right now are dance lessons." Payton said.

"Really?" I asked.

"I've never actually danced with anyone before, unless you count yesterday with Payton. Apparently, I've got two left feet." Lucy said.

"You can always just stand on my feet and I will sweep us across the dance floor." I told her.

"I'd be happy to give dance lessons in the ballroom today." My father offered.

Lucy's face lit up. "Oh, that would be great! Thank

you, Alpha." Lucy said.

"Maybe we should join as well, I'm a little rusty too." Payton laughed and Max agreed.

"I have a business video meeting with our branch in Japan and needed to head to my office, I'm going to have to sit this one out." I said, feeling Dukes disappointment pulse through me.

"Easy boy, we're still going to swim with her in the grotto today." I told Duke to help calm him. He hated being away from our mate and so did I.

"Not to worry, she's in good hands." My father said.

A few hours later, I was done with the business meeting and made my way over to the ballroom. I cracked the door open and stood quietly to observe for a moment. My father and Lucy were in the middle of the ballroom surrounded by a dozen other couples, including Max, Payton, Elliot and Megan. Our house manager, Tonia, was controlling the music and calling out the step counts *"one..two..three, one..two..three, spin..two..three.."*

I stood there watching for a moment longer thinking about how everything has changed so much in the last two months. Lucy has changed everything for the better. Watching my father and Lucy dancing together showcased the special bond they had developed. She had seamlessly fit right into my life and into the pack. I've also never seen Payton so happy, first with the arrival of Lucy and now her mate and Megan.

The hair on the back of my neck suddenly stood up

as the scent of fresh cut grass and oak hit my nose. It was faint, but it lingered in the hall where I stood. I walked around and ripped opened a large coat closet near the ball room entrance where the scent was strongest. Nothing. The closet was empty. The mystery scent did not belong to anyone in my pack and I was irked at the thought of anyone sneaking in and out of the castle. Maybe I had a traitor in the pack I wondered and made my way back to the ballroom door.

I heard Tonia call out, "Wonderful! You all look wonderful out there. Thank you for joining us and a special thank you to Alpha Knox for teaching today." Everyone applauded and started thanking my father.

I walked over to Lucy who was smiling at me and kissed my beautiful mate. "How was it?" I asked.

"My feet are a little sore, but it was great. Your father is a wonderful dance partner." She beamed up at me.

"Would you like to go down to the heated pool and grotto? I could massage your feet for you or anything else you want." I grinned.

"Sounds great." She blushed.

Twenty minutes later, we were sitting in the cave grotto in the heated pool. I had locked the door in the basement that lead to the pool to ensure we would not be interrupted during Lucy's swim lesson. I was teaching her how to float first and moved on to kicks and strokes. Once she was at ease in the water, she did very well. She picked up the doggy paddle first and was quick to learn how to swim on her back.

She tried to splash me in the face, but I quickly redirected the water back at her with my element. She also tried to dunk my head underwater and I was able to part the water. "No fair." She pouted. She's so cute, its fun watching her get all worked up.

"Little one, if you don't behave yourself, I'm going to be forced to take you right here." I'm sure my eyes darkened with desire.
I felt her heart start racing and heat climbing. I pulled her to me and started kissing on my mark. She moaned and started running her fingers through my hair. That was all I needed to come undone.

I had to have her. I lifted her out of the water and set her on the edge while I was still standing in the warm pool water. I peeled her swimsuit down and started trailing kisses down her chest. I took my time kissing and sucking on her beautifully full breasts.

I reached down between her legs and stroked her before sliding two fingers into her wet heat. The scent of her arousal hit me, and my hungry mouth moved lower on a mission to consume her. I trailed kisses down her stomach and just as I was ready to move lower, I heard the strangest fluttering sound coming from her. I laid my head on her abdomen and listened hard. Is that what I think it is?

Duke started howling with pride and joy as he understood what was happening.

CHAPTER 33 – DOUBLE SURPRISE

This man is going to be the death of me!

Diesel just stopped in the middle of heated passion to tease me. He was resting his head on my stomach, not moving or making a sound. What is he doing? Taking a nap on me?

I felt Lia stir inside of me and suddenly she was howling with joy. I looked down at Diesel and he looked up into my eyes with so much emotion, not the kind that says, *I'm going to rock your world.* Nope, this look was the kind that says, *I love you so much.*

"Little one, is there something you want to tell me?" He asked.

I wasn't sure what he wanted to hear. "Umm, Thank you for the swim lessons." I said.

He let out a chuckle. "No, not that, anything else?"

I wanted to ask why he stopped suddenly, but Lia was driving me crazy. "Lia, I can't think with all the howling." I told her.

"Mate is so happy." She howled back.

"I'm sorry, Lia won't pipe down and it's driving me crazy." I told him.

"She's probably just as happy about our pup as Duke is!" He said.

"OUR WHAT?" Did he just say... pup?

Diesel pulled me into his chest and buried his head in my neck. He inhaled deeply. "That would explain the change in your scent." He smiled.

"Is it true?" I asked Lia.

"Oh yeah!" She howled back.

"How did I not know?" I said in disbelief.

Diesel smiled from ear to ear and was pulsating happiness in his powerful aura. I froze with fear and uncertainty. What if something happens to my pup again? What if something is wrong with me and I can't carry a pup? What if Diesel hates me when I'm big and fat?

I started crying and Diesel lifted my chin up. "Lucy look at me, nothing is going to happen to you or our pup." He said.

I wondered if he was reading my thoughts again. "And I think you're going to look irresistibly sexy with a rounded belly, carrying my pup." He grinned at me. Yep, he's reading my thoughts again!

"Come on, let's go put your mind to ease and visit Dr. Ross, I just mind linked him to expect us."

Diesel wrapped a big fluffy robe around me and a towel around his wet swim shorts. He scooped me up and carried me upstairs to the south wing to see Dr. Ross. We were greeted by nurse Nelly who escorted us into an exam room.
Dr. Ross stepped into the room and started examining me. He took my temperature, pulse, and blood pres-

sure. He then asked nurse Nelly to draw a vile of blood for testing. Diesel stood next to me the entire time watching every little move.

"Are you ready to see to see this little guy or girl?" Dr. Ross asked as he wheeled over an ultrasound machine next to my bed. I nodded my head and laid back while Dr. Ross squirted some gel on my stomach. "Have you been having pregnancy symptoms?" He asked as he turned on the machine.

"A little bit of nausea recently and feeling a little tired." I said.

"Well that's normal." He said and placed the paddle on my stomach moving it around. "Alpha pregnancies are shorter than other wolf pregnancies and take more energy. You're about three weeks pregnant and should be holding the pups in about three more months." He smiled.

"Pups?" Diesel asked.

Dr. Ross smiled at us. "Congratulations, you have two healthy looking pups on the way."

"TWINS!" Lia yipped.

I was still in shock when Diesel carried me back to our bedroom and laid me on the bed. He started a warm fire and just as he finished, there was a knock at the door. "I had Helga send dinner up so we can stay in and get some rest." He told me.

Dinner smelled great; I was feeling famished. Diesel sat on the bed with me and he fed the both of us.

We had roast beef, with potatoes, carrots, celery and onions, spinach salad and chocolate mousse for dessert. I laid on Diesel's chest as he rubbed circles on my back. My tummy was full, and my eyes were heavy with sleep. I felt him jerk and tense up. I opened my eyes and Diesel's eyes were glazed over while he was mind linking with someone.

"Lucy, I need to head to the southern border we have a rogue problem. It shouldn't take me too long, but just in case, Payton and Megan are on their way to stay with you."

There was a knock on the door and Payton walked in followed by a smiling Megan. Payton jumped on the bed. "Slumber party." She laughed. Megan also joined her.

I was rarely ever left alone. Now that I'm pregnant, Diesel was definitely going to be overprotective. I mind linked Diesel, "Don't tell anyone about the pups yet. I want to do it when we're all together."

"Sounds like a plan, now get some rest." He linked back and kissed me before he left.

"I've arranged to have Ana from the spa come over with a few others tomorrow for a girls spa day." Payton said as she fluffed pillows next to me.

Megan also laid down on the other side of me. "Ohhh, sounds wonderful." She squealed.

I fell asleep almost as soon as my head hit the pillow, but I didn't stay asleep for very long. I was dreaming of the hole again and woke up. I looked around the room in a daze for a moment and then remembered that Diesel was away at the southern border.

I thought I had imagined hearing the doorknob shake, but when I looked, I saw that it was clearly jiggling. Someone was trying to open the door from the other side. Payton must have locked the door. I didn't want to wake anyone up, it was probably just Diesel checking up on me. I mind linked him. "Hi."

"Hi, you're awake? Is everything okay?" Diesel linked back.

"Yes, I'm just trying to slide out from between Payton and Megan to open the door for you." I said.

"Lucy, I'm still at the border." He said.

"I think someone is outside the door. The handle was jiggling." I told him.

"Don't open the door." That was the last thing I heard before a loud howl rang out from the southern end of our territory.

Payton quickly jumped out of bed and shifted mid-air into her black Alpha wolf! She went to the door and sniffed, she was snarling and growling. I had absolutely no idea what had just happened, and I couldn't mind link with her yet. Payton stood in front of the door as if expecting someone to come through it. I walked over to her.

"It's okay, anyone comes through that door and I will light them up." She nodded her wolf head at me.
"It's that scent again." Lia told me and she was on edge ready to attack. I took a deep breath and she was right, fresh cut grass and oak! But how?

"Lucy, were here." Called Diesel from the other side of the door.

I unlocked the door and was instantly pulled into Diesel's chest. Megan was hugging Elliot and looked confused. Max looked around the room and grabbed a blanket to cover the black wolf standing with us. Payton shifted back and wrapped the blanket around herself while max held tight to her with his head buried in her neck.

"Zeke is running perimeter right now; someone must be working with him!" Diesel growled.

"With who?" Megan asked.

"I'll fill you in, in the morning." An exhausted looking Elliot told her.

I felt like everyone knew something I didn't. Was Ranger here? Was he able to change his scent or was there a traitor in the castle helping him? Why would he work with rogues, they killed his mother?

I saw a crumbled up piece of paper in Diesel's hand. "What is that?"

"It's nothing, we need to get you back to bed and I'm going to have a guard placed outside of our door." He said and shoved the paper in his pocket.

It was just after midnight and I was exhausted. Diesel locked the door and laid in bed behind me, spooning me. His head was buried in my neck scenting me as he calmed himself down, and his hand slid over to my almost flat stomach.

The sun was rising, and Diesel joined me in the shower before we go down to breakfast. I wanted to take my time and finish what he started yesterday in the grotto, but Diesel was on edge and seemed to be lost in thoughts. The Luna ceremony was tomorrow, and we had so much going on today.

We sat at the breakfast table and Vannica went over the check list for today. "The caterer wanted to know which melons we specifically wanted in the fruit trays, the team assembling the outdoor stage and seating is preparing for snow removal, the band and DJ have been confirmed and wanted a list of any specific songs we want played, the cake will arrive tomorrow at noon..." She droned on and on.

I couldn't really focus, and Lia was pacing on edge. Something was off and Diesel had left without eating breakfast. Payton and Max sat with us and I couldn't shake the feeling that something was wrong. I needed to talk to Diesel, so I excused myself to go to the bathroom. I walked out of the dining hall and towards Diesel's office. There were two warriors standing by the door, I didn't wait for them to tell me I couldn't go into the office. I was going to be Luna of this pack tomorrow and this was my mate's office.

I opened the door and walked right in! I stood frozen for a moment and tears swelled in my eyes. Diesel was in his chair with his back to me and Athena was naked and straddled over him. His head was leaned back, and she was riding him hard, moaning. I turned and started to run down the hall. How could he do this to me, to our pups! I can't stay here; I need to leave. My head was spinning and suddenly I ran right into a brick wall. It was Diesel's chest and his arms wrapped around me.

"Baby, what's wrong?" He asked with a worried look on his face.

"I was in your office! I saw you—" wait a minute, how did he get out here so fast?

"You saw what?" He asked.

"I-I saw, I don't know." Now I wasn't sure what I saw.

"We would have felt the cheating pains if it was our mate." Lia reminded me.

"WAIT A MINUTE!" I said and turned back around and walked towards Diesel's office.

"Baby don't go in there. There's a rogue in my office the warriors captured this morning who wants to talk to me." He said.

"That's not a rogue!" I said and pushed the door open.

Diesel saw what I had, and his fists clenched tight. **"RANGER!"** He growled.

CHAPTER 34 – ARRANGEMENTS

"So ... Athena, you're the traitor we've been looking for." Diesel growled.

"Oh, come now little brother, all's fair in love and war." Ranger said, then he looked at me. "Hello little mate!"

"DON'T YOU FUCKING TALK TO MY MATE!" Diesel roared. **"AND PULL YOUR FUCKING PANTS UP! I'M GOING TO HAVE TO BURN THAT DAMD CHAIR NOW."**

I noticed coals in the fireplace that were dying down. "Allow me." I waved my hand and the whole chair lit up in flames.

"WHAT THE HELL?" Ranger jumped back.

After the leather chair was charred, I waved my hand again and the flames disappeared.

"You're elemental too?" Ranger asked.

"And if you come near me, I will not hesitate to burn you alive!" I said and could feel Diesel's pride radiating.

It was strange seeing him; I remember a time when the sight of him made me nervous and fearful. A time when I would have given anything for his love and affection. Not anymore. Diesel was everything Ranger could never be, even though they looked so much alike, they were completely different.

Payton and Max appeared behind us and Ranger let out a low growl. "First you steal my mate and now my Beta?"

"He didn't steal your Beta, I did." Payton said. "He's my mate dummy." She said pointing to her mark. Ranger looked at her mark and looked at Max's mark too.

"Speaking of mates, how is Miranda doing? She is your chosen mate after all." Payton asked.

Ranger let out a low growl. "Lucy is my mate!"

"Is that why you rejected her, beat her and starved her?" Payton snarled at him.

He looked at me. "Lucy please, I'm sorry, I need you."

"It's *Luna* to you! And in case you missed it, the Moon Goddess gave me someone who loves me for who I am, not what I am." I said and pointed to my mark.

A few more warriors appeared. "Take them both to a cell, we'll deal with them later." Diesel ordered.

"What? I'm not getting an invitation to the ceremony?" Ranger sneered at Diesel.

"GET HIM OUT OF MY SIGHT!" Diesel growled.

We went down the hall to the library. Diesel's eyes were glazed over mind linking with someone, I tried to listen to his thoughts through the link but couldn't. His wall was up. I remembered why I had gone to Diesel's office in the first place.

"What's going on? What are you not telling me?" I demanded.

Max looked to the wooden floor as if it was the most fascinating thing. Payton shifted uncomfortably looking at Diesel and Diesel look me right in the eyes with uncertainty. They were all clearly hiding something from me, I lifted my eyebrow and waited.

"I received a note a few weeks back, it threatened to take you from me. It was taped to my computer screen here in the office and smelled like the mystery scent." He said.

"And you didn't tell me?"

"I didn't want to worry you." Diesel said. "Then last night, I found another note taped to our bedroom door. It was similar to the first and had the same scent." He continued. "Ranger must have been creating the diversions with the rogues so he could slip in and out of the castle, with the help of Athena."

"But we still don't know who the scent belongs to." I said.

"It could be artificial to confuse us. When you were dancing in the ballroom, I caught the scent again. It was coming from the coat closet next to the ballroom entrance, but no one was there. I feel like I'm chasing a ghost." Diesel said and ran his fingers through his hair.

"Well now that Ranger and Athena are both in a cell, I'd say the issue has been neutralized. Let's focus on something happier, like getting ready for tomorrow!" Payton said.

"How long will he be in the cell?" I asked.

"We'll leave him there for a few days. Maybe even turn off the lights and leave him in complete darkness, naked, with no food or water. I'm seriously considering going in there to deliver some nasty lashes across his back!" Diesel growled thinking about all the terrible things Ranger did to me.

"We're better than that, that's what makes us so different from him." I said. "Let's worry about him after the ceremony."

"Fine, but I have to go speak to my father and take care of a few things. I believe you girls have a spa day scheduled." Diesel said as he pulled me into his chest.

"Yes, we do!! Ana should be here soon!" Payton said excitedly. "And don't forget, we have dinner reservations at Vito's tonight."

Payton, Megan, Vannica and I, spent the rest of the morning and early afternoon being pampered with spa treatments. Ana and her team gave us facials, scalp treatments, waxing's, fully body massages, mud wraps, manicures, pedicures, salt and oil scrubs. Salads and sandwich wraps had been served to us for lunch.

Payton was on her cell phone talking to her Cousin Alexis Ivy, who was expected to arrive early tomorrow morning with her husband. She was married to a human, who was also the Prince of an island nation.

"We're going to have royalty here tomorrow!" Megan

said in awe.

"Her husband may be royal, but Alexis is far more special than that. She's a very gifted seer, highly sought after, her prophecies are legendary." Vannica told us.

"Have you decided who's going to escort you down the aisle or if you're walking alone?" Megan asked.

"I'm not sure, there's been so much going on, I haven't really thought about it." I said.

The escort was equivalent to the person who would give away a bride. In a mating or Luna ceremony, it was usually your previous Alpha if you were switching packs or your father or brother. My previous Alpha was currently locked in a cell and I had no other living family. The more I thought about it, the more obvious it became. I had a pretty good idea of who I wanted to escort me and I would ask him tonight at dinner.

After all the pampering, I took a late afternoon nap. I felt the bed dip down and the delicious woodsy pine and musk scent of Diesel flooded my senses. I heard him talking to someone and opened my eyes. "How are my little Alpha's doing in there? Daddy can't wait to hold you." He said to my stomach.

I looked down at Diesel and he planted a kiss on my stomach. "Daddy can't wait to hold mommy too." He said with a mischievous hungry look in his eyes. He trailed kisses all the way up my body, to my neck and then my mouth. After two hours of much needed love making, we finally stepped into the shower to get ready for dinner.

I wore my long wavy hair down and applied a little

bit of makeup. Then I slipped into a beautiful blue colored tunic dress, with little white flowers, black leggings and black boots. I stood in my closet and looked around at all the options I had to pick from. I was reminded of that plastic tub that held about five raggedy changes of clothes I had in the basement at Dark Moon. What a horrible life I had lived those four years with Ranger as Alpha.

I stepped out of the closet and had my long cardigan in my hands when Diesel told me to grab my warm coat.

"Do I really need a warm coat? I might get over heated in the car." I asked.

"We're not going in the car." He said.

"Are we taking the snowmobile?"

"Not in your condition! Come on, it's a surprise."

"As long as we're not walking." I said and he laughed.

We stepped outside and I was speechless! I stood in complete shock taking in the sight before me. There was a beautiful white sleigh with a gray and white Clydesdale horse ready to pull. I walked towards the horse in awe and he seemed completely calm.

"I thought horses were afraid of wolves?"

"This is Charlie, he was born here and is very gentle. Wolves don't seem to bother him, he's a big lover boy." Diesel smiled and stroked his neck. "Come say hi, let him smell you."

I reached for Charlie and he gave me a gentle nay of approval as I rubbed his head.

"We'd better get going, the others are going to meet us there." Diesel told me and I stepped inside the two seat sleigh. He laid a warm blanket over our laps and grabbed the reins.

"Mate is so romantic." Lia purred in my head.

He sure is, I thought. I looked behind us as the castle grew smaller and smaller. The moon was almost full and cast a beautiful light on the snow. Charlie was so strong and gentle as he gracefully pulled us in the snow towards the village.

If someone had told me months ago, I'd be living in this fairytale, I would have never believed it. I laid my head down on Diesel's chest and could feel Duke purr contently. We eased into the village and a young man came out of Vito's Italian Ristorante. "Good evening Alpha, Luna, I will take care of Charlie for you, the others are waiting inside."

"Thank you Benito." Diesel said and we walked inside.

We were greeted by Alpha Knox, Payton, Max, Zeke, Vannica, Elliot and Megan. Once we sat down at the big round table, the servers brought in a big family style dinner. There were several platters, Bruschetta, Tortellini, Meatballs, Chicken Cacciatore, Parmigiana, roasted vegetables and Diesels favorite, Black Ink seafood Linguine.

The restaurant was quaint and charming, like everything else in this village. We started eating and a waiter made his way around the table pouring wine. He made it to my glass and Diesel waved his hand.

"None for the Luna." Alcohol didn't really affect wolves so easily, but Diesel wasn't taking any chances.

Payton looked over a Diesel, "Why not? It might help ease the jitters for tomorrow."

Diesel looked into my eyes and lifted my hand to his face; he kissed my open palm several times. "I don't think wine is good for our pups."

The table exploded with joy! "I'm going to be an Auntie!" Payton squealed. "Did he say pups? How many grand pups am I getting?" Alpha Knox asked. "How wonderful, baby Alpha's!" Vannica clapped. Once the table settled back down, we filled everyone in on the details of the twins.

Dessert was served and Alpha Knox was sitting next to me. "Lucy, I cannot tell you enough how proud I am to have you as a daughter." He beamed at me. "Your parents, I know are smiling down on you. You've made us all so proud." He said as he pulled me into a hug.
"Thank you. If it's not too much trouble, I have a favor to ask of you." I said.

"Anything, anything at all." He smiled.

"You have become such a special person in my life, and I was hoping that you would be my escort tomorrow?" I asked.

"It would be my honor!" His eyes glistening with so much joy and emotion. He pulled me into a hug again and kissed the top of my head.

I heard a roar rip out of Payton and looked to see her eyes locked with Diesel's. They were speaking through the mind link. I felt Diesel radiating anger. "What's wrong?" I asked.

Zeke spoke first. "Ranger escaped!"

CHAPTER 35 – READY

Today was finally here!

Diesel and I slept in this morning, we had breakfast served in our room. I wasn't really hungry and felt nauseous. Diesel rubbed circles on my back, and I waited for the nausea to pass.

"Should I ask Dr. Ross to come check on you? Maybe he can give you something for the nausea?" He asked.

"I'm okay, it should pass."

"Would you like to sit in a warm bath?" He asked.

"Only if my favorite lifeguard joins me." I smiled.

Diesel added more wood in the double sided fireplace and ran the bath. We slipped into the tub and I rested against his back. "This reminds me of the first night I spent here." I said.

"The first night you almost drowned in this tub." He chuckled. "I knew I wanted to slip this on your finger the moment I laid eyes on you." Diesel said and held out an absolutely stunning blue sapphire and diamond ring.

"Oh Diesel!"

"Werewolves don't traditionally exchange rings and wedding vows, but this ring belonged to my father's mother and then to my mother, I would like you to have it as a reminder of my eternal love." He said as he kissed my neck.

"It's beautiful." I managed to whisper as he slipped it on my finger.

"And a perfect fit." He added.

It was almost time for lunch, and I was due to have lunch with the ladies, so we went down stairs. The castle was bustling. The ballroom was still being decorated, the stage and seats were being set up at the big clearing in the woods. More twinkle lights were being brought in and the bar was being stocked up in the ballroom. The band and DJ were wheeling in equipment, while the florist was bringing in beautiful flowers. Some of our guests had arrived and were resting in their guest rooms.

"Here come the love birds!" Payton called out.

"You are glowing." Vannica added.

"And you should be resting Vannica, that baby looks like it's going to pop any minute now." Payton told her and we all laughed.

"Why don't you ladies go and have lunch, I need to go to the office and see if my new chair arrived." Diesel kissed me goodbye.

Payton had arranged a luncheon for the ladies in the family dining room. "Right this way ladies, some of your guests are already seated." Tonia led the way.

We entered the dining room and the ladies stood up to greet us. Payton began the introductions. "Everyone,

I'd like you to meet our new Luna and my sister-in-law, Lucy Michaels, soon to be Lucy LaRue."

"Thank you for coming." I smiled at them.

"Lucy, this is our cousin, princess Alexis, and her younger sister Ayana. Zeke's sister Claudia and our dear friend Jacqueline" Payton said.

"Please, call me Jackie."

"My grandmother's ring looks lovely on you." Payton noticed and everyone gushed at the ring.

Lunch was served and I enjoyed getting to know everyone much better. Getting comfortable with some of the guests helped ease some of my anxiety. Zeke's sister Claudia was a music major and played the harp and piano. Ayana was traveling the world, visiting other packs in search of her mate. And Jackie, was recently mated to Tyler Ross our pack Doctor. As we were finishing lunch, Alexis stood in her chair and the brown pupils of her eyes became white. She looked like she was in a trance and she when she spoke her voice sounded eerie.

"There is a war coming and a lost wolf. Only the one born from Gods can set the course. In a hundred years, a descendant will possess the power of all four and save us in the Great War to come."

Alexis's eyes turned back to their brown color and she sat down looking exhausted. "Sister, are you ok?" Ayana asked.

"Yes, I need to go lay down. Please excuse me Luna, prophecies take a great deal of energy and there's no controlling when I see them or not." Alexis said and left the room.

"Did you understand what she said?" Jackie asked Payton.

I replayed what she said over and over in my head so I could share it with Diesel. After lunch I made my way to my room to rest before I had to start getting ready. The pups were taking a lot of energy from Lia and I. The sun was setting when Payton knocked on the door and woke me up. The guard at the door was still there, with Ranger and Athena on the loose, Diesel wasn't taking any chances.

Payton started rolling my hair with a big curling iron in long ringlets. She used hairspray to help hold the curls and braided a beautiful crown on the top. The rest of my hair draped down my back. She finished it with small flowers in the braid and pulled a few loose ringlets to frame my face. Megan came into the room dressed in a beautiful blue gown carrying the garment bag that held my dress. Payton worked on my makeup, she used bronze and cream eyeshadow to complement the amber color of my eyes. She applied a thin line of eyeliner and two coats of mascara. She brushed on some blush and finished my lips with a fawn colored lipstick.

"Lucy, you look like a masterpiece." Megan said smiling at me.

"We need to get you dressed and downstairs in twenty minutes. My father will be waiting at the entrance hall to escort you."

A few minutes later, I was standing in front of the full-length mirror and I hardly recognized the girl staring back at me. The light ivory colored dress complemented the warm tones of my eyes and dark hair. The only thing missing was my mother's amber necklace. I reached into my nightstand drawer and pulled it out.

"It's beautiful, allow me." Payton said and hooked it around my neck.

Payton slipped into her black gown and we went downstairs to the entrance hall. The castle was quiet at the moment, everyone had gathered at the clearing in the woods for the ceremony. "We're going to leave you right here and get to our seats. My father is just outside and will be right in to get you." Payton smiled and squeezed my hand.

I stood anxiously waiting in the entrance hall, Lia stirred inside of me and she seemed alert. I had a funny feeling I wasn't alone. I looked around and didn't see anyone. I looked towards the ball room and the doors were closed. The closet door next to the ballroom was open, I heard some rustling coming from inside the closet and stepped closer.

"Hello." I called out. "Someone there?" I sniffed the air and caught a hint of fresh cut grass and oak.

"Hello Luna." A young girl about fifteen years old bowed.

"What are you doing in the closet?" I asked.

"My Aunt Tonia is the house manager. She's hired me to work the coat check tonight, I'm Sophia." She told me.

I took another sniff, she smelled like strawberry and lilac. "Is there anyone else in the closet?" I asked.

"No. It's just me." She said.

"Thank you for working this evening Sophia, I know you will do a great job." I smiled at her.

Just then, the front door opened up and a very dashing, older version, of my mate stepped in. Alpha Knox was wearing a tuxedo and a warm smile. He placed his hand over his heart. "Lucy, you look stunning and so much like your mother. I see you still have her necklace; it suits you." He kissed me on the cheek.

"Thank you." I blushed.

"Now, are you ready to go make my son the happiest wolf on the planet?"

"Let's do it!" I smiled back. I considered telling him about the scent, but maybe I just imagined it.

We stepped outside and the white sleigh was decorated with ribbons, flowers and twigs. "I believe you already know Charlie." He smiled and helped me into the sleigh. The clearing in the woods wasn't very far away, but I sure was happy not to have to walk in these shoes out there. Alpha Knox took the reins and Charlie started pulling us.

We entered the woods and the trail was lit with beautiful candle luminarias. Up ahead towards the clearing, I could see the glow from all the twinkle lights. As we got closer, I heard the sound of a harp being played. Charlie stopped when we reached the clearing, and everyone stood up. My breath hitched as I looked around, what kind of fairytale have I stepped into? The full moon hung beautifully over us, the twinkle lights in the trees gave a magical feel and the floral decorations were amazing.

"Are you ready?" Alpha Knox asked.

"I sure am." I smiled at him.

He stepped out of the sleigh and came around to my side to give me his arm. He escorted me to the aisle, and we stood for a moment. Zeke's sister Claudia was playing the harp and changed the tune for our entrance. Pachelbel's Cannon rang through the clearing as we started walking down the aisle. Up ahead my handsome mate stood under a wooden arbor decorated with flowers waiting for me. Alpha Knox escorted me down the aisle, there were happy faces smiling back at me that I recognized and many that I didn't.

A slight breeze rippled in our direction and I caught the scent of fresh cut grass and oak. I felt Alpha Knox tense next to me and knew he smelled it too. Diesel's eyes started roaming the crowd. The owner of the mystery scent was here, hidden amongst our guests and pack, making it difficult to single them out.

CHAPTER 36 – CEREMONY

Diesel's POV

She looked breathtaking! My own Goddess and Luna. Duke was howling in my head with such pride and adoration for his mate. I don't know how I got so lucky or what I did to deserve her. Claudia started the music, and everyone turned to watch them walk down the aisle. My father was beaming, I can't remember the last time I saw him so happy and he couldn't wait to be a grandpa. Lucy was going to be a perfect addition to the pack and a wonderful Luna.

My father mind linked me and told me that he scented the fresh cut grass and oak. That whoever it was, was here tonight in the crowd. I started looking around for anyone that seemed out of place. What a brazen move, to actually be here tonight blending in with our guests.

"It's actually not a bad idea." Duke told me. "Trying to scent someone in a crowd is hard. If anyone gets near my mate I will rip their throat out!" He snarled and started pacing.

"Let's get through the ceremony and when Lucy takes the pack on the moon lit run tonight, I should be able to scent our remaining visitors then." I told my father. I'll take care of this bastard once and for all. They finally reached me, and Lucy gave my father a hug before she turned and took my hand. My father sat in the front row with Max and Payton.

"Good evening Crescent Moon Pack." I called out.

"Good evening Alpha." They called back in unison.

"We also extend our welcome to our distinguished family members, guests and the light of the Goddess with us tonight." I continued.

"The power of the December full moon shines down upon us as we welcome our new Luna into the pack and bind my beautiful mate to me for eternity. We ask that the Moon Goddess continue to shine her light and love on Crescent Moon, who has been blessed with one of her own descendants as Luna."

Whispers buzzed through the crowd as some realized that I had just confirmed Lucy was a descendent of the Moon Goddess. "We are not only the largest pack in the world, we are also the strongest. Tonight, we accept the strongest of them all. We accept Lucy Michaels and her wolf Lia, daughter of Peter and Alice Michaels, as our Luna."

The pack applauded and some even howled for their new Luna. Payton walk forward with a small tray that contained an ancient Crescent Moon dagger and silk ribbon. I removed the dagger and held it up towards the moon.

"Oh, mighty Moon Goddess, Selene, bless this dagger as an instrument of your will." Then I turned to Lucy. "Do you Lucy Michaels, willingly and proudly accept the title and roll of Luna to Crescent Moon pack with all of the rights and responsibilities?"

"Yes, I do." She called out.

"Do you pledge to remain faithful and true to the pack and support the Alpha in any way possible?"

"Yes, I do."

"Do you pledge to defend and protect the pack to the best of your abilities and with your life if necessary?

"Yes, I do."

I brought the dagger down to my palm first and sliced it open, then I did the same to her. Max stepped forward with the silk ribbon and tied our bloodied hands together. The binder was something an honored guest does; it was equivalent to the human weddings best man role.

Max smiled proudly after he tied our hands together and lifted them in the air towards the moon. "Bound by the Moon Goddess in love and to the pack by blood." He called out.

The pack members knelt to their knees and those in wolf form standing on the outer edges bowed their heads.

"LONG LIVE LUNA LUCY! LONG LIVE LUNA LIA!" They called out in respect.

The light from the moon seemed to shine down brighter for a moment and then dimmed back down to normal. The crowd was gasping and pointing, stunned faces looked at us in awe.

"Looks like the Moon Goddess has definitely blessed your union; I've never seen anything like that." My father linked me.

I kissed Lucy and the pack started howling and applauding. Lucy's eyes were glazed over as the pack link was formed and she could now mind link with everyone else. She smiled up at me and my heart melted. She was all mine.

I raised my hand and the crowd fell silent. "Before our Luna takes the pack for the traditional moon lit run tonight, I would like to first welcome and add the two newest members to our pack." The crowd applauded again.

"Maximus Taylor, from Dark Moon pack, has found his mate, Payton LaRue. He will be joining us as our second Beta. Megan Taylor, also from Dark Moon pack, has found her mate, Elliot Rivers and will be joining us as our female Delta. Max and Megan please step forward."

I untied my bound hand and both Lucy and I had already healed. Payton handed the dagger to me once more. I sliced my other palm and did the same to Max and Megan.

I held Max's hand in mine. "Do you Maximus Taylor, break all ties with Dark Moon pack? Willingly and proudly accept the title and roll of Beta to Crescent Moon pack, with all of the rights and responsibilities? To remain faithful and true, defend and protect the pack to the best of your abilities and with your life if necessary?"

"Yes, I do." He answered.

I did the same with Megan and introduced their

wolves, Milo and Miley.

"We'd like to invite everyone to return to the castle, dinner will be served in the grand ball room followed by this evenings celebration. The pack will join the Luna, behind the castle at ten to midnight for the traditional moon lit run led by the Luna at midnight."

Claudia started playing the harp as I led Lucy back down the aisle towards Charlie. I picked her up and placed her on my lap in the sleigh. Charlie started pulling us back to the castle.

"Diesel, he's here, whoever he is, I scented him again." Lucy said to me.

"I know, I have the warriors on alert and they're going to scent everyone as they enter the ballroom. I don't want you leaving my sight for a second. When you take the pack out for the run, I have to stay behind and should be able to scent them if we haven't found them by then."

We reached the castle and I carried Lucy up the stairs. "By the way, you look absolutely ravishing tonight." I said and kissed her before setting her down.

"You know, we could just skip the festivities and go up to our room to celebrate naked." I grinned.

She giggled and kissed me back. "Alpha, we don't want to be rude to our guests, do we?"

I pulled her to me and inhaled her scent. I really wanted to take her upstairs and lock her in our room while I hunt the bastard. Lucy was strong and could handle almost anything, but she was also carrying my pups and that made me overprotective.

We made our way into the ballroom and Lucy's eyes filled with awe as she took in the splendor of everything. The band was playing classical music to start, and the DJ would take over later for the dancing. The ballroom started filling up with guests and our trackers were positioned by the doors scenting everyone who walked in.

I mind linked Sam, our chief tracker. "Remember, it's fresh cut grass and oak. Anyone who sets foot in this castle with so much as a blade of dead grass on their shoe, I want to know about!"

"Yes Alpha."

The Beta, Gamma and Delta couples sat at our table with us. My father was seated with our cousins and was deep in conversation with Alexis about a prophecy she made today. Dinner was served, I selected the steak and Lucy had the salmon. We continued to eat and tried to look as normal as possible. We didn't want to alert the mystery person that we were aware of their presence.

I leaned over to kiss my Luna on her neck, and she smiled at me. "Lucy LaRue. I like the sound of that. How are the pups doing?"

"They're doing great." She giggled back at me.

Max mind linked me. "Alpha, I've asked the trackers to be sure and scent the workers and kitchen staff as well." Max was on it.

After dinner, the cake was served along with a fruit tart that our pastry chef Byianca had prepared. Max lifted his glass to the table, "Lucy, Milo has always recognized you and Lia as our true Luna and tonight I am honored to be part of your pack."

"Thank you brother." She lifted her glass of water back.

The lights dimmed to cue the first dance. Lucy and I took the dance floor and other couples joined us for the opening slow waltz, Lucy did wonderful.

"I need to use the restroom." Lucy mind linked me.

"I'll have Payton go with you." I told her and linked Payton.

I walked out of the ballroom with them and waited outside the ladies room on the other side of the coat closet. The young girl working the coat check was sitting at the podium in front of the closet reading a book. She was the house managers niece, so I invited her to take a break in the ballroom and have something to eat.

"Thank you, Alpha." She squeaked and went to the ballroom.
I walked a little closer to the big closet and the smell of fresh cut grass and oak hit my nose. I stepped inside the closet and the scent was stronger, I reached for the light switch and heard a rustling sound behind me.

There was a sharp stinging sensation in my neck, and I turned to see a shadow swimming before me. My vision was blurry, and I fell to my knees. Before I could mind link Max, my world went dark.

CHAPTER 37 – REX

It's been almost an hour and Diesel is still nowhere to be found.
"Something is wrong, mate needs us." Lia said anxiously.

I tried to mind link Diesel again. "Diesel are you there? I'm worried, where are you?"

Nothing.

"Please Diesel, answer me."

Still nothing.

Payton had checked his office and was going upstairs to our room to look for him. "Check the astronomy observatory as well." I linked her. "Will do, stay with my father, we'll find him." She linked back.

Max and Zeke had slipped out of the ball room to check the perimeter for any signs of him. I linked Sam our chief tracker. "Sam we can't seem to find the Alpha and he's not responding to the mind links. I need you to track him."

"Yes Luna, I'm on it." He replied.

"Lucy, have a seat, I'm sure he's okay, all this worrying can't be good for the pups." Alpha Knox told me.

"But what if he found Ranger and something happened?"

"Ranger is no threat to Diesel without his wolf. Even with Rex, he was never as strong as Duke. You know, my wolf Kruz, can feel his pup's connections and Rex doesn't have much time left. He's almost completely faded, and Ranger has no one to blame but himself." He told me.

"Will Ranger die if Rex dies?" I asked though I wasn't sure that I really wanted to know the answer to that.

He paused a moment. "There's a good chance that will happen. He chose a path of envy, power and greed. Every time he had a choice, he made the wrong one. I tried to guide him, but he pushed me away. He could have accepted his brothers gift as a blessing in his pack, but he didn't. He could have challenged my cruel brother for this pack, but he chose not to, and Diesel did. He could have helped expand the company internationally and chose not to. Diesel did and quadrupled his wealth and company shares."

Alpha Knox looked up into my eyes. "Ranger could have accepted his mate from the Moon Goddess, but he chose to reject her, and Diesel loved her. At every step, at every turn, my boy made the wrong choice." I couldn't help but notice the sadness in his eyes.

"Soon you will hold two beautiful pups in your arms Lucy, the bond between you and your children will overwhelm your heart. You will love them both the same no matter how different they are. My love as a father never changed for Ranger, but my disappointment continued to grow. I prayed to the Goddess that he would finally change when he found his mate, but we both know how that worked out." I could feel the pain in his aura. "Now, I'm afraid he's lost forever."

We were interrupted by Elliot who had just returned from the prison cells. "There's no sign of him. We have an hour until the midnight run, I'm sure he'll be back for that." He looked over at his mate Megan who was sitting with an anxious looking Vannica. I felt a wave of nausea come over me and really needed some fresh air but first I might need to throw up in the ladies room.

"I'm going to the ladies room, I'll be right back" I excused myself.

I stepped out of the ballroom and walked towards the nearest restroom. I saw Sophia sitting at the podium next to the coat check closet. "Hello Sophia." I called out.

"Hello Luna." She bowed.

"You haven't by any chance seen the Alpha this evening have you?"

"It's been over an hour since I last saw him, he told me to take a break and get something to eat." She informed me.

I could smell Diesel's scent coming from the closet. I knew he would not have a coat checked in, but maybe he went into scent people's coats?

"Thank you." I said and she resumed reading her book. She would not have noticed much with her head buried in that book. I stepped inside the closet and Diesel's scent was strong, he had definitely been here. I also caught the familiar scent of fresh cut grass and oak. I looked around the closet and slid coats around on the racks looking for any clues.

"Mate was here." Lia said.

The closet had four rows of coats and I continued to look around. My hands reached to the back wall behind a few coats and found some kind of lever. I pulled it expecting more lights to come on, instead, I fell forward and lost my balance when the wall unexpectedly moved and turned. I looked around, I had fallen into another chamber and the door closed behind me.

"It's a secret passage." Lia said.

I tried to open the door again, but it was no use, I couldn't find another lever or figure out how to open the passage. I tried to knock but the door seemed thick with iron.

"Mate, I could smell mate." Lia paced.

I could too. Maybe he found the passage and followed it. I wonder if it leads to other parts of the castle? I tried to mind link Max but couldn't, the iron and stone may have been blocking the link. The passage sloped down beneath the castle and I followed it. "Lucy, you may want to hold a flame in your hand so we can see a little better down here. And if anyone tries to attack we can light their asses up!" Lia suggested.

She was right, I removed the small lighter I kept in my bra and flicked it on. A moment later I slipped the lighter back in my bra and held a ball of fire in my hand. The tunnel seemed to go deeper with a few twists and turns. We came to a fork and I wasn't sure which tunnel to take.

"Lucy, the one to the left seems to be a little colder, which means it could lead out or into a mountain. The one to the right is a little warmer, it could lead back to the castle or another chamber." Lia explained to me.

She was right, but I wasn't sure which way to go. "Which way should we go?" I asked Lia.

"If mate made it out, he would have responded to the mind link, he might still be down here."

We took the tunnel on the right and continued walking. I listened for any sounds but heard nothing. A short while later, Lia was alert and on edge.

"What is it?" I asked her.

"He's here!"

"Diesel?"

"No, Ranger."

She was right, I could smell cinnamon, apples and honey in the air. I sniffed again, there was also a metallic rusty scent in the air. I turned the fire down to a tiny flame and tip toed ahead. I saw the opening to another chamber and listened for noise. It was quiet. I slowly peaked my head over to look. There was a cell with a single occupant, chained with silver to the wall. He looked lifeless but his heart was still beating.

"Ranger?" I called out his name.

He didn't respond. I stepped into the room and called his name again.

"Ranger?"

"Lucy." He whispered.

He was beaten and his face was so swollen, he was hardly recognizable. He had cuts all over his body and had clearly been tortured. The silver had made him weak and with the absence of Rex he was not able to heal.

"Ranger what happened?" I asked.

"Lucy." Ranger was struggling to breathe. "You ... you, n-need to leave before he — he comes back, you're not safe here." He managed to say.

"Who? Before who comes back?"

"Run Lucy." Ranger couldn't even hold his head up.

"He's dying." Lia whispered to me.

I looked around for keys but couldn't find any. The flame in my hand grew into a large ball and I used it to melt the lock on the cell. I kicked the door open.

"Wha- what are you doing?" He asked me.

"Getting you out of here." I said as I thought about what Alpha Knox had told me earlier and the sadness in his eyes for his oldest son.

"No Lucy, jus-just let me die here." He gasped for air.

"You're not going to die Ranger." I said.

"I don't have Rex ... I've be-been injected with some

kind of wolfsbane an-and night shade. My legs won't even work."

"Who did this to you?" Ranger was unresponsive and slipping away quickly.

"Lucy, I can still feel Rex." Lia said.

"Rex? Rex please, are you there?" I called out.

Ranger's head started moving side to side. "Rex, can you hear me?"

"Lucy?" His voice called out, but his eyes darkened to a near black as Rex surfaced.

"Yes Rex, Lia and I are here." I said.

"I'm so glad I could see you one last time before I die." Rex said and I felt a pain in my heart for him and for Alpha Knox.

"Rex, please, you don't have to go. You don't have to die. Your father loves you very much and has been worried about you." I said.

"I'm so sorry about what this bastard did to you and to our pup. I tried to stop him, but he always blocked me out. Now that we've lost you, I blocked him out." Rex said.

"I know Rex, I know you tried. It's not your fault, please don't let yourself die just to punish him. You were born to be a strong Alpha wolf; your pack needs you. You can choose a worthy mate and have strong pups."

"Lucy, the Moon Goddess had us paired together." He

said.

"Maybe I was destined for a different path, I'm a unique wolf. The Moon Goddess gave me a second chance mate."

"I've always known Lucy; I knew Lia was something special. I didn't tell him because I didn't want him to use her for her power. Duke will take good care of you and your new pups." He said.

"You know about the pups?" I asked.

"I can hear their strong heartbeats." He said.

"Rex, if I can forgive Ranger and move on, I know you can. The Moon Goddess gave him a strong Alpha wolf to help guide him, not to just give up on him. Don't leave him here to die. You deserve better than this." I said.

"My brother is lucky to have you." Rex said as he dropped his head.

"Rex? Rex?" I called out. He opened his eyes again and the beautiful blue eyes that run in the LaRue family stared back at me.

"Lucy! Rex is back!" Ranger told me. "Rex is back!"

"I'm glad, now let's get you out of here." I said.

"These are silver chains, they will slow my healing, don't touch them or they'll burn you." He warned me.

He still didn't know about my golden wolf, I was immune to the effects of silver and wolfsbane. He wasn't going to be able to walk out of here and I needed to continue to look for Diesel. I would need to shift so he could ride on my back and Lia was strong enough to rip the chains out of the wall. I started taking off my shoes and gown to shift. Ranger was about to receive the shock of the century!

"Who did this to you?" I asked.

"My cousin, Alpha Titus's Bastard!"

CHAPTER 38 – COUSIN

Diesel's POV

I opened my eyes and the room was spinning. I could hardly hold my head up. I could feel Duke, he was weakened. What the fuck did he inject me with?

I looked around the room to try and figure out where I was. It definitely wasn't the coat closet. I was in a rocky dungeon or cave. The only light came from a single torch on the wall. My wrists were burning from heavy silver. I heard someone moving and felt a kick to my ribs.

"Look who's finally awake." I heard a gruff voice say. I recognized that voice and his scent, his scent was fresh cut grass and oak.

My eyes focused and his face became clear. "YOU! IT WAS YOU?" I growled in disgust.

"You can call me cousin." He said and punched me in the jaw.

"Uncle Titus didn't have any children." I said as I struggled against the silver chains he had around my wrists. I wanted to rip his fucking throat out.

"Funny, your brother said the same thing before I killed him." He laughed.

He killed Ranger? If he had killed Ranger, Duke would

have felt the connection break. Maybe we didn't feel it because Ranger was wolfless.

"My mother was his mistress, Jessica Monroe. I may not have the filthy LaRue last name, but I am still Alpha born and his only heir. He was so obsessed with having elemental born pups that it made him mad. After you killed my father, I made it my mission to take this pack and castle back."

"You should have been brave enough to challenge me if you wanted Crescent Moon, Alpha Jordan." I spat.

"How would that be fair? You have elemental power. Oh no, I was waiting for you to find your mate so I could kill her and weaken you before I challenged you. While I waited, I took over the Eclipse Pack. I made alliances with rogues and I discovered a perfect combination of wolfsbane and night shade to poison even the strongest of Alpha's."

"My Luna is stronger than you Jordan. She won't let you have Crescent Moon." I growled.

"Oh, my dear cousin, after the abuse your brother put her through and after the devastation of losing you, I will be the comforting friend and Alpha she remembers. With the help of a love potion she will be mine soon." He oozed.

"Lucy would never." I growled back. He was a delusional bastard.
Lucy will light his ass up as soon as she smells him!
Jordan picked up a silver blade and sliced the side of my waist. The warmth of blood ran down my side and the deep cut burned.

"My father had searched for an elemental wolf to breed. I had heard about Lucy's mother being elemental, but I wasn't sure if Lucy would have the gift too. I paid Ursa to keep tabs on her over the years-"

A roar ripped through me; I was going to rip Ursa to shreds as soon as I get out of here!

Jordan smiled at me. "When I visited Dark Moon, I had Lucy stay for lunch and sat her on my lap. It was so much fun watching Ranger struggle with his wolf as I fed her lunch. I was able to shift her hair to the side and saw the mark on her neck. Just like yours."

I growled at him and he plunged the dagger into my thigh, twisting it. Duke howled in my head as the pain burned.

"Your asshole brother nearly killed her before I could get my hands on her. When she ran away from Dark Moon, I put out a bounty on her, but she escaped my rogues. As luck would have it, she turned up at Crescent Moon and is now your mate. I have paid Ranger back for all the abuse he put her through. When they find your body, I will plant Ranger with you. It will look like he killed you and then died from his injuries after or vice versa."

"Where's Ranger?" I asked.

"What's wrong? Missing your big brother all of the sudden? HE'S DEAD!"

"How did you convince Athena to help you?" I asked.

"Athena? ... I almost forgot about Athena. She wasn't

working for me, the only thing she's guilty of is fucking your brother. She's actually being held by the
rogues as entertainment." He laughed.

"Why are you working with rogues? You have a good
sized pack?"

"Eclipse is only a quarter of the size as your pack.
Rogues could be very useful allies when compensated
nicely and always willing to get their hands dirty.
When the Luna goes on the traditional midnight pack
run tonight, they will attack the beloved elders and
pups first to weaken your fighters. Without an Alpha
to lead them, they will be weak enough to submit."

"If you want this pack, why would you kill the people
and pups you're supposed to protect?" I asked.

"Because they willingly accepted you four years ago
when you killed my father. They should have turned
on you and they showed him no loyalty." He growled.

"I challenged him and beat him fairly; you know our
laws." I said.

"YOU ARE ELEMENTAL! HOW IS THAT FAIR?" He yelled
and plunged the silver dagger in my other thigh.

"I didn't not use my waterpower at all, it was a fair
fight. You can ask the elders—"

"LIES!" He screamed.

"Before I kill you, I want you to know how much I'm
going to enjoy fucking your mate over and over again,
until she bears my seed."

A roar ripped through me and I felt it reverberate off the walls and echo back. I realized we were in a cave. The mountains in my territory are covered in snow this time of year, surely there had to be some water dripping into the cave or some snow near the cave opening.

"Don't you already have twin pups?" I asked.

"Two girls, worthless like their mother! I killed her right after their birth. Then last month, the Moon Goddess thought she'd have a laugh at my expense, and I met my second chance mate."

"You have a second chance mate? The Moon Goddess blessed you a second time?" I asked with obvious shock in my voice. Very few people received a second chance mate, why would she give him another mate after he killed the first?

"Shocking I know! I could hardly believe it myself. Miranda was all too happy to leave Ranger after he lost his wolf. I accepted her to torture him, but it didn't seem to have an effect on him. She will of course have an unfortunate accident once I secure Lucy."

This guy was just as unhinged as my uncle Titus. Maybe they were related after all? Miranda was still Max's sister, even though she was a power hungry bitch, she still didn't deserve Jordan. I wanted to know if anyone else was working with him and how he was getting in and out of the castle.

"So, Athena wasn't working with you? Then who was? How did you get the notes into the castle?"

"The castle has secret passages. It was fun watching you send the patrols out looking for an intruder when I was hiding right under your nose."

There must be one in that damn closet, that's why I kept scenting him there. I started to feel Duke stir a little. "Duke are you there?" I asked.

"Yes, I'm trying to heal you quickly, the night shade was strong. Don't let him see we're getting stronger." He told me.

"Jordan, if you kill me, there's no need to attack the pack, those people are innocent." I said and started coughing.

"Your Luna should be getting ready for the run and the attack should be starting in the next ten minutes. I'm going to have to give you another dose of this miracle juice, so I can join in the fun and make sure you don't escape. I'd like to rip your fathers head off to honor mine."

Another growl ripped through me; this bastard wanted to kill my father. "Are you even sure Titus was your father? You don't seem to have a resemblance to him or even the LaRue genes. Every male for generations has had the raven hair and blue eyes." I told him.

"MY MOTHER WAS NOT A WHORE!" He growled.

"Of course not, just a mistress right?" I replied.

"Duke it's now or never buddy." I told him hoping he could give me the extra push I needed to draw some water into the cave and fight this bastard.

I closed my eyes and tried really hard to pull the element; Jordan noticed. "Nice try Diesel, I have just the right thing for you." He said as he held up a syringe. He stepped forward to lower it and I kicked my legs out and knocked him down. He rolled over and picked up the syringe again and stalked towards me.

A thunderous angry roar ripped through the cave and I could feel the whole mountain shake. I saw two eyes in the shadows of the entrance, and they looked like they had flames burning in the pupils. The eyes moved forward, and a big angry golden wolf stepped into the cave.

"THAT'S MY MATE!" Duke barked in my head, so happy to see her.
Jordan stood speechless for a moment taking her in.

"Is this some trick?" He wasn't sure if this was an illusion. She bared her teeth at him and growled. Lia radiated such power and anger that it made me want to kneel and submit. I could see Jordan struggling with the same feeling.

"She's going to rip your head off." I said.

Jordan was eyeing the exit and considering his escape. Lia moved closer to let him know there was no way out. He was still holding the silver knife and in a flash, he threw it at my chest aiming for my heart.

Lia leaped in front of me and the knife plunged into her side. A howl ripped through me as my mate landed at my feet. **"LUCY!"**

CHAPTER 39 – RESCUE

"Your uncle Titus has a child?" I asked Ranger.

"Apparently no one knew, Jordan Monroe is Jordan LaRue." He said as he struggled against the silver chains.

"I'm going to shift, close your eyes. Once I shift, I won't be able to communicate with you. I'm going to pull the chains down and you can ride on my back." I told him.

"I don't want to hurt you." He said.

"Oh, trust me, you can't. Now close your eyes."

I shifted and moved to the silver chains on the walls. Lia grabbed the chain and yanked the bolts right out of the rocky wall. We'd have to figure out how to get them off his wrists soon, they were slowing down his healing.

Ranger was unable to use his legs at the moment and crashed to the hard stone ground. He looked up at me and struggled for words as he took in the sight of Lia. "What the hell?"

I barked back at him; I really didn't have time for this. I needed to get moving to find Diesel. Lia picked up the lighter in her mouth and lowered us down so Ranger could climb on.

"I can't believe what I'm seeing!" He said and laid his

head down on my back.

I went back out the tunnel and towards the fork, I was going to try the tunnel on the left this time. I sniffed the air for any signs of Diesel and kept walking until we reached the fork. "I think this tunnel leads out." Ranger said and I nodded my wolf head.

"I think he's bleeding on my fur; you owe me a bath after this." Lia said.

"How are the pups doing?" I asked her.

"They're doing just fine; all they need is our mate." she said.

The deeper we went into this tunnel, the colder it got. I could feel Ranger shiver on my back, he was struggling to regulate his body heat while Rex was trying to heal him. I heard a faint sound from the end of this hall and then a familiar growl.

"MATE! We found him!" Lia yipped.

I heard the sound of clanking chains and realized that Diesel might also be in the same position I found Ranger.

"Let's go save our mate." Lia said and wanted nothing more than to run to her mate.

Then I heard the familiar voice of Alpha Jordan yelling. **"MY MOTHER WAS NOT A WHORE!"**

"Of course not, just a mistress right?" Diesel's voice rang back.

I slowly and quietly lowered myself down and set Ranger on the ground before I entered the chamber to rip out Jordan's throat. Diesel's scent was strong, and it was mixed with blood.

"Mate is hurt!" Lia said and she was livid.

I looked into the chamber and could see Diesel chained to the wall on the ground. Jordan had a syringe in his hand and was moving quick. Lia roared and they both turned to the shadow we were standing in. I stepped forward and Diesel smiled at me. Jordan's eyes were wide open, and the color drained from his face. He looked as if he had just seen a ghost.

I could hear his heart racing and stepped closer. I saw a flash of silver in his hand and in a second he had tossed it at Diesel's chest.

"NO!" Lia roared in my head and we lunged to protect our mate.

"LUCY!" I heard Diesel yell.

The blade was lodged in my lower rib and I fell to the ground. The silver had no effect on me but would have been fatal if it had come into contact with Diesel's heart. My mother had died with a silver bullet to her heart.

"Lucy, can you hear me?" Diesel mind linked me.

"Yes."

"Don't shift, Lia will heal faster in wolf form and protect the pups." He said.

"The pups are okay." Lia said in my head.

"We need to get the blade out." He said out loud.

Lia turned her head and tried to bring her mouth to the blade but couldn't really grip it to pull it out from this angle.

"Let me get that for you." Ranger said as he dragged himself across the floor. He was still unable to walk, the broken bones in his legs were healing slow. The silver chains dragged behind him as he crawled using his elbows.

"Where the hell did you come from?" Diesel growled.

"Lucy don't move, I'll pull it out." Ranger's ragged voice said.

"DON'T FUCKING TOUCH MY MATE!" Diesel roared as he pulled against the chains.

"It's okay Diesel." I mind linked him.

"She just saved my life and helped bring back Rex when she could have let me die. I'm not going to hurt her." He said.

I looked at Ranger and nodded my head. He reached for the knife and pulled it out, then he dropped it on the floor. The wound closed in a matter of minutes and Lia stood up to pull the silver chains out of the wall that shackled Diesel. We were engulfed in a big hug by Diesel and Lia purred. He kissed me all over my wolf face. "Don't ever scare me like that again, little one."

"I missed you too." Lia gushed in my head and Diesel

laughed because he could hear her.

"Duke is happy to see you too." He said out loud.

"Any idea how to get the silver shackles off? Neither of you are going to heal fast while the silver stays on." I mind linked him.

"Jordan left his jacket in the corner; the keys are in the pocket." Diesel said as he limped over to check the pockets.

"Bingo!" He inserted the key and unlocked each shackle. Then he walked over to Ranger and tossed the keys down to him. Ranger unlocked the shackles on his wrists and breathed a huge sigh of relief as he rolled over on his back and stared up at the ceiling.

"You know the bastard is going to try and kill dad." Ranger said.

"And attack my pack." Diesel said.

"We need to get out of here and warn them." I mind linked Diesel, though neither of them looked like they could make it far in their current condition.

"He has rogues on the outskirts of the territory ready to attack the elders and pups. They're going to strike when the Luna takes the warriors and the rest of the pack members on the midnight run. But seeing as the Luna is here and we're both missing, I'm sure the pack is on full alert right now." Diesel said out loud.

"He'd be stupid to attack now, especially after seeing Lia, but then again, he seems a little crazy." Ranger said.

"Almost as stupid and crazy as that Alpha who threw his pregnant mate into the hole after whipping her." Diesel snarled.

Ranger hung his head in shame.

"Now's not the time, we need to get out of here." I linked back.

"Can you walk?" I asked Diesel.

"Yes, Duke is feeling much stronger now that you're here." He mind linked me.

"Great, now have Ranger climb on my back so we can get out of here." I linked back.

"I will not have that asshole anywhere near you and potentially harm our pups." Diesel growled out loud.

"Lia is much stronger than that, we're not going to leave him here!" I replied.

"I swear to the Goddess, if you even try anything!" Diesel said to Ranger.

"I won't, I promise." Ranger said.

"I'm only allowing this for Rex!" Diesel growled.

Ranger climbed onto my back and Diesel rested his arm protectively around my neck and we left the cave. Diesel had taken the fire torch off the wall and held it in the other hand.
"Where the hell have you been anyway?" Diesel asked Ranger.

"Getting Jordan's special treatment after he broke me out of your cell. He used wolfsbane and night shade on me. I woke up chained to the wall down here."

"Did you know about him?" Diesel asked.

"No. Never even suspected it." Ranger replied.

"When this is over, I need Ursa's head. She's been working with him." Diesel said.

"I'll personally deliver it to you myself." Ranger replied.

We made our way through the tunnel and could feel the temperature dropping. We reached the end of the tunnel and it appeared to be closed off with a wall of snow.

"Think you have enough energy to move that?" I asked. "Or should I try to melt it with fire?"

Diesel spoke out loud. "If we melt it, we risk the chance of flooding this tunnel because we don't know how much snow is on the other side. Let me try to move it first."

Diesel closed his eyes and tried to focus, he waved his hands and I could see the snow tumbling back. He paused a moment and tried again, after a few more attempts, I could see a dark hole in the snow. The hole grew larger and we were able to walk through it.
We were finally standing outside beneath the full moon and looked around at our exit point. We could see the castle from where we were. We were in the southern mountains and there was snow that seemed

to cover the pass to the castle.

Diesel fell to his knees. "Lucy I think you caused an avalanche when Lia unleashed that powerful growl. The entire pass has been sealed off with snow. No one can get in or out without climbing over the mountains." He said.

"Does that mean the rogues are stuck on the other side?" Ranger asked.

"I think so, but Jordan won't give up so easy." Diesel said.

I tried to mind link Payton. "Payton, are you there? I found Diesel."

I heard a howl rip through the air from the castle, it was Payton! I howled back into the night. My howl was returned with hundreds of pack wolves howling back to their Luna. Diesel suddenly shifted and Duke rubbed up against Lia before he let out a howl that echoed through the territory.

A war is coming.

CHAPTER 40 – CODE RED

Duke and I descended down the mountain with Ranger still on my back. The full moon's light was bright, and I could see what looked like a thousand wolves rushing towards us. In the front leading the wolves was a large black Alpha wolf with blue eyes. I instantly recognized Kruz, Alpha Knox's wolf. The other wolves came to a halt as many set eyes on Lia for the first time, they lowered their heads. Kruz walked up to Duke and nodded his head, then he turned towards me and sniffed the air.

"What happened to Ranger? Where have you been?" He asked us through the mind link.

I looked at Duke and his eyes glazed over; his Alpha voice rang through the mind link to every pack member. "Attention Crescent Moon, we have found the traitor! Earlier this evening, Alpha Jordan Monroe, attacked your Alpha and Luna. He has gathered rogues just outside our territory who planned to attack our most vulnerable pack members first, the elders and pups, while the pack took their traditional midnight run with the new Luna."

Angry howls rang out across the territory.

"Alpha Jordan has escaped and could be hiding in the territory; his scent is fresh cut grass and oak. I order the launch of CODE RED."

"What's code red?" I asked through the mind link.

"Let's get to the castle and I'll explain." He linked back.

The other pack wolves started moving with purpose and we ran towards the castle. Payton was standing at the castle doors with the guards and tossed us blankets to shift. Max came running down the stairs and lifted Ranger off my back.

We shifted and I draped the blanket around myself. Megan appeared at the stairs with shirts and sweatpants for all of us.

"Tonia, our guests stay in their rooms and lock their doors." Diesel said to our house manager and she nodded her head. "Everyone else to my office."

"What should I do with him?" Max asked while holding Ranger up.

"Take him to Dr. Ross and get back to my office."

Our chief warriors and trackers joined us in the office. We had five chief warriors but without Athena, we were down to four. The chief warriors all led squads of warriors and trained pack fighters, having about three hundred wolves on each of their teams.

"Dad, do you know if the castle has construction plans or any maps or charts? It seems the castle has secret passages the bastard was using." Diesel asked.

"I'll check with Tonia." Alpha Knox said and mind linked her.

"Sam, I want every corner of this castle checked and

scented for him. I don't know if Jordan returned to the castle through a passage or if there's another exit point.

"Why would Jordan do such a thing?" Max asked.

Diesel explained everything, who Alpha Jordan really was, what he did and what his plan was.

"There isn't a shred of evidence in him that would suggest he's a LaRue." Payton said.

"Code Red is in effect; we are preparing for war. The patrols have not picked up any sign of rogues in the territory. If they climb over the mountain it could be morning before they breach." Diesel said.

"With any luck the avalanche buried some of them." Zeke said.

"After everyone is in position let's make sure the backup defenses are ready. I also want the archers on the rooftops before sun rise." He said. Our sixteen and seventeen year old teens were all required to master archery since they didn't get their wolf until eighteen and could not shift.

"The elders, pups and vulnerable are being moved to the bunker under the arena." Elliot said.

"I'll want a bonfire burning nearby." I said.

"You're not fighting." Diesel said.

"Like hell I'm not!" I replied.

"Lucy please, the pups." He reminded me.

"I'm a golden wolf, nothing is happening to the pups."

"You're right, nothing is happening to them because you will be in the bunker with the vulnerable and Vannica." He said.

"I'm not going anywhere!" Vannica said and we all turned to look at her. "My water just broke."

Zeke carried Vannica to the infirmary and Payton was currently at the infirmary with Alpha Knox, talking to Ranger. Diesel was reviewing old castle plans and maps with Sam, our chief tracker and Elliot, trying to find any other secret passages we may have at the castle. I wanted to go with Payton to the infirmary and check on Vannica, but Diesel wouldn't let me out of his sight.

I stood at the fireplace and stared at the flames. I could hear Lia purring now that we were safe with our mate again. Megan came and stood next to me. "I've been thinking." She said in almost a whisper.

"About?" I asked.

"The prophecy from Alexis yesterday, a war is coming and a lost wolf." She recalled.

"Do you think she was talking about this?" I asked.

Megan nodded her head. "Yes, and maybe Ranger is the lost wolf." She added.

"Or it could be Jordan since he might be Titus's son." I said thoughtfully.

She paused for a moment. "You don't think it could mean literally losing a wolf ... as in death? Do you?"

"I sure hope not."

"Lucy, you're the one born from Gods who will set the course." Megan said giving me a nervous glance.

"I believe I already have." I said and rubbed the tiny bump on my belly. "I think my great grandchild will possess all four elements in a hundred years."

"It looks like there are two passageways." Diesel said. "One is in the grand coat closet."

"And the other?" I inquired.

"In this office." He said.

We began searching for anything that could look like a button, handle or lever.

"The one in the closet is a lever." I said.

"Like this one?" Megan pointed to the light fixture on the wall that had a small lever tucked in next to it. It almost looked like it was a part of the light fixture. Diesel pulled the lever and a section of the bookcase turned open.

"Should we follow it?" Elliot asked.

"I don't think we have time, but I also don't want any surprises coming through them." Diesel said thinking out loud.

"Alpha we could send a few trackers together down

both of them." Sam suggested.

"We could try to disable the opening lever from the other side, so that it could only be opened from the inside." Max said.

"We need to know where this one leads out to, Sam, assemble a team. Elliot, get to the coat closet and find the lever on the other side, see if you can disable it. Max, check the arena bunker, I want it secured in ten minutes and everyone accounted for. Paul, make sure the archers and lookouts have what they need." Diesel instructed and they all moved.

We walked to the kitchen where Diesel insisted I eat. "The pups are growing fast Lucy; twin Alpha's will deplete Lia's energy quick."

"I'm famished." Lia said practically drooling.

Diesel pulled out sandwich meat, cheese, bread and other condiments. He sat me down on top of the kitchen counter to watch as he worked on the sandwiches. He piled the layers of meat on the sandwich. Then, he lifted a slice of cheese to my mouth and I took a bite before he placed the other half in his mouth.

When he was done, he left me on the kitchen counter and stood between my legs pulling me into a hug. He dropped his head to my neck and inhaled deeply. "How are my pups doing?" He asked as he moved his hand to my stomach.

"They're doing great." I said and he brought his lips to mine. His lips tasted so good and all I wanted to do in this moment was spend the night wrapped up in Diesel's arms tasting every inch of him.

"Who do I have to kiss to get a sandwich around here?" Alpha Knox said walking into the kitchen.

I flushed red and Diesel returned to the sandwich making. He also made one for Alpha Knox. We finished eating our sandwiches and Diesel was called into the hallway to speak with Sam.

"Lucy, Ranger told us what you did for him. As an Alpha, I would have let him die. As a father, I'm thankful for your mercy." He said with warm eyes and hugged me.

Diesel stepped back into the kitchen and his aura had changed. "What is it?" I asked.

"Sam found the exit point of the second chamber. It's in the southern mountains as well, not too far from the first exit point."

"Then the exit points are on our side of the mountains, so that's a good thing. The castle sits in the valley, with the avalanche closing the pass, they won't have a way in unless they climb over and we'll have the advantage of seeing them." Alpha Knox said.

"That means that Jordan will still be somewhere on our side." I said.

"That's not all they found." Diesel told us. "They found the bodies of the missing prison guards who were on duty when Ranger was taken in the tunnel. They also found Athena, battered and abused."

I wasn't sure if I wanted to know the answer to my next question. "Is she ... alive?"

"Barely. She's in the infirmary." He said.

"Son, is there something else?" Alpha Knox asked.

Diesel nodded his head. "When Sam pulled Athena down, he recognized a familiar scent on her. It was Ramos, he's working with Jordan."

I could feel the energy between the two Alpha's radiating power and anger. Diesel was trying hard to control Duke and Alpha Knox's blue eyes had turned dark. Kruz was on the surface and a low growl rippled in his throat.

"Who's Ramos?" I asked.

"Payton's first mate!"

CHAPTER 41 – WAR

"Who's going to tell Payton?" I asked as we walked over to the infirmary.

Alpha Knox and Diesel exchanged uncomfortable looks as if trying to decide how to tell her. I know that Payton had taken the rejection very hard. Ramos had rejected her on sight, because she was Diesel's sister after Diesel challenged and killed Titus. Ramos was one of the best warriors Crescent Moon had at the time. His blind loyalty to the previous Alpha had turned him into a rogue.

We reached the infirmary; Dr. Ross was going to have a busy night. We walked by the first room and I could smell Ranger. I could hear whimpers coming from the second room, Vannica was still in labor. The third room had a great deal of commotion going on, Dr. Ross and nurse Nelly fluttered around the room stabilizing Athena.

Payton stepped out of Vannica's room. "The pup is almost here." She said smiling.

"What's wrong?" She asked noticing the uncomfortable glances she was receiving.

"We have a situation." Diesel said with a matter of fact tone.

"What kind of situation?" Max's voice came from behind us; he had just entered the infirmary as well. He walked over to Payton and pulled her into his side, placing a kiss on top of her head.

"Ramos is working with Jordan. His scent was all over Athena." Alpha Knox said.

"Her first mate?" Max let out a low growl.

Payton instinctively laid her hand on his chest to calm him. She seemed unfazed but Max was ready to rip his throat out. I wondered if her reaction would have been different if she had not found Max. I felt nothing towards Ranger, and it was thanks to my second chance mate. Diesel was everything I could have ever dreamed and more.

Diesel had been holding my hand and brought it up to his lips. He placed a kiss on my hand, and I realized he had been listening to my thoughts. A knowing grin flashed on his face.

Dr. Ross stepped out of Athena's room and gave us an update. She was stable and expected to make a full recovery. Zeke opened the door to Vannica's room, and we heard a newborn pup crying.

"IT'S A BOY!" He smiled proudly.

A round of hugs and congratulations were passed around. We waited for the midwife to finish before we went inside to greet the newest addition to our pack. Vannica gave us a big smile as she turned the little bundle to face us.

"Alpha, Luna, meet Zachary." She beamed.

He was absolutely perfect. His little hand was laying against his chubby little cheek, clenched in a fist. He had the same thick tuft of hair his father had. I looked at Diesel and his eyes were glazed over in a mind link. He spoke the words we were all anxious to hear...

"They're at the top of the southern ridge."

The tension in the room was thick. "Zeke, you're on castle watch, the team is on the roof and guards at the door. No one comes in or out."

Zeke protested. "I'm the Gamma, I need to fight with you."

"You need to ensure the castle is not breached and keep our pack safe, including my new Godson." Diesel smiled and Vannica breathed a sigh of relief.

We stood at the front doors of the castle. The sun was starting to rise but the sky was still dark from the snow clouds rolling in. There was a chilling bite in the air and the sound of shifting wolves could be heard. I looked up and saw Megan on the roof top leading the archers. Elliot was already in wolf form and stood in position before the pack. We had a bonfire burning on the field for me and I could feel the flames pulling me. The energy and power of fire was pulsing through me.

Diesel looked at me and pulled me into his arms. "I love you." He whispered in my ear and inhaled my scent before he shifted.
Alpha Knox shifted and his clothes were left in shreds. His wolf Kruz, was as big and husky as Duke. They looked identical, with the exception of a few gray hairs around Kruz's muzzle and Duke had a small scar above his right eye. Payton's wolf, Poppy, was a slightly smaller and thinner version of the other two

Alphas, making her faster and more agile. All three had black shiny coats and piercing blue eyes.

Max's wolf, Milo, was just as big as the Alpha's and had a dark brown coat. Diesel moved to the front and was flanked by Payton and Max. I walked behind them with Alpha Knox at my side. I wasn't going to shift yet; we didn't want Lia to be the main target to start.

There was a line of about fifty rogue wolves standing at the top of the ridge. "This can't be all of them?" I asked Alpha Knox. "Who would be foolish enough to start a war with us when we have almost fourteen hundred fighters?"

"They must have more on the other side." He answered back and let out a growl. I saw a man in human form standing at the top, but it wasn't Jordan. He lifted his arm up and dropped it back to his side. The rogue wolves started running towards us.

Diesel's Alpha voice came through the mind link. "HOLD YOUR GROUND! We wait for them to get near enough. Archers stay hidden, this is not the bulk of their rogues." We watched as they continued to run down the ridge in our direction.

"Is that Ramos?" I asked Alpha Knox, eyeing the man who had dark hair, dark skin and a bulky physique. He had lifted his arm up again and another fifty rogues appeared at the top of the ridge. He dropped his arm and they began running towards us too.

"Yes, that's him!" Alpha Knox growled.

The first line of rogues was almost to the bottom of the mountain and the second line was just behind them. I reached my hand out towards the flames and felt them grow. They would be within range for Diesel's element soon and he could bury them in snow. I would be able to reach them with fire at about one hundred yards.

The first line of rogue wolves neared the end of the field and suddenly turned back around. They had rogues in human form riding on their backs who launched smoking canisters at our fighters. Fifty canisters landed on the field and purple smoke emitted from them.

"LOOK OUT! IT'S NIGHT SHADE!" Diesel roared through the mind link. Nearly three hundred fighters dropped to the ground and others moved back. They were knocked out cold before they could even react.

The second line of rogues also did the same and launched another fifty canisters. I immediately shot flames out to try and incinerate as many canisters mid-air as I could. Diesel did the same and buried them with snow. The second round of canisters that actually landed, knocked out another hundred fighters.

Ramos shifted into a large brown wolf and started charging down the mountain towards us. He let out a howl and a large group of wolves appeared behind him. Judging by the size of the group, it had to be Alpha Jordan's Eclipse pack and hired rogues.

They had about eight hundred wolves and we had roughly a thousand left. They were almost to the end of the field and would be within reach of the archers. We had a team of fifty archers on the roof of the castle and twenty on the roof of the training arena guarding the bunker.

"CASTLE ARCHERS READY!" Diesel called through the mind link.

Megan's voice rang next. "READY. AIM. **FIRE!**"

The silver tipped arrows hit most of their marks dropping about forty wolves.

"READY. AIM. **FIRE!**" Megan called again and dropped about thirty more rogues.

"Come on Lucy, lets light these flea bags up!" Lia snarled.

I held my hand out and a big ball of fire appeared in my hand, I looked at Alpha Knox who gave me an approving nod of his head. I launched it, aiming for Ramos and hit the wolf next to him who howled in pain and dropped. Ramos locked eyes with me and let an angry howl out.

"Bring it! I've got plenty more where that came from." Lia said.

Our warriors and rogues clashed, and the battle broke out. Snarls and roars echoed all around us. The white snow was blood stained as wolves lunged at each other. Diesel used his element to trip up wolves and bury some. I continued to launch fire balls at rogues. Some burned alive and others dropped in the snow to roll out the fire.

Payton and Max were fierce, they moved together quickly ripping out throats. Milo jumped on their backs and Poppy quickly went in for the kill. Elliot was fighting off a rogue when another rogue tried to attack from behind. I was about to launch a fire ball at the rogue when Megan shot an arrow right through his skull helping her mate. The archers remained on the roof trying to pick off rogues who were not standing in close proximity to our fighters.

Two warriors from Eclipse pack tried to leap at me but Alpha Knox took them down before they could touch me. I looked around, there was still no sign of Alpha Jordan. Something felt off. I continued to scan for Jordan but found Ramos. Ramos was charging at me with a dozen other wolves and a determined look on his face.

I crouched down, my clothes ripped to shreds and I unleashed Lia.

CHAPTER 42 – LOSS

An earth shaking growl ripped out of Lia's mouth and her teeth were bared. Wolves across the field turned their heads mid-fight looking for the source of the God like growl. Some even stopped dead in their tracks, unable to move, in awe of the mythical wolf standing before them.

Ramos seemed to lose his confidence the closer he got to me. Lia radiated power beyond any Alpha. Payton took advantage of this distracted moment to jump on Ramos and sink her teeth in the back of his neck. He growled in pain and managed to throw her black wolf off. Payton rolled back up and was ready to charge again when Max let out an angry growl, snarling and challenging Ramos. Ramos circled slowly taking in the size of Max's wolf, Milo, they were almost the same size. He reared up on his hind legs and lunged at Max.

I threw out a ring of fire that trapped three of the charging wolves and pounced on the others. Lia fought several rouges at once, clawing and ripping out throats with ease. I was able to manipulate fire in wolf form and continued to set rogues on fire. Diesel was sending balls of snow flying into the faces of the enemy to distract them momentarily, for an easy take down.

Alpha Knox was fighting three rogues at once and howled in pain when a rogue ripped some flesh from his shoulder. Lia pounced higher than I've ever seen her jump and landed on the rogue, knocking him off. She grabbed a hold of his neck and ripped his head right off. Alpha Knox plunged his claws in the neck of the rogue under him and Lia did the same to another.

"You're bleeding a lot. You should get back to the castle." I mind linked Alpha Knox.

"It's just a scratch. I'm not leaving my grand pups." He linked back.

Elliot and Payton were fighting back to back. Diesel was fast and ruthless. Rogue bodies were falling quickly, and our fighters were winning. The fighters from Eclipse pack put up a good fight, but they were outnumbered. Without Alpha Jordan here, they will not surrender.

Max and Ramos were still fighting. Ramos had his claws in Max's back and Max sent him flying in the air. Ramos crashed into another fight and landed on a rogue. He jumped back up and lunged at Max trying to sink his teeth into Max's neck. Max's claws extended and he dug them deep into Ramos's chest. Ramos fell lifeless to the ground and Max ripped his head completely off before he went to help his mate.

I turned my back to find the bonfire had been tipped over and a few warriors from Eclipse pack were trying hard to bury the rest of the fire with snow. I let out an angry roar and lunged at the warriors. Diesel growled and jumped on two of them. He noticed the source of my power was out and mind linked Zeke.

"Zeke we need some fire out here, can you light a torch?"

Zeke's voice came back weak and panting. "Alpha, I-I've been shot. Silver bullet. Jor-Jordan is in the castle."

I turned and started running back to the castle. I could feel Diesel and Alpha Knox running behind me. The castle doors were open, and Jordan stepped out. He had at least a dozen Eclipse warriors flanked behind him. How did he get in the castle I wondered? Was he hiding in the castle this entire time?

"There must be another passage we haven't discovered yet." Lia said.

Jordan stood in human form on the castle steps, holding a gun in his right hand. His warriors shifted and lunged towards us. Diesel was fighting off four warriors and three others jumped on Alpha Knox.

"Shall we make this a fair fight?" Jordan smirked at me.
He lifted his right arm and pointed the gun at me. A single shot fired off and it hit my shoulder. I felt a slight sting, but silver had no effect on me. A big black Alpha wolf, with piercing blue eyes came running out of the castle from behind Alpha Jordan and lunged at him. It was Ranger.

Jordan fell down the stairs and shifted into his wolf. He was black with brown patches and his eyes were green. He looked absolutely nothing like a LaRue Alpha. Ranger snarled at him and lunged with his claws extended. I did not have a fire source, so I pounced on the warriors and plunged my claws in. I heard a yelp coming from Diesel, a warrior had clamped down on his back leg.

"OH, HELL NO!" Lia snarled. She quickly ripped out

the throats of the other warriors and lunged to help her mate.

Ranger was attacked by another warrior while fighting with Jordan. Jordan rolled himself on the ground and shifted back to human form. He reached for the gun at the bottom of the stairs. Ranger dropped the lifeless body of the warrior and turned towards Jordan. Ranger was emitting a dangerous aura and was ready to send Jordan to hell.

Jordan scooted back on the ground and raised his right hand towards Ranger. Jordan held the gun up and pulled the trigger before Ranger could pounce on him. In a flash I saw Kruz, Alpha Knox's wolf, jump towards Ranger, pushing him out of the way. The bullet hit Kruz in the chest and he dropped on the ground, shifting back to human form.

"NO!! PLEASE MOON GODDESS, NO!" I screamed in my head.

Ranger stood motionless and a low sorrowful howl came from Rex. Diesel dropped the last warrior and Duke stood next to me. I frantically searched his chest for the wound and wondered if I could pull the bullet out with my fingers. Silver inside the body was toxic to a werewolf. I shifted back to human form. "Alpha? ALPHA, can you hear me?" I asked.

"WE NEED DOCTOR ROSS!" I yelled out to Diesel, but he knew nothing could be done.

Ranger lowered his wolf head to his father's shoulder and whimpered.

Alpha Knox's voice was low. "It's okay Lucy." He took

a shaky breath. "I-I'm going to be with m-my Clair soon. Tak-Take care of them for-for me."

"Alpha, Alpha, stay with us ... please." My eyes filled with tears. This man who had become a second father to me, laid dying before me. Taken away just like my mother. Stolen from us before he had the chance to hold his grand pups. This isn't fair.

My heart was racing. The grief was unbearable. Alpha Knox always believed in me, even when I didn't believe in myself. He was patient and kind. He loved and respected all of us. He was the center of our family. Alpha Knox drew his last breath and painful howls ripped out from Diesel, Payton and Ranger at the loss of their father's connection. My heart ached and I could hardly contain it.

I stood up and stepped back. A half scream half growl ripped out of me. A storm was brewing inside of me. My body was pulsing and there was a burning in my chest.

"Lucy your eyes are glowing." Diesel mind linked me.

A bright light engulfed me, and I looked down to my hands as sparks shot from my fingertips. Fire! I had internal fire, a gift from Apollo. I was a true descendant of the Gods. Alpha Knox always told me I could do this.

I imagined fire shooting out from my palms and it happened. I was able to generate my own flames. I willed the flames to surround me and they did. I was a walking ball of fire. A small burning sun, radiating power and no one could touch me. No one could hurt me. I wasn't going to let anyone hurt my family again. I looked to find Jordan and saw that coward running away towards the woods in wolf form.

"JORDAN!" My voice rang out across the territory, shaking the ground, emanating the power of the Gods I had tapped into.

He turned his head and looked at me, I could sense his fear. Rage burned through me and flames shot out of my eyes towards Jordan. His wolf was immediately engulfed in fire and howling in pain. He dropped and shifted back, screaming as he burned.

It wasn't enough, I needed more. The pain was too much to contain and revenge was mine. I saw Ramos's decapitated body on the ground and burned it. I looked around and saw other rogue bodies, I burned them too.

The remaining rogues and Eclipse warriors stopped fighting and started running back up the ridge. My heart was full of pain and I couldn't seem to find compassion for those trying to escape. They had come all this way with the intention of first attacking the vulnerable members of our pack and helpless pups. These were monsters and they did not belong in this world. Fire continued to pour out of me as I set the remaining cowards on fire.

EVERY LAST ONE OF THEM BURNED.

I let out a scream, that shook the ground. I was burning with rage and grief. I wasn't sure how to control it. A power so great, it could destroy armies. The power and wrath of the Gods pulsed through me.

"Lucy?" Diesel called out my name.

I looked at him, he was back in human form. He reached out his hand and his eyes were swimming with so much emotion. I felt his pain, his grief, his guilt, his fear, his admiration and his overwhelming love. I looked around and the war was over. We may have won, but we had also lost.

"Lucy, Please." Diesel called to me again. Desperation in his voice to hold me. He needed me and I needed him. I closed my eyes and willed the fire to stop. His arms immediately embraced me, and I collapsed.

CHAPTER 43 – RETURN

Diesel's POV

I was seated in the back of the Escalade, looking down at Lucy's beautiful sleeping face. Her head was resting on my chest and my hand was rubbing circles on her belly. She was always at ease listening to my heart drumming.

Dawn was breaking on the horizon. We had about two hours left, and our caravan of black SUV's made its way towards Dark Moon territory. Max was driving and Payton was sleeping in the front passenger's seat. My mother was Luna of Dark Moon and was buried there. We held a funeral at Crescent Moon for my father yesterday and he would be buried this afternoon next to my mother at Dark Moon.

It's been three days since the war. Lucy spent the first two days sleeping. Tapping into her full power was exhausting and grief weighed heavy on all of us. Looking down at her face and those full cherry lips, I'm reminded of the first time she took my breath away. The first day I pulled her out of that river after she had escaped from Dark Moon. Now, she was willingly returning to her personal hell hole, to help lay my father to rest.

Our pack had suffered thirty-four deaths including my father. Alpha Jordan and the eight hundred others that breached our territory, had been turned to ash. My gamma, Zeke, was lucky enough to be outside the infirmary when Jordan shot him. Dr. Ross was able to act quick and remove the silver bullet in his abdomen before it poisoned him.

Zeke had stayed behind to run things at Crescent Moon while I was away. Vannica and the pup were doing great, holding baby Zach made me excited for my pups. I was lost in thoughts thinking about my pups and praying to the Moon Goddess that I would be half as good a father as mine was.

I was admiring the familiar territory when Max broke the silence. "We're almost there."

I caught sight of the big lake we used to swim at when we were pups. My father used to hold big family barbecue's out there on warm summer nights. I thought about the time I used my element to flip Max and his first mate, Olivia, over in a canoe, because I was secretly jealous that he had a mate and I didn't.

While I had wonderful childhood memories here, Dark Moon never felt like home. Crescent Moon was my home and I hope Lucy will feel the same way soon. She may have been born at Dark Moon, but it held painful memories for her. I was going to make it my life mission to fill her life with nothing but happy memories.

We pulled into the long drive leading towards the main pack house. Ranger had come back in my helicopter after yesterday's service with our father's casket to make arrangements. Athena traveled back with Ranger and had requested permission to switch packs. I granted it. They had both rejected their first mates, so they would both most likely not have second chance mates. Miranda had left Ranger for Jordan, so Ranger was free to find a new Luna.

I kissed the top of Lucy's head and spoke in her ear. "Wake up little one, we're here."

"You won't be calling me little one next month when my belly is huge." She whispered back and kissed my lips. The thought of her round with my pups made me want to have a dozen more!

Ranger was standing in front of the pack house with a few others waiting for us. Our family home was on the north side of the property and we would be spending the night here before we drove ten hours back. We also had some unfinished business I wanted to take care of at Dark Moon. Our seven vehicle caravan pulled up in front of the pack house and we all stepped out of the cars.

"LUCY?" Beth the bully and Lucy's previous tormentor called out. Duke felt the urge to rip her head off right here.

Ranger growled at her. **"IT'S LUNA LUCY AND YOU WILL ADDRESS HER AS SUCH."**

His Gamma and Delta twins, Blake and Cole, looked so much alike, I had a hard time distinguishing who was who sometimes.

"Hello Luna, it's good to see you again" Blake, I believe, bowed his head at Lucy smiling. Then he turned to me. "Welcome back Alpha Diesel." He said and I nodded my head.

We went inside for breakfast in the main dining hall.

All these years and nothing had changed. It felt kind of strange and yet so familiar. I sat at the table and pulled Lucy to my Lap.

"Alpha Diesel, how good it is to see you Sir." Davis said to me.

"Davis, the pleasure is mine. Tell me, is Rose still in the kitchen?" I asked.

"Yes Sir, she still is." He smiled.

"Please tell her I'm requesting two of her delicious T-bone steak breakfast meals. My mate is eating for three and needs her strength." I said and kissed Lucy who blushed.

"Coming right up and congratulations Sir."

We ate breakfast and many curious eyes wandered in our direction. So many familiar faces and the elders all took turns coming to greet me. The one person I was hoping to see, had yet to show her face.

"Where's Ursa?" I asked Ranger.

Everyone seemed to have hushed down and their ears were perked. The room was full of people who had mistreated my mate over the last four years. They could feel the powerful aura fill the room and assumed it was mine, when it was really Lucy's.

"I'm holding her in a cell for treason, we will deal with her tomorrow." Ranger said.

"And the family home?" I asked.

"It has been in Lucy's family for generations and is

rightfully hers." Ranger told us.

"We will keep it as a vacation home for visits." Lucy said and Ranger nodded his head.

I was a little surprised that Lucy wanted to visit Dark Moon. But, her parents were buried here and Ursa never let her go to cemetery hill. After breakfast, Lucy took my hand and wanted to show me something. We excused ourselves and I followed her towards the kitchen. She opened a door that appeared to lead down into a basement.

There was pain in my heart, and I understood where she was taking me. I may have grown up here, but this was a place I had never been. I held tight to her hand and entered the big laundry room. She stood quietly and looked around. The dog bed was gone and there was no sign of anyone living down here. It was so cold and dreary; I honestly don't know how she did it for four years. I pulled her into my chest and after a moment, we silently left the basement.

We went back to the family home to get cleaned up and rest. Some of the others who came with us stayed in the guest rooms at the pack house. I took Lucy upstairs to my old room to get some shut eye. She was the first female to ever sleep in my bed and it made Duke happy.

It was late afternoon when we arrived at the cemetery. A large crowd had already gathered including allies from other packs. My father was a great Alpha, he was loved and respected by many.
Several of the elders who knew him well spoke. His casket was lowered in the spot next to my mother, her

headstone was also adorned with flowers. Howls of goodbye rang out and he was finally at rest and with my mother. His beloved mate and Luna.

We went back to the car and Max took some flowers out of the back. He handed them to Lucy. "I thought you'd like to see your parents."

Lucy took the flowers and hugged Max before we walked over to her parents. I was surprised to see Ursa had allowed them to be buried next to each other. Then I remembered what my father had told us about Ursa being a chosen mate. I'm sure it was my father who had them buried together.

Lucy asked to have a few moments alone with her parents so Payton, Max and I walked back to the car to wait for her. I waited anxiously, I could feel her emotions through the mate bond, she was experiencing everything from grief to anger. This was the first time she had been allowed to visit the cemetery. She had so much grief locked away. I saw her walking towards us, hair blowing behind her in the wind and her fists clenched.

Her eyes were swimming in tears and then I noticed her amber colored pupils were flickering. I leaned in closer and saw flames in her eyes. "Lucy, what's going on?"

She responded with one word. "Ursa." We obviously had some unfinished business with Ursa.

We woke the next morning in my bed at my old room. Lucy was still sleeping, so I took Duke out for a quick run before we made the long trip back home in the car.

The trees in the forest at Dark Moon, were some of my favorites. I ran towards the river to my old swimming hole. There was a rustling noise behind me, and Rex stepped out. We were still able to mind link because of our family link.

"Rex is looking better." I told Ranger.

"Thanks. How's Lucy doing being back?" He asked with hesitation and guilt.

"She's stronger than we give her credit for." I said.

"Certainly stronger than I ever thought. I never deserved her."

I wasn't going to argue with that. He didn't deserve her. He was lucky that she took mercy on him and saved Rex. She could destroy his entire pack if she really wanted to, but her love for my father stopped her.

"She also didn't deserve the treatment she got in her last four years here. No one does."

"I know, believe me I know. She was able to bring Rex back and give me a second chance that I didn't deserve." Ranger said.

"Dad always believed in you and was very disappointed. There's not a day that he didn't miss you or worry about you these last four years. He gave his life to give you a second chance too. Don't let him down."

"I'll try not to." He said.

"If you fail to produce an heir, I expect you to pass

Dark Moon to one of mine." I told him and he nodded. Since my parents were buried here, it was important that a LaRue had Dark Moon.

We gathered at the pack house for breakfast before we left for home. Ranger called a pack meeting outside and Blake asked us to attend. Delta Cole appeared holding an angry looking prisoner.

"Good morning Dark Moon." Ranger called out.

"Good morning Alpha." They rang back in unison.

"I've called you here today because we have recently discovered a traitor in the pack." Ranger said and a few pack members growled.

"Ursa Taylor, has admitted to conspiring with Alpha Jordan, to gain power with the intent of killing the LaRue Alpha's and taking over their packs. She is also found guilty of lying to her Alpha and the abuse of Luna Lucy Michaels LaRue."

Ursa struggled against Cole as he restrained her. "That trash doesn't deserve to be Luna." She growled.

I could feel Lucy's anger flare and her eyes started burning with fire. Fear covered Ursa's face in recognition. Shocked looks and gasps swept through the pack as they set eyes on Lucy. She radiated such great power.

"Ursa Taylor, you have been sentenced to death." Ranger called out.

Lucy walked towards Ursa who cringed back onto Cole

trying to step back. "Alpha Ranger, I have a more suitable punishment for her."

"Anything you wish Luna." He answered back.

Lucy's eyes returned to their calm color before she spoke...

"Throw her in the hole and leave her there to rot."

EPILOGUE

Two years later

The summer was coming to an end and we were enjoying one last family picnic before the fall weather set in. Crescent point had become one of my favorite spots in the territory. This was the exact spot Diesel brought me to on our first date, when he saw Lia for the first time.

Diesel was entertaining our son's with water using his element. The water flowing from the waterfall was dancing and swirling in the air. The show was wonderful, and the boys were squealing and clapping. Knox was born first, and Peter followed ten minutes later. We named the twins after both of their grandfathers.

I sat under the tree with our newest pup at my breast. She was a demanding little thing and needed to be fed on a schedule. Like our boys, baby Raven also had the signature LaRue jet black hair and blue eyes. I looked down to admire her beautiful little face and felt the tingling gaze of my mate on me. I could always feel Diesel's gaze when he looked at me.

Diesel leaned down and placed a kiss on my neck and then another on the top of Raven's little head. "Can I get you anything?" His husky voice softly asked against my neck.

"I'm ok. Let's wait for the others."

"How's my princess?" He smiled at Raven who clearly

had her daddy wrapped around her little finger.

"Hungry." I smiled back and switched her to the other breast.

Diesel showed the boys how to pick wildflowers and they crawled around in the grass plucking the flowers. The boys were strong Alpha males and had the energy to go with it. I sat wondering if they would get an elemental gift or if it was possible to get both. The prophecy always seemed to drift in my mind, half had come true already.

Raven let out a coo and had just finished eating. She was satisfied and ready for a nap. I looked up to see Payton waddling her way to us, she was ready to deliver their second pup in the coming weeks. Max smiled hello with their daughter Clair clinging to him. She was six months younger than her twin cousins and the apple of her father's eye. Max set Clair down in the grass with the boys, she looked like she could have been their sister. The LaRue genes were strong.

Max was holding a big pillow and plopped it down next to me so that Payton would be comfortable on the blanket. He took her hands and gently helped her get comfortable. I couldn't have been any happier to have my best friend as my brother-in-law.

"I'm hungry, let's eat!" Payton said, practically demanding.

Diesel chuckled. "Now we know where Raven gets it from." Payton glared at him.

"I'm not responsible if she kills your mate." Max whispered to me and I couldn't help but giggle.

Helga had packed our picnic with fried chicken, baby back ribs, potato fingers, corn on the cob, biscuits, mixed fruits, and brownies for dessert.

"Ohhh brownies!" Payton practically drooled as she reached for one and we all burst out laughing.

Raven opened her beautiful blue eyes and started crying. I tried to calm her, but she was having none of that. Her little fists were clenched tight and she was angry.

"See, she wants a brownie too." Payton joked and shoved the brownie in her mouth.

"Awww, my princess wants her daddy. I'll take her." Diesel cooed and stretched out his arms.

Raven squirmed in my arms and cried even louder. I thought it might be gas and was ready to hand her off to her father, her knight in shining armor. From the corner of my eye, I saw something unusual. I thought I saw an amber flame flicker in her little eyes.

I stared for a moment longer and they were still blue. Maybe I imagined it? Or it was a trick of the light? I handed her to her father, and she settled back down, drifting to sleep.

Printed in Great Britain
by Amazon

56857263R00180